THE AFRICAN POISON MURDERS
by Elspeth Huxley

"This is a whirlwind job, Grade A."
—Will Cuppy, *Books*

"This book is not to be judged merely as a crime puzzle, although it is a baffling one. Its chief merit is the convincing manner in which the author pictures the background, with which she is thoroughly familiar, and the way in which the various characters fit into that background as if they belonged there and nowhere else."
—*The New York Times*

THE AFRICAN
POISON MURDERS

ELSPETH HUXLEY

PERENNIAL LIBRARY
Harper & Row, Publishers
New York, Cambridge, Hagerstown, Philadelphia, San Francisco
London, Mexico City, São Paulo, Sydney

A hardcover edition of this book was originally published by Harper & Row, Publishers.

THE AFRICAN POISON MURDERS. Copyright 1939 by Harper & Row, Publishers. All rights reserved. Printed in the United States of America. No part of this book may be used or reproduced in any manner whatsoever without written permission except in the case of brief quotations embodied in critical articles and reviews. For information address Harper & Row, Publishers, 10 East 53rd Street, New York, N.Y. 10022. Published simultaneously in Canada by Fitzhenry & Whiteside Limited, Toronto.

First PERENNIAL LIBRARY edition published 1981.

ISBN: 0-06-080540-4

81 82 83 84 85 10 9 8 7 6 5 4 3 2 I

THE AFRICAN POISON MURDERS

CHAPTER 1: ALL THE WAY UP THE ROUGH,

bumpy road Vachell wondered why the woman at his side had been so insistent. He judged that she was not the sort of person who generally pressed her point. Her manner was curiously detached, almost indifferent, as if her mind had windows of its own from which to stare at secret views. But there had been a note of urgency in her voice when she had invited him to spend the night on the farm. She lived alone there with her husband, Dennis West, raising cows whose cream, duly processed, travelled six thousand miles to its market on British breakfast-tables.

The car jostled and lurched over the rutted surface. Headlights threw into sharp relief deep holes dug by ant-bears, ruts made by farm wagons sticking in the mud, and tufts of stiff grass between the wheel-tracks.

"Afraid our approach isn't exactly a speedway," West, at the wheel, remarked. "I ploughed it all up last year and it was fine for a bit. But it's gone again now. Nothing you can do, short of spending a packet."

"You don't need to apologize," Vachell said. "There's boulders on the main road a mountain-goat would puzzle over, and one swamp where you get leeches in the carburettor."

The car skidded sideways around a sharp bend with a big acacia tree in the angle, and climbed steeply to reach the homestead. Clouds of dogs swarmed like giant red mosquitoes around the headlamps as Dennis West swung the car up to the front of the house, straight on to the lawn. The road petered out among the farm buildings behind in a shed shared by the car, two carts, some seed-boxes and an old incubator. Vachell got out clasping a six-months-old bull terrier called Bullseye. He had brought her with him from Marula, the capital, on his up-country tour. She was an impulsive dog, at the tom-boy age, and he felt nervous about her reception; but the setters sniffed around amiably and flattened their bellies on the ground in apparent ecstasies of self-abasement. They seemed friendly, unsuspicious dogs, with no grudge against strangers.

Commander West led the way into the living-room and began to pour out drinks. Vachell looked at him more closely in the strong light. He had never met his host until an hour before. West was a tall, broad-shouldered man with the unmistakable look of the naval officer about him—clean-cut, healthy-skinned face, clear eyes with wrinkles at the corners, tidy brushed-back hair. His face and arms were deeply sunburnt and he looked somehow incomplete without a pipe. But his dark, thick hair was streaked with grey, although he could not yet be fifty, and there were deep lines in his face, as though worry or suffering had left a mark.

"Need a drink after listening to all that gup," he remarked, handing a whisky and soda to his guest. "God knows I don't often agree with Munson, but he was plumb right this time. Norman Parrot's a bloody fool. Doesn't know the first thing about stock."

"He only does it to annoy, because he knows it teases,"

West's wife remarked. "Give me a drink, please, Dennis. Mr. Vachell must have thought he'd got into an insane asylum—or else been very bored."

They had been to a meeting of the district farmers' association at the local club. A debate on East Coast fever policy —to dip cattle and let the disease remain endemic, or to eliminate the infection—had occupied most of the evening. Vachell wasn't interested in cattle disease, but he was interested in the people who discussed it—in one of them, at least. He had come up from headquarters to find out more about this man. It was strange that he should have been asked to stay so pressingly by the people who owned the next-door farm, people he'd never even met before. The more he thought of it the stranger it seemed.

It was Mrs. West who'd invited him. He looked at her as she took her drink and walked over to the fire to warm her hands. Again he felt the faint disturbance in his blood that had come over him when he first saw her in the meeting-room at the club, standing silently amid the hum of talk and the haze of tobacco smoke, her face white and grave, but her eyes so startlingly alive. She was very slim, dressed in navy corduroy slacks and a white silk-shirt, open-necked, and she moved as lightly as a dancer. Her cheekbones were wide and high, her chin pointed. There was something of the Slav, he thought, about the shape of her face. But she was American; her voice told him that. It was her eyes that fascinated him most. They were the colour of dark honey, very large, and they affected him in a way he could not classify or describe. It was as if they held a personal message for him that he could not read, but whose purport he had known a long time. He lit a cigarette impatiently. Africa was giving him a lot of dumb, screwy ideas.

They talked about the meeting for a little, and he listened with only half a mind while West explained how East Coast fever could be cleared off a farm by grazing the land for eighteen months with native oxen who'd recovered from the disease. After that the ticks would no longer be carriers of the infection. It was something to do with the life-history of the parasite and the blood of immune cattle, but Vachell had forgotten it all by the time he had finished a hot bath and put on an old flannel suit for dinner.

After his bath and a change he took a quick look at the lay-out of the place, to get it fixed in his mind. It resembled most East African farm-houses: it looked as if it had reproduced by budding, like certain kinds of bacteria. The nucleus was the living-room, with a stone veranda in front: a long untidy welcoming room, warmed by a big open fire stacked with cedar logs. At one end was a large round table where all meals save breakfast were served. The whitewashed walls of the house were made of timber, wire-netting and mud, which had flaked away on the outside to leave bare brown patches. They were plastered inside with a mixture of skim milk and flour, and distempered a bright cream. The roof was corrugated iron, concealed from within by a celotex ceiling. The room was full of sagging easy-chairs, red setters, old magazines, fishing-rods and tins of cigarettes, and the floor sprinkled with skins of leopards and bushbuck.

The kitchen quarters were out at the back, and a series of

thatched mud huts of varying shapes and sizes was dotted inconsequently about, like weavers' nests around the crown of a tree. One of them was connected by a covered way and a cement path to the veranda of the living-room; this was the Wests' bedroom. The other and unconnected huts might be bedrooms, offices, or stores. Vachell's own room was a square, roughly-plastered hut equipped with home-made furniture and electric light. It was clean and comfortable, with bright printed curtains and bare white walls. While he was dressing a native servant brought a plate of meat and rice for Bulls-eye, and a basket for her to sleep in. He was glad that hospitality was extended to dogs.

For some reason that he could not analyse he began to feel a queer sort of excitement, as he had as a child when confronted at a party with a bran pie. The whole thing was strange: the sudden invitation, his acceptance, the feeling of constraint he had already sensed between the Wests. He could not take his mind off her eyes. They seemed to be looking at him, while he fixed his tie, from the open window, from behind his shoulder in the room. She had a curious deep voice, slow and a little husky; she spoke as if a subtler meaning lay behind the words. Vachell frowned as he folded a clean handkerchief into the breast pocket of his grey suit. It was dangerous for a policeman to imagine things.

At dinner West did most of the talking, replying to questions about his farm with a mixture of enthusiasm, bitterness and resignation common to men on the land. The food was excellent, with more thought behind it than was usual in a farm meal. There was a salad of a crispness and subtlety that

Vachell could not remember meeting since he left America. You could always tell a British colony by its salad, he thought (if they existed at all): flabby lettuce, sliced tomatoes, saddened beet.

"I've only got about twenty milking-cows," West wound up. "With cream at eighty cents that doesn't bring in much. It takes so long to build up a decent herd. One needs capital —always capital. If I could only buy in fifty high-grade heifers. . . . It's fellows like Munson, who do things on a big scale, that make the . . ." West checked himself abruptly and switched the conversation on to the well-worn tracks of the European situation. There had been bitterness in his voice.

Mention of Munson seemed to bring a new tenseness into the air. Vachell saw Janice West—he had heard some one at the club use the name—glance at her husband over a low bowl of red Barberton daisies in the table's centre, her face expressionless and yet strained. He tried not to look too obviously at her thick black hair lying in soft waves back from her forehead, and at her cool carved face.

"Let's have coffee by the fire," she said. "It gets cold up here after dark."

Her voice was deep and husky; the words fell into silence like drops of ice-cold water on to a hot stove.

They moved over to share the sofa and chairs with the dogs. Janice West pushed a sleepy animal off the well-worn settee and told Vachell to sit down quickly before another one took the place. After the coffee had come West said suddenly:

"It's really about Munson we—my wife—wanted to talk to you. To ask your advice. That is, if you don't mind. If it isn't asking you to do something unprofessional, I mean."

Vachell stretched his lanky legs and squinted at the fire. "I hope it is," he said. He leant back and prepared to listen with more attention than he showed.

His host gulped down a cupful of hot coffee and filled a pipe. He was obviously ill at ease.

"It's a bit difficult to explain," he began, hesitation in his voice. "God knows there's enough gossip in this district already without my weighing in. All the same . . . the law protects everything here but the poor bloody fool on the land. You mayn't touch the hair on the tail of an elephant, or say boo to a wild goose, but there's an open season on farmers. Anyway on those who live next door to Karl Munson."

Vachell nodded, and dribbled cigarette smoke out of his nostrils. His lean, bony face remained impassive, his eyes fixed on the crackling wood fire. Karl Munson was the man he'd come up to the district to find out about. A good deal was known already, recorded on the file at C.I.D. headquarters in Marula. All aliens had a dossier of sorts. Germans and Italians in particular had been carefully investigated, and as Munson was not only a German but high up in the hierarchy of the local Nazi Bund, his activities had been checked by the C.I.D. as closely as possible. That, in the circumstances, was not closely enough. Vachell was very much in the market for information about Munson.

"You reckon the guy's anti-social but keeps within the law?" he asked.

"No, I don't," West said bluntly. "I think he breaks the law. But you know yourself that a working farmer can't spend half his life in the magistrate's court bringing petty cases."

"What's the trouble?" Vachell inquired.

West hesitated a little, as if uncertain where to begin, and then dived into a stream of explanation.

"I could go on all night talking about Karl Munson. Not personally, though there isn't a bloke in the district who doesn't think he's a tick, but as a neighbour. He does everything he can to make things difficult for all of us. He won't keep up his fences, for instance. So his cattle wander off into other people's crops and demolish them. A year ago they ruined forty acres of my maize. Last year they walked into Jolyot Anstey's beans and cleared off the lot, a week before harvest. Anstey has the farm above Munson's, you know—he's another of the suffering neighbours. We fence, of course, but the cattle break the fences—so Munson says. Of course they don't. His boys pull up the posts. I've seen evidence myself."

"You could bring an action for that."

"Oh yeah? Ask Jolyot Anstey. He tried. I dare say we could if we could catch Munson's cattle red-handed, or red-hooved, rather. But when you go down there in the morning, all you see is a trampled waste of maize stalks, or whatever it is, and a lot of hoof-marks. How the hell are you going to prove it? One of Anstey's boys caught them at it, and recognized Munson's herdsman. And what happened? Munson brought his head herd and half a dozen witnesses into court and they swore black and blue that the cattle were safely shut up all night, and that what Anstey's boy saw was a herd of buffaloes or a flock of satyrs or something. Of course the case was dismissed, and Anstey was landed with the costs. And there was a sequel to that story, too."

Janice West looked up quickly and said: "Dennis, please, it makes me sick to my stomach to hear that."

"You can hear it all the same!" West said explosively. His eyes were snapping as he looked across at her. "This was your idea, to bring all this up. You know I said . . ."

Janice got to her feet in a single motion. Her face in the shaded lamplight was white as the petals of a frangipane.

"I don't want to listen," she said. "Mr. Vachell, please excuse me. I hope you have everything you want."

The room suddenly seemed flat and empty after she had left it. She had spoken little, yet Vachell could remember every inflexion of tone. He had to make an effort to concentrate on what West was saying.

"It's a beastly story," his host went on, "and I've no proof, but it shows you the sort of fellow Munson is. Soon after the case, that boy of Anstey's—the one that gave evidence against Munson—went on leave. About a week later he came back—carried in by some other natives. He'd been found in the forest behind Munson's farm. His feet and hands were swollen the size of melons and stinking with gangrene. He was a pretty awful sight. When Anstey got him into hospital the doctor found loops of baling wire somewhere deep down inside all the pus. His wrists and ankles had been wired together and he'd been tied to a tree. He'd managed to twist himself free, but the wire dug into his flesh and I suppose he'd tripped up and stunned himself on the way, or something. Anyhow, by the time he got to hospital it was too late. The doctor amputated his feet and hands, but luckily the wretched devil died."

"There was no proof it was Munson," Vachell said.

"None that a magistrate would accept. The boy never got coherent enough to make a statement, but Anstey swears he babbled Munson's name. Of course Anstey was livid with rage. He's tremendously keen on the natives anyhow, knows their customs and all that, and when the police found themselves up against a brick wall he raised a tremendous stink, and even went down to see the Governor about it. But it didn't do any good. Munson's boys are far too terrified to give him away."

Vachell lit another cigarette and leant back in his chair, his long legs stretched out straight in front. The fire toasted his soles and made his bony face with its deep-sunk eyes look gaunt. West, his hands clasped tightly between his knees, glanced up and decided that his guest looked like a Scot, as so many Canadians did. He had the sandy hair and long jaw of the true Scot. He looked young, too, to be head of the C.I.D., but of course one of the things a Scot seldom gave away was his age.

"Granted Munson's the sort of guy who ought to be pushed down the bath-tub waste," Vachell remarked, "what do you reckon any one can do?"

West hesitated, stroking a sleeping setter with a thick, heavy hand, staring into the fire.

"It was really my wife's idea to tell you all this," he said finally. "She thought you might know of some way to put a spoke in his wheel. At the moment, you see, we're having another row. Some of Munson's cattle have been dying rather mysteriously, presumably of poison, since the vet can't think of anything else. Munson has accused me of putting some poison plant or other on his land, to kill them. Accused me, the damned swine." His voice shook a little with anger. "Well, isn't it criminal, or something, to make accusations like that?"

"Sure, you can file a suit for slander. If you can prove it, that is."

"Proof! That's the whole damned trouble. How can one prove anything in a country like this? I heard about Munson's latest effort at the club; he'd said something one evening in the bar, but suppose I tried to get any one to swear on oath ———"

Footsteps came down the stone-flagged veranda and Janice West opened the door. She wore a black silk dressing-gown with a white monogram on the lapel. Her dark hair was rumpled; there was a look of fear in her eyes. Vachell's heart missed a beat and his throat felt suddenly dry; it was a long time since he had seen a woman who did so much to him. As he stood up she said:

"Dennis, I can't find Rhode anywhere. He came out with me and I heard him barking way down towards the vegetable garden, but he hasn't got back yet. Maybe you'd better go out and look for him. There might be a leopard around. . . ."

West jumped to his feet and said:

"I'll just get a lamp." He was out of the door in an instant.

Alarm had sprung up like a flame; there was something seriously wrong. Vachell looked across the room at his hostess and asked:

"How long is it since a leopard took one of your dogs?"

She turned her head slowly to face him and he saw nothing but her eyes. Their pupils were wide and black and he thought again that they were almost frighteningly alive. She shook her head faintly and answered:

"We've never lost one that way yet, but there's always a chance a leopard might come around."

Vachell gave a little twitch to his shoulders and walked over to offer her a cigarette. She fumbled as she took one from the box. When he lit the match he saw her eyelashes reflected in faint shadows on her smooth, high cheek.

"Why are you scared?" he asked.

She drew on the cigarette and looked up at him. He could not read the expression in her eyes. There was something hard in them and hostile, like an animal behind bars. He thought that if she were angry her face would turn as cruel and cold as a stone gargoyle on a Gothic church.

"Because of Rhode. I told you there's always a chance of a leopard," she answered, "and sometimes the natives set traps. He's the pride of the pack. We call him that after Rhode Islands. They're such good setters."

Vachell didn't smile or answer. After a pause she spoke again, reluctantly, he thought. "There's been some queer things going on around here lately. You may hear talk and gossip. But there's probably a perfectly rational explanation to everything. It just makes me nervous, that's all."

Vachell nodded, and walked over to the fireplace to throw away the match. "Suppose you tell me about it," he suggested. "That's what I'm here for, isn't it?"

She hesitated, looking at her cigarette end, and said: "No—not exactly—well, I guess so, in a way. Most likely it's all imagination. The fevered fancies of a disordered mind. After all, there weren't any footprints." She seemed to be talking half to herself.

Vachell looked at her face with narrowed eyes. "Listen, what is this, a poltergeist or something? Or do I have to guess? Animal, vegetable, mineral . . ."

"Or things that go bump in the night," she added, and smiled. Little creases formed at the corners of her lips; he noticed that her mouth was wide. "Lately they've been bumping outside my window. Last night something knocked against the pane. Three nights ago I thought I heard something breathing outside. I didn't get up, I was too scared. Now morning we looked in the flower-bed, but we couldn't see any footprints. It was kind of—well, you know how it is when you feel as if spiders were crawling up your spine?"

Vachell nodded. "Sure. Sounds like a native burglar looking the ground over. Have you missed anything lately, or had any one break into the store?"

She shook her head. "About a week ago there was another queer thing. It hardly seems—" She hesitated, and Vachell, watching her face, said gently:

"Go ahead all the same."

"It was the garden—my delphiniums—I raise good delphiniums, you know; I've taken prizes. Well, one morning I found them all decapitated—the blooms were lying around in the dirt. They'd been cut off with a knife. It was so senseless, so . . . malicious."

Vachell ran his long fingers over his chin. "Some one has it in for you, maybe. You'd better lock the door before you go to sleep."

"The goblins will get you if you don't watch out." She smiled again, but the shadow of fear did not leave her face.

They sat on the sofa for twenty minutes, talking idly and listening for any sound. The night was still and windless. A waning moon had risen over the forest above the farm, but the sky was hard and brittle with stars. Out of the window Vachell could see a square full of them, sharp and unwinking in the clear mountain air. There was a tension, a feeling of expectancy, in the silence of the night. He felt restless and ill at ease. He had only to put out his hand a little way to touch her arm. Mohammedans, he thought, managed these things better. If women were kept in purdah, wrapped up in thick black veils, they couldn't go around doing a lot of damage among reluctant strangers. And with belly-dancers you'd know just where you were.

At last they heard West's voice giving a sharp order, and saw the light of a hurricane lamp bobbing over the lawn. Janice caught her breath and her hand went up to her throat, a white V below her black silk robe. West's boots clanged on the stone steps outside.

"Janice!" he called. His voice was like a knife-blade rasping on a brick wall. "Get the permanganate and some hot water. And bandages. Don't come out here."

She put out a hand to steady herself on the back of the sofa. Vachell could see that she was feeling sick. In three strides he was across the room and on the veranda. A native was holding a hurricane lamp above his head and West was bending over a limp brown form on a garden settee. Dark stains covered the front of his shirt. Vachell felt his stomach contract. He leant over the settee and looked down at the red setter. Its mouth was open and its tongue hanging limply out, but life still flickered in the desperate pain-racked eyes. Both the fore-paws had been slashed off clean above the joint, and a thin trickle of blood oozed on to the cushions.

Vachell swore in a low voice, and then saw West's dark line-graven face. The expression made his blood run colder than the sight of the dog's raw bleeding paws, and its look of agonized betrayal.

"By God," West said softly. "I swear to God I'll get the swine for this."

CHAPTER 2: BREAKFAST WAS SERVED ON THE
veranda, with morning sunlight streaming gaily on to a
blue-and-white check tablecloth, and the honeysuckle that
smothered the stone pillars scenting the air. In front of the
house were beds of delphiniums bluer than the sky, set in a
deep green lawn shaded by tall junipers and flowering native
trees. Beyond lay a view that, Vachell reflected, people
might travel across half the world to see if it wasn't in a
British colony, and therefore taken for granted at home and
unknown abroad. A long wide valley carved away the earth
beneath, lakes shone like bits of fallen sky in its hollow
shimmering depths, and, beyond, range upon range of purple mountains rose to meet the bases of cloud mountains piled
in the sky above. The air was clear and cold as iced water,
and the sun had warmth but not savagery in its rays.

But Vachell's first breakfast at the Wests' was not a cheerful meal. The injured setter had not survived the night. A
rug to hide the bloodstains had been thrown over the settee
where he had died. While West and Janice had bandaged the
dog's mutilated legs, Vachell had searched the garden and
paddocks beyond in the half-hearted moonlight, without reward. He had slept a little, Bullseye within reach of his hand,
and searched again at sunrise. But he had found no traces of
the night marauder. The house's surroundings were all under
pasture or light bush. Besides the road going down to the

club and railway station, two wagon trails branched out from the farm buildings, one leading to the cattle dip and the river, the other to the cultivated land. A footpath wound away towards the other side of the farm, taking off from the bottom of the garden.

"Goes to the Munsons'," West told him. "It's only about a mile—our boundaries adjoin. We're getting very suburban here."

They ate, for the most part, in silence. Janice was looking paler than ever; she had hardly slept at all. West's face was grey as that of a sick man. Vachell noticed that the two avoided each other's eyes. They nibbled at their food, but his appetite was not affected and he felt half ashamed to eat so much. The pawpaw was ripe and firm, the scrambled eggs light and full of flavour, the toast crisp and hot. After an excellent meal he lit a cigarette and said:

"Of course, Commander West, this thing has to be looked into. I've a little time in hand, and I'd be glad to take up the investigation myself. I hope you'll allow me to question any of your boys, and generally nose around."

West looked at the table and mumbled: "Of course."

"I'll need your co-operation in another way," Vachell went on. "Naturally I know pretty well what's in your mind. But it doesn't do to jump at conclusions. I'll have to ask you not to go over to see Munson about this. I'll handle that end myself."

West didn't argue. After a pause he said: "I'd better not see him. I wouldn't answer for the consequences if I did."

Janice said quickly: "But you must do something. You can't

leave a maniac like that loose, free—it isn't safe. He—or some one—has gone crazy; next time he might . . ."

"I'll do all I can," Vachell promised. "But I have to get proof."

"Proof!" West snapped, and swore. Then he apologized and left the table, looking distraught. The calf-feeding had yet to be done. It was obvious that he was having to keep a tight hold on himself, and Vachell felt sorry about it. He seemed to be one of those reserved, disciplined men who didn't invite sympathy, but there was something likeable and a little pathetic about him now that he was faced with a situation where direct action couldn't be applied.

Vachell telephoned to the local town and told Prettyman, one of the two white policemen stationed there, to come over with his car. While he was waiting he questioned West's house-servants, but got nothing useful out of them. About the dog they shrugged their shoulders and said: "Perhaps a leopard. They come often to the forest." Leopards, Vachell retorted, didn't sever dogs' legs neatly through the joint; the job had been done with a sharp knife. The boys had strong views on Munson. "A bad European," the head boy observed. "When black men go to his farm he catches them and ties them up to trees with ropes. He eats meat that crawls with maggots, after it has gone bad. He had a case against Bwana Anstey and he promised his herd-boys a cow each if they told the judge what he instructed them to say. In court they did as Bwana Munson had told them, but when they asked for the cows he threatened to beat them. That is very unjust."

Vachell found Janice in a lean-to shed attached to one of the stores, filling the incubator lamps with the kerosene. The incubators were well-worn and rather battered contrivances, of an old and clumsy model. The eggs were spread out neatly in rows, a pencilled cross on each brown shell.

"May I join you in a game of noughts and crosses?" he inquired.

She looked up smiling, her hands glistening with oil, as slender and graceful as a Chinese girl. She was dressed in brown corduroy slacks and a bright orange shirt.

"I see you never raised chickens," she said. "You know eggs have to be turned twice a day, morning and evening. You make a mark to show which side up they are."

He looked down at her and grinned, just for the pleasure of seeing her turning eggs in the incubator shed. What's the use, he thought, when he'd come to say good-bye. But as soon as he began to thank her for the hospitality, she protested and pressed him to stay on until the mystery was solved.

"I guess I sound like a baby afraid of the dark," she added, "but I'm scared. I can't help it after . . . after last night. Couldn't you just stay a few days longer? There's another thing, too—while you're here you can help keep Dennis on ice. I'm so scared of what he might do, alone here with me, thinking of Rhode."

Vachell took a deep breath; he saw the roads of duty and inclination meet. The Wests' farm was a fine lookout post from which to make a closer study of the Munson *ménage*, too. He could spare two days.

"Right now there isn't a thing I'd like better," he said.

"You're very kind. I'll find that maniac for you, Mrs. West, if I have to use black magic and spells."

With an unfamiliar mixture of excitement and misgiving he heard a car in second gear climbing the hill towards the house. It was his, coming over with Prettyman, the young policeman from Karuna, at the wheel.

Although Munson's house was a mile from West's by path, the dirt road went down to the railway station and up again and made the distance eight. On either side were big pastures spattered with remnants of the bush and forest that had once clothed the slopes. There had been rain recently, and grass and brush were a vivid green starred with orange-flowered creepers, clusters of small mauve lantana and, close to the earth, the brilliant blue of hounds-tongue.

"Looks like swell farming country," Vachell remarked.

"First-class, sir," Prettyman agreed. "Blokes like Munson do nicely, thank you, in spite of prices and ticks. All the same, I'm jolly glad I'm not a farmer. Stuck in one place all your life, tied down to a lot of cows. Makes a feller awfully narrow, I always say."

He was a slight, dapper young man with blond hair brushed straight back from a narrow forehead, and a small moustache which he was apt to finger while he spoke. His chief worry was his name, which filled him with deep resentment. Head-quarters believed him to be hard-working when on the job, and new enough not to have lost his ambition.

"You're for the big cities, like Karuna."

"Oh, it's not such a bad little spot, sir. We get a game of rugger every week-end, except in the dry weather. There's quite a decent movie, and nearly always a dance at the Black Buffalo on Saturday night."

"Be careful not to get the rush and bustle of city life into your blood," Vachell advised. "You might get a frontier post next tour."

When they drove up to Munson's place Vachell thought for a moment that they had reached a clump of Indians hops. Straggling, untidy brown hovels were scattered about on the top of a rounded hill, like dog-biscuits upset out of a packet. There was a lawn of sorts, but it was littered with farm implements and gear, and five gaunt-boned oxen were cropping the grass. A little way off a herd of donkeys wandered about nibbling at the unmown grass around some of the huts. Chickens picked their way in and out of buildings, and several natives in patched unwashed shorts were strolling about.

"Well, we missed the circus," Vachell remarked. "Looks like the elephants and tigers have moved on."

Prettyman laughed. "You'll still see plenty of freaks," he said.

He drove up to the only hut which possessed a veranda. Unexpectantly, it had a flagpole in front. It was a tin-roofed cabin made of uncut stone and mud, unplastered. They got out of the car and Prettyman shouted, "Hodi." There was no reply, so they went up the steps on to the veranda and into the living-room beyond. The mud walls were concealed by hanging strips of native rush matting. Otherwise little attempt had been made to make the room look habitable. Roughly carpentered sofas and chairs were covered with skins flung over the ox-hide webbing. Some dirty tea-cups stood on a big bare table in the centre of the room. There was a dry, unpleasant smell of badly cured hides, and another smell that Vachell diagnosed as pure dirt. The whole room looked as if it hadn't been swept in a month. Prettyman remarked: "Careful of the little strangers," and scratched an ankle resentfully.

After a long interval Mrs. Munson came in. Her squat, lumpy figure was dressed in a khaki twill skirt and a bushman's shirt with big bulging pockets. Long strands of hair escaped from the bun into which it was screwed at the back. The idea passed through Vachell's mind that she was wrapped in fat as a dancer might be swathed in shawls. It did not seem to be an integral part of her; there was something essentially jovial about fat, but nothing so easy-going as joviality about the woman who stood in front of him, her feet squarely apart, darting her small eyes from one visitor to the other like a chameleon flicking its long tongue at a couple of flies.

"Good morning," she said abruptly. "What do you want?"

By arrangement, Prettyman answered: "I'd like to see your husband, Mrs. Munson. I'm checking up on any unregistered vagrants, looking for a couple of blokes we want for theft. I'd like to see a list of the boys he's signed on lately.

Mrs. Munson grunted. "You won't find any vagrants here. My husband is always careful to make proper inquiries. Unlike some round here, who'll sign on any native that comes along with a pack of lies and a wheedling manner."

"Well, if you'll tell me where I can find Mr. Munson, I'll go and have a chat with him," Prettyman persisted.

She glanced at an ornate china clock on the mantelpiece,

filmed with dust. "He isn't back to breakfast yet," she said. "He's very busy. Farmers don't sit about twiddling their thumbs at half-past nine in the morning; they're out at work."

"Well, we'll follow his example," Prettyman answered. He led the way out into the sunlight, and asked a native where the bwana was. They found him in a store, mixing a ration for pigs. He was a tall man, broad-shouldered, with a poker-stiff back. His mouth was a thin line across a leathery face, sunburnt to a brick red. He had a big nose and wore a monocle in his left eye. His hair was cropped short and his face was totally devoid of humour. Vachell judged his age to be about forty-five.

He seemed to be on the defensive when he saw Prettyman's uniform, but he was civil enough, and took them over to his office to show them the labour register. His German accent was unmistakable, but his English good. "Strange natives may not roam over my land," he said. "I keep guards to watch my fences. You see I am also raising steers, so I try to make my land clean from measles. You will find that all boys here are signed on according to the law. If you look for vagrants you'd better go to Commander West," he added. "All bad-hats are welcome there. Any one with a black skin, that is a passport."

After they had made a pretence of inspecting the labour register, Vachell extracted an invitation to see the farm. The place had a cheese-paring and ramshackle and yet, at the same time, an organized look. Nothing was tidy, but plenty was going on. He was shown the pedigree bulls—Carnation

Friesians, muscled like Olympian athletes, imported from Seattle—the pure-bred heifers, the Large Whites, the movable calf-rearing pens, the silo pits, the dairy, and a host of other things. Farther on rows of hessian-bottomed trays were spread out in the sun, each tray white with the half-withered flowers of pyrethrum, one of Munson's principal crops. The flowers were dried and ground up to make insecticide powder, Munson said. He took Vachell into the drying-shed, built on the principle of oast-houses used to dry hops in Kent, but square, tall, and made of logs. There were two floors. On the ground floor a number of charcoal braziers gave off heat and thick acrid fumes, and on the first floor a layer of flowers was spread out thinly to dry. The atmosphere was like that of a hot-house, about 90 degrees, and so stifling that Vachell's throat tickled and his eyes ran and he had to come out coughing.

"The air's thicker than a fat girl's ankles," he remarked.

"There is ventilation at the top," Munson explained. "A slit in the roof. A boy once stopped it up with a sack because the rain came through; he was thinking to be clever. Next time he entered the gas made him faint, but he recovered, and now he does not stop up the hole any more. Ha! ha! But the pyrethrum, I have little to do with it myself. I am busy always with the stock. To look after it is the business of my nephew and assistant, Edward Corcoran. To-day he superintends the sowing of some oats."

They walked back through a paddock full of movable hen-houses with covered runs attached, made of wire-netting and canvas washed over with cement.

"The hens, they are for women," Munson observed. "To them goes the greater part of my skim. Mrs. Munson keeps also turkeys of a very good breed. Eggs came first by air from Holland, and then Mrs. Munson successfully hatched."

"That's all right," Vachell said. "I guess I'll skip the turkeys and hens."

"Miss Adams also assists. I see that she is in the mash-room. She will demonstrate to you the hens." Munson, having undertaken to show Vachell around the farm, was going to complete the job. "Miss Adams is governess to my two children," he explained.

Miss Adams was indeed in the mash-room, a dark and smelly shed, mixing a new supply of middlings, maize and bone-meal feed for her charges. Sacks of potatoes and grain lined the walls. Three incubators, some spare braziers and a few empty petrol tins occupied most of the remaining space.

The governess was a tall, long-limbed girl with a thin, pale face and straight, mouse-coloured hair badly cut and innocent of wave. She was not attractive, and her skin was an unhealthy colour, but when she came into the sunlight Vachell noticed that she had interesting eyes. They were light blue, with unusually pale irises, and very restless. He thought that she looked hungry, and wondered how much Munson employees were given to eat. She seemed nervous in front of Munson, and ill at ease with the visitors. She wore a pair of khaki slacks that had been washed into a threadbare faded condition, a yellow sweater darned a good many times, and no hat.

She said her piece about the chickens in a jerky yet monotonous voice, self-consciously, keeping her eyes away from Vachell's face. He felt sorry for her, she was so painfully shy. Directly it was over, she turned her back to attend to an incubator in the corner of the shed. The top had jammed, however, and she couldn't get it open. Vachell stepped quickly forward with an offer of help. It was a home-made contraption; the lid, constructed of boards, had swollen and refused to budge. He dug at it with his pocket-knife and then asked for the big sheath-knife he had seen hanging from Munson's belt. When Munson handed it over he ran his thumb down the cutting edge. It was sharp as a sliver of glass, and so bright it must have been recently cleaned. He prised the lid open and noticed that the eggs inside had crosses on their uppermost sides, and that reminded him again of Janice West.

Outside, in the bright sunlight, he said: "Thanks a lot, Mr. Munson. There's just one more thing. There was a little trouble over at Commander West's place last night— an accident to a dog. The boys thought they saw some one, they don't know who, make a getaway along the path that goes to your farm. I'd like to know if you can account for all of your household around, say, ten o'clock last night."

Munson scowled, and readjusted the monocle in his eye. "What do you think—that one of my household goes at night to cause an accident to West's dogs? What has occurred to the dog?"

"Some one cut its paws off with a knife."

A slight sound, it might have been a stillborn gasp, caught

his ear, but Munson had halted and swung around before he could get it classified in his mind.

"Why do you listen, Miss Adams?" he barked. "What business has this of yours?" The girl was standing in the doorway, her eyes fixed on Munson, a curious expression, half of fear and half enlightenment, on her face. She shook her head. "None—none at all. I—I'm sorry, I didn't mean to hear. I was thinking of the wretched dog."

"Wretched dog," Munson repeated. "You think of West's dog, what of my heifers? Three die of poisoning. Poison plants, the vet says. Where do those plants come from? They do not grow on my farm. They are put there at night, in the paddock by the boundary of West's farm. Why will not the police attend to that? But no, they will come here to tell me that I cut off dog's paws with a knife!"

"I'm asking, not telling," Vachell said. "Where were you at ten o'clock last night?"

"In bed, of course. What do you think? That a farmer stays up to midnight playing beggar-my-neighbour, perhaps?"

"Perhaps," Vachell said equably. He glanced around at the cluster of huts, like a glorified native village, and sighed inaudibly. It was a hopeless proposition. Everybody slept in a separate hut; no one could check another's statement. After bedtime—around 9.30, he found—any one could slip away without being seen. The native boys slept way out at the back, and they wouldn't be worrying, anyway, about the comings and goings of the Europeans. His eyes came back to Munson and he caught the tail end of a wolfish grin on the German's long, rigid face. There was something malignant in that look. He felt vaguely disturbed, as if the light had dulled suddenly with no cloud over the sun. A memory of Mrs. Munson's suety face, with its hard little eyes, increased his disquiet. A pair of trouble-makers right enough. A foreboding came to him that the trouble wouldn't end with the death of a dog.

CHAPTER 3: "You know, sir, I shouldn't take too much notice of all that West says about Munson," Prettyman remarked confidingly on the way back to Karuna in the car. "He's what you might call prejudiced. For one thing, he was a prisoner in the war, and as a result he's convinced every German commits atrocities in his sleep. Of course that's rot. In spite of Hitler and all the rest of it, there are some jolly decent Germans round here. One of them's a damned good full back. I think it's a silly attitude myself."

"Narrow."

"Yes, exactly. And then, of course, there's all this business about West's wife."

Vachell pushed in the electric lighter on the dashboard and held it to the end of his cigarette without comment.

"It must cut both ways having a wife like that," Prettyman went on. "Hell of a good-looker, isn't she? You can't blame half the blokes in the district for wishing they were in West's shoes. Anyway, Munson's a stiff-necked beggar but apparently he's sound at heart underneath; he fell for Mrs. West and got it pretty badly, they say. What I can't understand is what the hell she can see in him. You'd think she'd give him the air as soon as look at him, he's got about as much appeal as a he-goat, and it isn't as if she couldn't have her pick if she wants to play around. There's Norman Parrot, for instance—one of the neighbours. He's a funny sort of bloke in some ways, to meet him you'd think he was a bit half baked, but actually he's very much all there. Well, he'd jump to it if she lifted her little finger, I should say. But there she is, letting this stuck-up bloke Munson show her his compost pits and take her for picnics by the reservoir and all that sort of thing. Women are damned queer, I must say."

Vachell was staring straight ahead at the dusty road and the graceful rounded shoulder of an extinct volcano crater ahead.

"If you want to hear the scandal, ask a policeman," he said.

"We always get it, sooner or later," Prettyman agreed. "Pretty useful sometimes, too. Well, you can't blame West for getting fed up. As a matter of fact I'm surprised myself that he hasn't cut up rough before now. He must know damned well what's going on, and I hear he did turf Munson off his farm once, and tell him he'd knock him to blazes if he—Munson that is—ever came near the place again. But I should have thought he'd do more than that myself. Now I hear Munson has accused West of poisoning some of his cattle. Well, I suppose people do funny things when they're worked up, but I must say it's the last thing I'd have expected of West. It's a bit . . . well, somehow . . ."

"Un-British," Vachell suggested.

"Yes, that's it exactly. After all, an old sea-dog like West. Still, perhaps there's nothing in it. I wouldn't trust Munson an inch, and they say his wife is the worst of the two. She's a dreadful old trout, isn't she, sir?"

Vachell grunted agreement, eyes fixed on the road. His arms were tense on the wheel. He was finding the conversation a bit of a strain.

"I had your report on Munson," he remarked. "I want to find out some more."

Prettyman smoothed his slight blond moustache with a forefinger and nodded sympathetically. "I thought you would, sir. With the situation as it is you must have to keep a pretty close check on Germans and their pals over the Abyssinian border. I bet they'll spring something pretty hot on all of us when the balloon goes up. So I ventured to do a bit of inquiring on my own."

"Fine," Vachell said. "Shoot."

"Apparently there's been quite a row going on in the inner circles of the Nazi Bund. Munson was the local Führer for years, as you know, sir, back in the good old days when pacts were pacts and Papa Hitler didn't give a hoot in hell for his far-away little colonial baby. In those days the Bund consisted of two men and a swastika, more or less, and Munson kept all the records and generally ran the show. But when things began to warm up, and the boys in Berlin sent out a proper home-produced young Nazi, all booted and spurred, to make things hum, naturally Munson wasn't any too pleased."

"We have all that on the file," Vachell pointed out.

"I know sir, I'm just leading up to the point. Well, as you know, this super-Nazi Wendtland duly took over and rushed about the country giving pep-talks to all the Germans and getting them signed up in the Bund. Everything seemed to be going according to plan, but apparently Munson never really learnt to love this bloke Wendtland, and they had a real dust-up about some papers—records and things, I believe—that Munson refused to hand over to the new boss. Not only that, but there's a rumour in Bund circles that Munson has managed to get hold of some dirt on Wendtland—what its nature is I don't know—and that he's trying to use it to get Wendtland unstuck. In fact, there's quite a flap going on about it, I'm told."

"Where do you get all this?" Vachell asked.

"Rather a roundabout way, I'm afraid, sir. The sister of a girl I know teaches in a bush school up beyond Mbale. A lot of Dutch kids go there, and some Germans, including the children of a bloke who's a sort of lieutenant of Wendtland's. The teacher speaks a bit of German and picked the gossip up. I don't suppose it amounts to much, just a sort of internal dogfight in the Bund, unless possibly . . . though I suppose it seems a bit far-fetched . . ."

"Go ahead," Vachell encouraged him. He could see the iron roofs of Karuna glistening on the plain in front, like pools of water lying under a vast cloud-packed sky.

"It's part of my job to issue permits to move cattle," Prettyman said, with apparent irrelevance. "Munson applied for one the other day. He sent Corcoran up to the Western Frontier to buy a batch of native cows, and bring them down. Probably that's all in order, but it struck me as just a little odd. He's never done it before, for one thing—I looked back through the records. He's never gone in for native cattle at all. He's got very high-class stuff, pedigree bulls and so on, and he grades up all the time. Why should he suddenly want to go right back to native stock? And why send Corcoran up there, anyway? There's a couple of breeders in the district he could buy good native cattle from."

Vachell ground his cigarette against the top of the door, to make sure that no spark survived, and flicked it out of the window. "You reckon Munson has a plan to sell out this guy Wendtland to the boys over the border," he remarked thoughtfully.

"It's only an idea, sir. The Bund are working hand in glove with Musso's little gang—we know that—and if Munson could get the Italianos suspicious, he might put a spoke in Wendtland's wheel. It does seem awfully far-fetched, I know, but then Munson's the sort of bloke who'd stick at nothing. And those small cattle-traders up on the Western frontier are obvious go-betweens, always popping over into Abyssinia and back again. I bet that's how communications between Germans and Itos here and Addis Ababa go through."

Vachell nodded. It was a shrewd guess. "Smart work," he said. "It's a thought, anyway. Corcoran's in with Munson, then?"

Prettyman shrugged his shoulders and put on his helmet. They had reached Karuna's one shop-flanked street. "Don't know, sir. He's half Irish. May have spent his early youth slipping bombs into public lavatories and tube stations, for all I know. He's a South African, though. His mother is Munson's sister, I think. I believe he was in the Air Force for a bit at home, before he came out here to be uncle's right-hand man."

"For a peaceful farming district, there seems to be plenty going on around here," Vachell observed.

Prettyman, unconscious of dangerous ground, remarked: "Anyway, sir, you've got a nice snug little billet to conduct operations from."

Vachell spent the rest of the morning in the police station, checking up on all aliens in the district and the arrangements for their disposal in the event of war. He found the young inspector intelligent and reliable, though well aware of his own virtues. At four o'clock he drove out to the Wests with two hulking native policemen, spruce in their uniform of khaki shorts, blue jerseys and puttees, sharing the back of the car with Bullseye. He arrived in time for a late tea on the veranda. His host was out supervising the afternoon separating, and he was left alone with Janice.

The sun was behind the house, and the hills across the great valley below looked quite different. They had gone from blue to purple, and were full of sharp detail unrevealed before.

Janice West showed no traces of the fear that had shaken her composure the night before. It seemed as if sunlight had brought reassurance, and the daily chores of a farm had calmed her nerves. They talked about America, about places they both knew; of her childhood in New York, and the summers she had spent in Canada after her father, a professor of psychology at Columbia, had made enough money out of a lucky venture in amusement parks to retire. He had taken his daughter on a trip around the world, and that was how she had met Dennis West, then in the China Squadron and stationed at Hong Kong. Acting with a decision and speed proper to the Navy, West had gone straight to New York on his first leave, and a month later they were married. Soon afterwards he had retired from the Navy and fulfilled his life's ambition to invest his small capital in a farm. He had first visited Chania when a sub-lieutenant in the East India Squadron, which paid it periodic calls, and had decided then and there to make it his eventual home. The climate was fine. Living was cheap and easy; the country still free from the more rigid fetters of convention, still with a tinge of the frontier about it. They had been happy there, Janice said, building a farm from the foundations and making a home. It had been hard work, full of the disappointments farmers always met with, especially on land untouched before by man; but it had been exciting enough at times, and a satisfactory job to do.

"I used to get homesick at first," she admitted, "but I wouldn't care to go back to the United States now, not to live in a city again. You get to depend on the sun, and the way the natives just sit around. They don't worry about stock market averages and the next war and the budget, and I guess they have the right idea. After a while you stop worrying too. If I ever get a little nostalgic I think about that professor's rats—the ones that went nuts when he made them jump off a plank and bump their noses, after he'd gotten them accustomed to finding the ground give way gently and land them on top of a piece of cheese. Being faced with an insoluble problem, that's what sent them crazy. Well, I guess there are insoluble problems here too, but you don't go crazy trying to figure them out, you just leave them over till next week."

"I've noticed it," Vachell said. "The Government does a swell job on that."

Janice laughed. "If the professor's rats had never jumped at all, they wouldn't have encountered any problem. That's the way the Government figures. The professor used to blow them over the edge with a gust of hot air. There's plenty of hot air around here, at that, but I guess there's no one who can work the bellows."

"You ought to come down to Marula more often," Vachell said, "and brush up your civilization. We have four movies now, a municipal slaughter-house, and the latest thing in high-powered street lights. And a hell of a lot of civic pride. Besides, sometimes there are parties that turn out to be fun."

"Dennis doesn't care a lot for parties. And then it's hard to get away—there's calves to feed, chicks hatching out, milk records, butter-fat tests—you know how it is on a farm. I like it all right, only lately it's been—well, I guess things have gone a bit sour."

Vachell didn't say anything to that. The peace of evening lay over the garden and the vast drowsing valley. The boles of acacia trees were reddish-gold in the slanting light. In spite of all the beauty he could feel the sadness too. A phrase of Prettyman's stung his mind like a persistent mosquito. "What I can't understand is what the hell she can see . . ." That coarse, arrogant bastard. He dodged the thought and focused all his attention on a shining emerald sunbird deftly robbing the flowers of a giant buddleia bush.

A tall figure rounded the corner of the house, walking with long strides. It was Miss Adams. She came up to the veranda and halted awkwardly below them on the deep-green lawn. Her face was a little flushed from the walk and she looked, somehow, less flattened, more three-dimensional, than she had in Munson's presence.

"Hello, Janice. Hope I'm not butting in," she said. "Edward's taken the children up to the top dam in the car, so I took the chance to slip away. I do hope you don't mind." Her voice had a new warmth in it; Vachell was vaguely surprised at the change.

"Of course I don't, Anita. Come right up and have tea. You've met Mr. Vachell?"

The girl muttered something and came on to the veranda, moving jerkily. She did not look at Vachell at all. She sat down and talked to Janice about the Munson children— there were two of them, a boy and a girl—and the rains. He could see that Janice was sorry for her rather uncouth and lonely visitor, but he couldn't imagine they had much in common. He gazed at the deepening view, hardly listening to the talk, until a sudden exclamation from Janice made him look round. She was gazing at Miss Adams as if she had just seen a ghost.

"Anita," she said, "I forgot. Your pigeons. You must tell Mr. Vachell about that." Her voice was urgent and intense.

The unexpected remark clearly disturbed the girl. She looked down at the table and ran her thumb over the cloth.

"I—I hate talking about it," she said.

"I know. I know just how you feel, Anita. But don't you see, it's all linked up with—with what happened to Rhode."

Anita Adams raised her head with a jerk and fixed her pale nervous eyes on Vachell's face. "I came over here to tell you, really," she said. Her sentences were abrupt and unshaded, like ant-hills on a treeless plain. "Only it—it seems such a small thing. And I've tried to forget about it altogether. It makes me feel sick."

"You'd better let me have the story," Vachell said. He tried to sound encouraging and soothing at the same time.

"About a week ago I lost my pigeons," she said baldly. "I mean their heads got bitten off. Clean, right off, like a guillotine."

"That's too bad," Vachell said. "That's the way mongooses act, isn't it, or civets; or any of those wild-cat things."

"Yes, but this wasn't a mongoose or a civet cat. The pigeons live in a coop that's raised off the ground on piles, and there's a big chicken-wire cage all round it. Of course they sleep in the coop, I always shut them in myself, and padlock the door of the pen. Well, some one must have let them out of the coop, because in the morning they were lying on the ground without heads. They couldn't have got out unless some one had opened the door. At least, I don't see how." She came to a full stop and looked at him with a puzzled expression, her light eyes steady, for once, on his face.

"Does any one have a key to the pen, aside from you?"

"Yes, Mrs. Munson. She has all the keys, but she lets me keep a duplicate for the mash-room and for the pigeons."

"None of the natives has a key?"

Anita Adams shook her head.

"And the lock wasn't forced or tampered with?"

"No. Of course I looked for that when I found them."

"Were the torn-off heads lying around inside the pen?"

Anita Adams looked down at the table again and her hand shook as she reached for a cigarette. It was an unpleasant little story, but Vachell wondered why she should be quite so upset. She swallowed twice before answering, and ran her tongue over her lips.

"No. They were found some way off, in the bush, where they'd been thrown. Torn and—" She left the sentence unfinished. Her face was very pale.

It was getting cold on the veranda, but Vachell felt a chill that was not due to the approach of night. Pigeons, heifers, dogs. Work for a psychiatrist, not a policeman. "Do you know of any native who has a special grudge against the Munsons?" he asked.

She gave a short harsh laugh that did nothing to lighten her colourless and uneasy face. "There are plenty of natives with grudges against Karl Munson. They tried to poison him once. But they wouldn't pull heads off pigeons, if that's what you mean. They wouldn't bother about a pigeon—they don't think of birds as valuable things. They'd go for his bulls and cows. Besides, they were *my* pigeons, not his. The hens are Mrs. Munson's, but she let me keep the pigeons. They were all I had."

The remark might have sounded silly, but it didn't. Anita Adams looked so bare of possessions the statement might be almost literally true. Only a girl who had no place else to go would be likely to stay in a job at Munson's place. That was her trouble, Vachell had learnt—no place else to go. Her father had died leaving a farm that fetched little more than enough to pay off the mortgage and Land Bank loan. Her mother had married again, soon after, and gone to South Africa; and the low level of commodity prices had hit the colony so badly that there weren't many people who could afford a European governess, or help, on a farm. She wasn't trained for anything else. Her last job had been with a Government official, but he had moved to the Falkland Islands and she'd been down and out in Marula for some time before she landed the Munson job. The Munsons probably paid her next to nothing, and were always late with that.

Janice West walked with her a little way along the path. Vachell sat alone, watching the dusky blue of night deepen in the valley below, and the lights of Karuna spring up far away. From the native quarters came the soft beat of a drum and the sound of plaintive barbaric chanting that was doubtless a free rendering of a Church of England hymn. Bullseye snored quietly by his side. West came in and sat beside him, puffing at a pipe and filling the air with a pungent flavour.

"Sorry to desert you," he said. "Bit worried about the bull. Had to drench him, and took a blood-slide to be on the safe side. Probably only indigestion, but you never know."

There was a scurrying in the darkness and the setters appeared, panting and waving long feathery tails and effusively greeting their master. Janice followed them up the steps.

"Anita's a pathetic creature," she said, half apologetically, as she sat down. "I guess she gets as much fun out of life as a turnip in a clay field in a wet December. This is about the only place she can escape to, so I haven't the heart to drive her away. But sometimes, I admit it, she's a weight in the middle, like too much suet pudding."

"She lacks sex appeal," Vachell admitted.

"She's got about as much sex appeal as a spike harrow left out in the rain," West remarked irritably. "I wish she wouldn't come over here. You're too good to her, Janice. I'm sorry for her, but I don't want any of that damned Munson lot over here. They'd better keep away. Even poor old Adams, with a face like a horse."

"She has to come up sometimes for air, Dennis. It's not her fault. The children like her, poor little brats. And she just adores them. That's why she stays with the job, I guess."

"She told a queer story," Vachell remarked.

"Yes, it wasn't pleasant," Janice agreed.

West grunted: "If true."

"Lock your door to-night," Vachell advised. "And keep a weapon handy by the bed."

"I'm going to sit up all night," West said. "If anything comes this time, by God I'll plug it as full of holes as a bar of aero-chocolate. Small shot, of course—I won't shoot to kill."

The air was cold on Vachell's face, and he was glad to see, through the open door behind, a house-boy come in with a glowing brand to light the fire. He stared thoughtfully out into the garden, already dimly lit by a vast company of stars. Apprehension had laid its cold fingers on his heart.

"Maybe you'd better hold your fire," he said slowly, "until you're certain that it's somebody you want to hurt."

CHAPTER 4: ONE OF THE POLICE ASKARIS KEPT watch until 2 a.m. in a clump of bush below the garden, where the path from Munson's farm came in, and the other took over until sunrise. Vachell himself slept lightly, with Bullseye by the bedside, and got up at two to see that the watch was changed. But no one came. The askaris spent a cold night wrapped in heavy overcoats and sustained by a thermos of hot tea. They saw nothing, they reported, except two duikers eating the Barberton daisies in the garden.

After breakfast, complete with kippers that came from Scotland wrapped in cellophane, Vachell smoked on the sun-flooded veranda and wondered what to do next. He seemed to have run into a blind alley. Investigations in Africa often did. In Europe or America people were generally at hand to be questioned; whatever a person did, there usually turned out to be a looker-on. But here in Africa life was lived on two levels, with a barrier between the two. Natives might see and hear and register, but to the police be blind and deaf and blank. What white men did was no affair of theirs; what they did was at all times to be hidden from the whites. The only chance was to catch this dog-slashing maniac, this psychopathic pigeon-killer, at the next attempt. He had a hunch that if he stood by and waited, something, soon, would break.

A little before ten o'clock the telephone rang. A house-boy put his head in at the door and announced: "The hole wants you," and disappeared. Vachell heard the excited voice of Prettyman at the other end of the wire.

"Sir, are you there?" the young policeman said. "Something extraordinary's happened. Corcoran—you know, Munson's nephew—has just come in by car. He says Munson's dead."

Vachell whistled into the telephone.

"Killed, or just passed on?"

"I don't know. He was found by a boy in the pyrethrum-drying shed this morning, about eight. Corcoran said there were no marks of foul play. He thinks Munson must have been overcome by fumes from the charcoal braziers and fallen down in a faint, and suffocated. But I thought, after yesterday, you'd want to look into it yourself."

"Sure thing. Did they leave the body out there?"

"At the farm, yes. Corcoran says it was no good getting a doctor, Munson was quite dead. He wants to know what to do."

"Load him into a car and take him back there right away, and bring out the first doctor you can corrale. Warn the doc if he can't certify cause of death he'll have to do an autopsy, and get the inquest arrangements under way. I'm going right over. Meet you there as soon as you can make it."

"Okay, sir," Prettyman said, and rang off. Vachell collected a box of gadgets filled with his detective apparatus, known locally as the abortionist's bag, got into his car, and bounced off over the lawn and down the drive inside three minutes. He made the Munsons' homestead in less than fifteen more.

There was a look of disorganization about the straggling

homestead. No natives were to be seen; probably they had taken cover in their huts, to speculate over maize-meal porridge and cups of black syrup-like tea. Vachell made straight for the living-room. At first he thought it was empty, but then he saw two white-faced, wide-eyed children sitting side by side on the sofa, their looks fastened on his face. The bigger was a boy of about ten, with freckled face and tousled hair; the other was a girl perhaps two years younger, a scrawny creature with cropped hair and a thin angular body.

"Hello there," Vachell said. "Seen your mother anywhere around?"

The boy got to his feet and answered nervously, in a voice so low that Vachell could scarcely hear.

"She's in her bedroom, sir. I'll show you, if you like."

He led the way across the rough half-grassed space that did duty as lawn and yard to a long mud building with four doors in it that Vachell would have taken for a stable. The roof was of corrugated iron, and big rainwater tanks stood at each corner. The boy knocked timidly on the end door on the left. In a moment the top half opened—the doors were in two sections, like those of horse-boxes—and Miss Adams looked out. Her face was paler than ever, and her eyes so faded that they looked almost white. Her hair was untidy and uncombed. When she saw Vachell she managed a smile and said:

"Thank God you've come. Mrs. Munson has had some sort of attack. She seems all right now—you'd better come in. Roy, run along back to your sister, I'll be over in a few minutes." The boy turned obediently and Vachell slid back the wooden slat that fastened the door, and walked in.

He was in a sort of sitting-room, with leopard skin rugs on the floor and many faded photographs on the wall. A mahogany desk of mammoth proportions squatted under the window to his left; it was entirely snowed under beneath a drift of papers. Against the wall to the right was a low couch and on it, covered by some dirty and dog-chewed rugs, lay Mrs. Munson. She was propped up against some cushions, and her black keen eyes were fixed with an undeviating stare on his face.

He drew up a chair, sat on the edge of it and offered his condolences. She inclined her head a little, never relaxing her stare. Then she said so sharply that he almost jumped: "Go back to the children, Anita. They must do their lessons as usual, don't forget that. You want me to tell you how my husband met his death. Why were you here yesterday with that conceited young whippersnapper, pretending to be interested in labour-sheets?" Her voice was sharp-edged with suspicion.

"I just happened to be passing through."

"You were here very quickly to-day." She put a bright check handkerchief to her lips and her eyes left his face and rolled up to the ceiling. Alarmed, he jumped up to hand her a glass of water from a table in the middle of the room; but she recovered, lowered her handkerchief, and nodded towards the chair.

"I can look after myself, thank you. I can tell you very little about Mr. Munson's death. One of the boys found him before breakfast, lying on the floor of the pyrethrum shed. He fetched our assistant, Edward Corcoran, but it was too late. He was dead before they found him in the shed."

"With no marks of violence?"

"Certainly not. There was no question of his being attacked. Edward thinks that he was overcome by fumes from the brazier in the shed. They are certainly strong, especially in the mornings when the doors have not been opened for fourteen hours at least. Personally, I have no doubt how my husband met his death."

Vachell looked his question, watching her face.

"He was poisoned." She was going to say more, but a fit of choking interrupted her. Vachell held the glass for her while she sipped a little water. It looked as though there was something wrong with her heart.

"You've made a serious allegation," he said. "Whom do you suspect?"

"That is for you to find out." She spoke flatly; he could see that her mind was made up.

"I'd like to know your husband's normal routine, if you please, Mrs. Munson. Starting from the time the house-boy called him in the morning."

She looked down at the coverings and said, as if she knew he was wasting his time: "Mr. Munson got up early, of course —we work for our living on this farm, unlike some I could name. He was called about six, or a little before."

"With tea?"

"Yes, with a cup of tea. Then he went out to the farm, generally to see to the milking first of all. Sometimes that was close at hand, at other times he would ride out on a pony to one of the movable bails, perhaps three or four miles away. Then he'd do the calf-feeding and enter up the milk records, and see the separating properly started. On days when they were dipping he would go out to one of the dips, or attend to whatever needed to be done. I can't tell you exactly what he did every day. It depended on what was going on."

"How much time did he give the pyrethrum, usually?"

She looked at him in surprise, and spoke with impatience. "Do you think these sort of questions help you to find out how Mr. Munson died? He didn't have a great deal to do with it. Edward Corcoran is supposed to be in charge of the crops, but you can't stick to hard and fast rules. Sometimes Mr. Munson looked over it to see that everything was all right. You've got to see to things yourself on a farm."

"And he'd come back to breakfast, I suppose?"

"Between nine and ten." She shot him an impatient look. "Why don't you question some of the boys? I can't tell you anything about it."

"I'll get around to that, Mrs. Munson. Did you see your husband this morning, before he went out?"

She looked down at her feet, two hillocks under the dirty plaid rug. Her podgy face was quite expressionless. He wondered if she felt sorrow underneath, or anger, or a sort of amorphous indifference to life.

"No," she replied. "The boy brings my tea at the same time, but Mr. Munson had gone out before I was up."

"Last night, when you saw him last, was he all right—his health normal, and nothing on his mind?"

"He was in perfect health. And if you knew anything about farming, young man, you'd know there's always something on a farmer's mind."

"And you dined alone—you four—you had no visitors or guests?"

For the first time she hesitated, and although her expression did not change he got the impression that the question had annoyed her.

"We had a guest," she said.

"I'd like to have the name."

She raised her black eyes to his face, and this time he had no doubt of her anger.

"Why don't you do your duty? Do you think all these silly questions will do any good? Mr. Munson's body has been taken to his bedroom. I should have thought that even an official of the Chania police would have known enough to have an examination made. But you sit here and badger me with questions. . . ." She closed her eyes and lay back on the cushions, her face a pasty grey.

"I'd still like to know the name of your guest last night, Mrs. Munson."

She moved impatiently on the settee. "A man called Wendtland came to dinner. A compatriot of Mr. Munson's, and an old friend. Now will you go and do your job? You've wasted enough time. . . ."

Vachell rose abruptly and said he wouldn't bother her any more just now. She told him where to find her husband's bedroom, at the other end of the building they were in. Her own bedroom was next door, opening out of the sitting-room where she was lying; then came a bathroom which they shared, and Munson's room beyond that again. "There's a doctor on the road," Vachell told her from the doorway. "I'll send him right into you, Mrs. Munson. He'll be able to fix you up."

Her beady black eyes had followed him to the door. "I don't need a doctor," she snapped. "They're a lot of thieves. I won't have him near me."

He smiled at her as if she had been a wilful, wayward child that had to be coaxed, and quickly shut the door. "Okay, sweetheart," he said into the fresh sun-sparkling air. "He should give you a shot of rat poison. That would be a tonic to you."

He had to walk along outside the building to enter Munson's room. He pushed open the door and went in. There was nobody on guard at the door, or in the room. Anybody would have got in or out, probably unobserved. He sighed, and walked over to the bed that jutted out into the room, its head against the opposite wall.

Munson lay flat on his back on a coarse calico counterpane dyed butcher-blue. His eyes gazed up at the white-washed ceiling in the glassy stare of death. The monocle was not there. His flesh was a colourless grey, and looked spongy as cheese; his mouth was open. He lay in an unnatural position, his legs straight and his arms like poles by his side. In death it was plain what a strongly built man he had been. His shirt had been opened and pulled apart, and a broad hairy stretch of chest showed below. He wore shorts, and nothing else but a pair of shoes made in the shape of moccasins. They were very old; at the toe, the soles had come adrift from the uppers so that they must have flapped when he walked, and one sole had a big hole in the ball of the foot. Vachell put out a hand and touched the dead man's flesh; it was cold as marble. He lifted the forearm by the wrist and found it stiff; rigor was well advanced.

The room had been cleaned and tidied since Munson had slept in it. The bed was made, the early morning tea removed, and the cup, no doubt, washed long ago. He looked around the room carefully from habit rather than from hope. It was cleaner than the rest of the homestead, or what he had seen of it. Munson's wardrobe was much as he had expected: a small supply of shorts and corduroy slacks, two heaps of short-sleeved, much-laundered shirts made of a cheap Japanese cotton material, a couple of flannel suits, and an old, considerably battered dinner-suit. There was a black tin box full of letters, old photograph albums, account books, and flotsam and jetsam of all sorts. Fishing tackle, two rifles and a shotgun leant against the wall, and some well-thumbed books on animal diseases and cattle-rearing lay about. The only pictures on the wall were photographs, two of prize bulls, and the third of an Arab stallion. The whitewashed celotex ceiling was stained yellow in one corner, where water from a leak in the roof had come through. It was a curiously soulless, characterless room.

Vachell paid special attention to the dead man's foot-gear. It stood in a row underneath the home-made hanging-cupboard. Munson was clearly not extravagant as regards his dress. He had one good pair of shoes, moccasin-shaped like those he had worn when he died, but new and recently cleaned; a pair of soft leather mosquito boots reaching to just below the knee; and a pair of leather mules. Wrapped up in newspaper in the bottom of a drawer Vachell found some old cracked evening shoes. There was a pair of gum-boots in the corner, and that was all.

He stepped outside and closed the door; there was no key. The sunlight was deep and reassuring. Trees cast cool black shadows on the coarse grass, but the day was not too hot. Big flat-bottomed clouds were beginning to swell over the hills across the valley. He sighed, and lit a cigarette. He had never struck a case that seemed so barren of clues. There were blank walls everywhere: motives lying around as thick as leaves in fall, opportunities for every one, the room cleaned, the body moved. And, beneath it all, an indefinable feeling of menace, of unexplained queer happenings, perhaps of an evil twisted mind at work under cover, like a maggot underground. He drew at his cigarette and muttered: "Something nasty in the woodshed . . ." and then pulled his thoughts back under control. Most likely it would turn out to be death by misadventure after all.

CHAPTER 5: THE NOISE OF A CAR IN SECOND gear came from beyond the living-room, and Prettyman, wearing uniform, drove up with Corcoran and the doctor beside him. Prettyman had brought two askaris. Vachell posted one by the door of Munson's room and sent the other around to the kitchen to find out anything he could. The doctor went straight in to make his examination.

Edward Corcoran, Vachell estimated, must be about twenty-eight or thirty. He was a nice-looking young man with clean even features and lively brown eyes. His hair was dark and curly and he had a small black moustache. But he spoke with a rather affected Oxford drawl that got into Vachell's hair. It seemed incongruous in a man half Irish, half German. He looked so British that it was hard to realize that he had no English blood, and was colonial bred. Now, however, the excitement and shock had undermined his self-assurance, and he answered questions eagerly, with every appearance of being anxious to help. He was an unexpected type to find at Munson's place, either in the capacity of employee or relation, Vachell thought. It seemed unlikely that farm life would meet all his requirements. It was easy to recognize the roving eye.

He was, Vachell established, employed by his uncle at a nominal salary of ten pounds a month, with the idea that one day he would have a share in the farm. His uncle wouldn't let him have much to do with the stock, but he was in charge of the cultivation side—pyrethrum, corn, oats, alfalfa and one or two other things. Vachell got the impression that Corcoran hadn't liked the arrangement, that he found the livestock the most interesting side.

"Munson was stepping over into your territory, in a sense, when he went into the pyrethrum shed this morning?" Vachell inquired.

"Yes, that's rather odd," Corcoran agreed. "Not that he mightn't have gone in any time, of course. He kept a general eye on things. But he didn't like going into the drying-shed; the pyrethrum gave him a sort of rash. He avoided the stuff whenever he could."

"He didn't say anything to you about checking up on the pyrethrum, then?"

"No, not last night, and I didn't see him this morning— I mean till . . . till I had to go in, and he was lying there, dead. And now you mention it, it *is* funny, because to-day was the day for hand-dressing the pedigree bulls, and he always sees to that himself. Always. It's the first time he's missed since I can remember."

"I guess I'm a city boy after all," Vachell confessed. "Hand-dressing. Could you explain?"

Corcoran looked a shade self-satisfied about his superior knowledge, and ran a hand over his dark curly hair.

"Well, all our cattle go through the dip every seven days. (We use five-day strength.) It's too risky to send valuable bulls through in the ordinary way, they might kick up a fuss and do themselves an injury. So we spray them with dip mixture out of a fruit spray, and then we go over them by hand to see that no ticks escape. You can't trust a native to hand-dress really properly, so Uncle Karl always saw that done himself. It's definitely odd, I must say, his going into the pyrethrum shed to-day. I suppose he just looked in and got overcome by fumes, and that was that."

The young man paused and cleared his throat, clearly anxious to say something more and uncertain how to begin. "By the way, I hope you won't take everything my aunt says too seriously," he began, using a man-to-man tone. "She's convinced that some one poisoned Uncle Karl. That's all rot, you know. She's got a sort of mania about being poisoned ever since they both got dysentery after the only time in history that they kicked over the traces and took a fortnight's holiday at the Coast. She wouldn't believe some native hadn't got at her soup. Uncle Karl's been out here twenty years and nobody ever tried to poison him before."

"Who knew about his getting this pyrethrum rash?" Vachell asked suddenly. "Did every one know?"

Corcoran looked surprised and answered: "I don't know, but I never heard him mention it. He's . . . was . . . one of these tough guys who can't bear to let on if anything's wrong with his health. Even when he had a go of 'flu he pretended he was bright as a daisy. He did tell me about the rash once, though, when he said I was to take over the pyrethrum."

Vachell saw the doctor come out of Munson's room, bag in hand, and walked out to meet him. The doctor shook his head. He was a tall, lanky man with a slouched walk and long, nervous hands. He had a reputation as one of the two best surgeons in Chania, but there might be more doubt as to his skill in diagnosis. He stood under a tree and wiped his spectacles.

"Can't help you much, I'm afraid," he said. "There's no way of establishing cause of death without an autopsy. It's none of the obvious things."

"How long ago did he die?"

The doctor squinted at the sun. "You ought to know how difficult it is to answer that here. Rigor's set in, but isn't complete. Say a couple of hours ago, or perhaps a little more."

Vachell looked at his wrist-watch. It said five to eleven. "That makes time of death around nine o'clock, or maybe half-past eight. He was found at eight o'clock, so that doesn't make sense."

The doctor, Lawson by name, blinked in a puzzled way and looked irritated. "Well, I don't understand that at all," he said. "If he'd been dead for three hours rigor would have been a great deal more advanced."

"You know he was found among a lot of braziers in a drying-shed?"

"No, I didn't," the doctor said. "That would delay rigor, of course. I could tell better if I could see what the atmosphere's like."

Corcoran led the way to the pyrethrum-drying shed. It was a little distance beyond the rest of the farm buildings: a queer-shaped, two-story building made of cut stone, taller than it was long or broad. It was perched up like a square church steeple without the church. A blast of hot air hit their faces as they went in. Sharp acrid fumes made them cough and choke.

"Whew!" the doctor exclaimed. "It's like a furnace. What's the temperature in here?"

"Ought to be kept between 85 and 90 degrees," Corcoran replied. "It varies a little, of course. You see, the braziers are all down here on the ground floor. They burn charcoal. The pyrethrum's spread out on the floor above, only about one flower deep. The heated air rises and dries the flowers, and the whole place is ventilated by those louvres in the roof. It's on the same principle as an oast-house in England, of course."

Vachell examined the building carefully. A ladder led to the second floor and he climbed up it and through a square hole cut in the ceiling boards. He found himself standing among withered white pyrethrum flowers, brittle and half shrivelled with heat. The atmosphere was still stifling, and as soon as he got among the pyrethrum he started to sneeze. Above him were bare timbers and then the unshielded iron of the roof. The ladder was not fixed. He hauled it up, set it against a tie-beam and climbed up to examine the louvres: long slits on each side of the ridge-beam through which air could come and go. By stretching up he could just reach high enough to run his fingers along the corrugated edge. He repeated this all the way along, but he could find no traces of anything recently stuffed into a gap to prevent ventilation of the shed. That was not conclusive, though. He glanced with annoyance at some old sacks thrown into a corner; just the thing for blocking the louvres.

The doctor was standing outside, drawing deep breaths of

air. "Can't stand that Red Sea atmosphere," he remarked. "If Munson'd had a weak heart, a sudden change like this might have brought on an attack. But he hadn't, so far as I know."

"How about time of death?" Vachell asked.

"Of course, this alters things. It makes it impossible to give a close estimate. All I can say is, he's not been dead much longer than four hours, even if he lay some time in this heat, and not less than two."

"That puts it between seven and nine o'clock. Gives us about an hour; we know he was dead by eight. Another thing, doctor. How about the fumes from these charcoal braziers—could they gas a man to death?"

The doctor looked at the braziers doubtfully through the open door. "If you'll tell me the composition of charcoal gas I'll give you a definite answer. I'm afraid you've found a hiatus in my knowledge. If there's enough CO in the fumes—there's certainly some—they could kill a man pretty quickly. And of course he'd be asphyxiated eventually in any case, by the removal of oxygen for combustion of the charcoal and its replacement by CO_2. But the shed would have to be made pretty well air-tight first, and a man couldn't be overcome so suddenly as to be unable to reach the door."

"In other words, you'd have to close up the louvres and lock the door."

"Probably," the doctor agreed. "But I'm not an authority on gases. You'd better get a book on A.R.P. Well, if that's all, I'll be getting along. I'll have some results from the autopsy this afternoon."

"Call up the station," Vachell instructed. "Prettyman will be there."

The doctor nodded and walked back past the cowbyres towards the house. Vachell relocked the door of the shed and slipped the key into his pocket.

"The next thing," he remarked, "is to try to check him into that shed. You didn't see him at all to-day?"

Corcoran shook his head.

"Where were you?"

"We were sowing some late oats. I went out to set the task, to see the boys started, and then on to the pyrethrum."

"How did you go? By automobile?"

"No, Uncle Karl wouldn't have cars used for farm work. I took a pony out. I'd just got back when Jerogi, the head pyrethrum boy, came rushing up and said Uncle Karl was ill— and then I found him in the shed."

Munson, Vachell learnt, had been found face downwards in the centre of the room, limp and sprawling, but not actually touching any of the braziers. It looked as though he had just crumpled up and pitched forward where he stood. Corcoran and Jerogi had carried him out, thinking he had merely fainted; Corcoran said the body was still warm, but then the heat of the drying-shed, about blood-heat, would have kept it so. Only after he had thrown cold water in his uncle's face did he think of feeling for the heart, and then realized that first aid had come too late. The native had run away in a panic and Corcoran had fetched a reluctant Christian head-man to help him carry the body into the house. He had broken the news to Mrs. Munson, and gone straight off to Karuna to notify the police.

Vachell listened with a wrinkled forehead, rubbing the lobe of one ear between finger and thumb, searching in the curiously uninformative information for something to catch hold of. No one seemed to have seen Munson go into the shed. It would be a tedious business, questioning all the farm boys. When they reached the lawn in front of the homestead buildings he remarked: "You had a visitor last night. Naturally you'll understand we have to check on all your uncle's movements in the last few days. What did this guy Wendtland want?"

Corcoran stiffened at once, and his face went blank. Vachell saw the warning signals out.

"Wendtland?" Corcoran said it too casually. "Oh, yes, he was here for dinner. I don't suppose he wanted anything, in particular."

"Just a social call?"

"Yes, of course."

"Did Wendtland often drop in for a meal?"

Corcoran hesitated. "It depends what you mean by often. He did come sometimes."

"When was he last here?"

"Good Lord, I don't know." There was an edge of impatience in his voice. "I don't keep count of these things. It was some time ago. Whatever has that got to do with my uncle's death?"

"I'm asking the questions." Vachell's voice had hardened

and his tone was brusque. "Can you remember the last occasion Wendtland was here?"

"No, I can't." Corcoran's face was flushed and his eyes bright. "And I don't see what it's got to do with you. Can't my uncle have his friends to dinner without having to notify the police?"

"So Wendtland was your uncle's friend. That's interesting, very. It's a shame two such old friends should have to quarrel the night before your uncle died."

The shot in the dark scored a bull. Corcoran's expression changed from anger to alarm. The hostility died out of his eyes and a look that Vachell could only regard as one of pleading took its place.

"They didn't quarrel, really," he said quickly. "It was only a disagreement over a business affair. It wasn't serious at all. Uncle Karl used to be leader of the Bund and Wendtland only wanted him to . . ." Corcoran broke off abruptly and stepped back, suspicion in his eyes. "Who told you they quarrelled? I don't believe you. . . . My God, if you've been trying to trap me, I'll . . ."

He left the end of the sentence unsaid. A car rounded the corner of the living-room suddenly and pulled up with a squeal of brakes. It had been coming too fast, and rocked when it was jerked to a halt. A man Vachell had never seen before was at the wheel. He was bulky and bareheaded with a fair skin and a round, heavy face. When he jumped out of the driver's seat and came towards them Vachell's first impression was that a pink seal was approaching, sleek and buoyant. The man's knees and arms were burnt a brick red.

Vachell looked at Corcoran with raised eyebrows, and the young man glared back with an expression of mingled humour and chagrin.

"Hermann Wendtland," he said.

CHAPTER 6: Wendtland was very polite. He clicked his heels—Vachell wondered whether he wore knee-long, close-fitting boots in order to do this with an air—and bowed and shook hands very formally, smiling broadly at the same time. He had a florid open face, small eyes, and was smoking a small Dutch cigar.

"I am pleased," he said. "But it is not good that I come now, no? Bad news is here."

"You've heard already, then?"

"Yes, captain, the news I in Karuna heard. I go to the town, I take to the shop a part of my plough to make repaired, I am told: 'To-day is bad news. An accident to Mr. Munson has occurred, Mr. Munson is perhaps already dead.' So my car I take, quickly I come to bring Mrs. Munson my sympathy. Mr. and Mrs. Munson, they are very old friends; I grieve with Mrs. Munson, I come to offer my condolences, my help, all I can do." He waved an arm, and his eyes were on Corcoran's face. He had stressed the phrase, "very old friends" so much that Vachell knew they held a message.

"My aunt will be awfully grateful," Corcoran began. "She'll want to see you, I'm sure. May I take you . . ."

"Mrs. Munson is sick and she's not to be disturbed," Vachell said shortly. "I'm sorry, Mr. Wendtland, but you can't see her to-day."

Wendtland's small eyes narrowed and the smile died on

his face. "So! That she is sick is bad. But I think, captain, to see me she will wish. It is good for friends to come when there is grief. I will stay only a few moments, I do . . ."

"Doctor's orders," Vachell snapped. "You can't see Mrs. Munson to-day."

Wendtland pitched his cigar to one side and stepped forward, fists clenched. Vachell was tall, but Wendtland had a two-inch advantage, a chest as thick as a barrel, and round muscular arms.

"You will tell me where is your authority . . ."

"Don't be a fool," Corcoran said. "I'll tell my aunt you came. Everything's all right at present, Wendtland. I can give her a message, if you like."

Wendtland relaxed, and nodded his head. "*Ach*, so. That is best, perhaps. I another day will come. Tell her, please . . ."

Vachell could feel the eyes of both men watching him for a sign. He pulled out his cigarette pack, extracted one slowly, and felt for a match, keeping a poker-player's face. It was Wendtland who decided to take the risk. He gave a stiff little bow, and said.

"*Ich bedaure lebhaft über den Tot von Herr Munson zu hören.*"

There was a slight pause. Vachell did not look up, but felt Corcoran's eyes on his face. Then Corcoran said:

"*Die Angelegenheit ist ganz in Ordnung. Die Witwe hat bekommen die Sache welche Sie zu haben wünschen.*"

There was no pause this time. Wendtland answered quickly: "*Sie muss dieselbe heute bis zum Rechtsanwalt in der*

Stadt bringen. Ich werde den Artikel von dort nehmen. Unter keinen Umständen muss man denselben hier finden."

"Ich werde ihr die Mitteilung erteilen," Corcoran said.

Wendtland clicked his heels again, bowed, and held out his hand. His expression was unquestionably a smirk.

"Good-bye, Herr Captain," he said. "I will not your patient disturb. I rejoice to see the care which to the bereaved is given. Like your so famous London police, the Chania police do not sleep."

"Auf wiedersehen," Vachell said. He was gratified to see a cloud of alarm pass swiftly over Wendtland's face, but he was afraid the accent wouldn't do. That was the only phrase of German he knew. "I have a feeling, Herr Wendtland, that we shall meet again."

"That I hope, Herr Captain." His pink face was wreathed in smiles as he climbed into the driving-seat, and he waved enthusiastically as the car swung out of sight around the living-room hut.

"Taking no risks, I see," Corcoran observed. He was smiling—a pleasant, spontaneous sort of grin. "You had no right to do that, of course. But I can't say I blame you. Wendtland does get one's back up a bit."

"Thanks," Vachell said dryly. Corcoran was right; he had no authority. Mrs. Munson would get the message, whatever it was. He glanced at his wrist-watch and did a mental calculation. Wendtland must have passed the doctor on the road. News had a way of leaking out quickly, but even so it was barely possible that the story of Munson's death should already be current in Karuna. And Wendtland, he recollected, lived at over an hour's journey from the town.

"You called Wendtland from Karuna when you went to notify the police," he observed, more as a statement than a question.

"Preposterous," Corcoran retorted, but without any heat. "Why on earth should I do that?"

"Just to cement a very old friendship."

It took a lot of patient questioning to get Munson's last movements straightened out. His personal boy was a young native called Mwogi with an intelligent face, and teeth filed into needle-points after the custom of his tribe. Vachell felt inclined to trust the boy's word, because when asked why he worked for such a bad master he grinned and replied: "There is so much land that I can keep all my goats here without trouble. Also, I can keep the goats of my sister's son and my father's brother's son's half-brother; and also many cattle die, so that we often get meat."

Mwogi himself had brewed the tea that he had taken to his master. No one else had come near it, or handled the packet at all, he said. The cup, as Vachell expected, had already been washed up and put away. Mrs. Munson issued a pound once every two months, Mwogi explained, for early morning tea; it had to last out the time. The packet was about half full. Vachell took charge of it, and Mwogi remarked:

"The mistress will be very, very angry when she hears that you have taken away her tea."

Munson had woken as usual and poured the tea while

Mwogi drew the curtains and took his master's working-clothes out of a drawer. Vachell was curious about the old shoes on the dead man's feet.

"Bwana wears the same pair every day," the native said. "He uses one pair only until they are dead; then he goes to the Indian and buys more."

"When do you clean them?" Vachell inquired.

"In the evening, when work is over, bwana takes off his shoes. He puts on the slippers, or sometimes, if it is wet, the long boots. Then I clean the shoes of every day and return them to bwana's room, where they are ready for him in the morning."

"And last night—did you return them as usual to his room?

"Yes, of that I am certain; I cannot be mistaken."

"Then why did your bwana put on the very old shoes, the pair that had died, if the new ones of every day were waiting as usual?"

Mwogi shrugged his shoulders.

"I do not know. How am I to know why Europeans behave as they do? But I am certain I put the shoes of every day into his room last night."

Vachell rubbed the lobe of his ear and puzzled a little over the point. It seemed irrelevant, and probably was, but all the same it was odd.

"The good shoes were in his room when you made up the bed this morning?" he persisted.

"Yes, bwana, I saw them on the floor when I entered,

after he had gone to the cows, as if he had thrown them away in anger."

Vachell released his ear-lobe and regarded Mwogi with a new interest.

"Come to the room and show me," he said.

Mwogi at first displayed extreme reluctance to enter the room, although he knew that Munson's body had been taken away. But after a little Vachell coaxed him in. He kept glancing uneasily at the vacant bed, but he put one of the shoes down on its side a few feet from the bed, and the other against the opposite wall. They did, indeed, look as if they might have been hurled away by a man seated on the edge of the bed.

"Perhaps he threw them at the rats," Mwogi suggested. "There are many here."

Vachell examined the shoes carefully, inside and out, but could find nothing wrong. They were roughly made out of thick stiff leather, but they seemed in good shape. Finally he locked them into a box in the car, together with the packet of tea, for closer examination later on.

Munson had gone out to the farm buildings soon after six. He had spoken to the milkers and inspected a cow with mastitis and another with a sore eye. At about half-past six, the boys said—their times were always vague—he had walked on past the bull-pens towards the pyrethrum-drying shed, which was screened from the rest of the farm buildings by scattered olive-trees and some tall bush. A cart track led past the shed door and down a slight hill towards the pyrethrum fields beyond. Munson had walked down this cart track,

and, so far as Vachell could discover, that was the last time
he had been seen alive. He'd said nothing to the boys of his
intentions, save that they were to start to hand-dress the bulls
and he would be back to see that the job was being properly
done.

That left an hour and a half to fill in. He might have gone
straight into the pyrethrum shed and died at once. Or he
might not have entered it at all for another hour. Or, of
course—if it was foul play—he might have died elsewhere and
been taken to the shed afterwards, though for what reason
it was impossible to say.

Prettyman was instructed to go over the shed with a fine-
tooth comb, using a magnifying-glass on the edges of the
louvres to search for traces of anything having been stuffed in
to block the ventilation system.

Vachell went through all the letters and papers he could
find in Munson's room, and the contents of the dead man's
pockets, without discovering anything beyond farm documents—bills, receipts, estimates, circulars—and a few personal letters which seemed of no special interest. A list of
recent cream cheques showed that Munson was dairying on
a big scale; at the present price of butter-fat he must be doing
well. There were plenty of pleas and threats from firms whose
bills he hadn't paid, and one or two lawyers' letters. But he
could find no trace of anything relating to the Nazi Bund,
nor communications of any sort from Munson's fatherland.
Of course, Mrs. Munson had had plenty of time to deal
with those, and he had no right to make a search. He sighed,
and put on one side for further examination the dead man's

passbook, some letters in German from an address in Natal and signed Kate, that he judged must be from Munson's sister, and two notes that looked worthy of closer attention. One would be easy to follow up; it had a date and an address and read:

"DEAR MR. MUNSON,

"I have not received your cheque for what you owe me. Unless I do so within one week I shall go to a solicitor. I do not think you would like to be sued in Court. I shall not hesitate to bring out things you would rather keep quiet for the sake of your Reputation and also the reputation of others who are without Protection as I am.

"Yours faithfully,

"DAISY PARSONS"

It was dated three weeks ago.

The other note bore no date, address or signature. It was scrawled in a large, rather childish hand, on a piece of paper torn out of a cheap note-book, and bore every sign of having been hurriedly written.

"I can't meet you this evening," it ran. "D. is being difficult, I'm afraid he'll suspect. Don't want him upset now. Be at same place to-morrow, same time, will get there if I can. You understand, don't you? It's all so difficult. Love."

Vachell read it with a frown and folded it carefully into his pocket-book. Munson's death, accidental or otherwise, seemed to have been a fine thing from every angle.

Finally, with a good deal of reluctance, Vachell went in search of the two children he had seen, briefly, earlier in the day. He found them in the schoolroom, part of yet another of the dilapidated mud-and-rubble buildings scattered about the homestead without design or plan. This one had a thatched roof. The walls inside were protected by papyrus matting that rustled and crackled faintly all the time, whether from gentle stirrings of the wind blowing in through the open door and windows, or from the seething insect life that doubtless went on in its recesses, it was impossible to say.

Roy and Theodora Munson were sitting at an ink-stained table, one on each side of their teacher, laboriously taking down dictation. Both looked white-faced and disturbed, but they were clean-looking, friendly-seeming children, and Vachell could not help feeling a sense of surprise that the Munsons should have offspring at all—it was illogically unlikely—or that, having them, they should be such nice-mannered kids. For this, he supposed, Miss Adams should be thanked. She rose when he came in, pushing her straight, soft hair behind her ears, and making an effort to smile. Her eyes looked apprehensive in her thin face.

"Mrs. Munson insisted that we should carry on as usual," she said. "It seems ghastly, but it does give us something to do."

Vachell sat down on a spare chair that wobbled dangerously, looked over the dictation, and tried to make the children feel at ease. It was, of course, a hopeless task. He put his questions casually, first about routine. Breakfast, he found, took place in the schoolroom at seven-fifteen; lessons began sharp at eight. Roy and Theo were generally up by six-thirty, and filled in the time before breakfast pottering around the farm buildings and playing games, while Miss Adams was busy with chickens and turkeys. That morning, she told him, she had gone out as usual about half-past six, let the young chicks out of their heated coops into the movable runs, fed them, turned the eggs in the incubators, and filled the drinking-troughs with skim milk. That had taken her till breakfast time. She had eaten, as usual, with the children, and started lessons punctually at eight. She had been in the schoolroom until a boy came to summon her to Mrs. Munson; and then she had heard the news. She remembered seeing Munson in the distance by the cowsheds when she first went out, but not to speak to; and that was all she knew.

Roy Munson suddenly became embarrassed when Vachell asked him how he had spent the pre-breakfast interlude. He wriggled and looked at the table and then at Miss Adams with a mute appeal for help. Beneath his freckles he was pale and his eyes were wide with alarm at the terrors of the morning. He was a well-built, sturdy lad, tall for his age. It seemed more of a mystery than ever that such unprepossessing parents should have given rise to such a promising product.

Miss Adams smiled at him and said: "I don't think you need worry, Roy. Mr. Vachell won't give you away."

With the children she seemed a different person from the defensive, awkward young woman he had seen at the Wests'. Her manner had softened and lost its prickles; the difference was that of a fish swimming in its native pond and a fish gasping on the bank. From their manner it was clear that the children, Roy anyway, liked her in return.

"Well, I was out shooting," Roy said defensively.

"Say, that's something," Vachell remarked, deeply impressed. "What did you use? An air-gun?"

Roy wriggled his shoulders again. "No, bow and arrows, but a proper real one, like the Dorobo have. Only don't tell dad or . . ."

Roy broke off and paused, horror-struck at what he had said. "I mean . . ."

"I won't say a word to any one," Vachell promised. "What kind of game do you go after?"

"Well, only birds so far, pigeons—but when I'm a good enough shot Arawak's promised to make me a bigger one and I can get buck, duikers and bushbuck even, and one day I shall hunt buffaloes. The Dorobo do, you know, or at least they used to. Arawak's father shot lots. So far I haven't hit anything but I've only had it a week, and I can't practise much as they'd take it away from me if they found out."

"This Arawak is a Dorobo mole-catcher who lives on the farm," Miss Adams explained. "He made Roy a bow and arrows just like his own, only smaller. But please don't tell Mrs. Munson or I shall get into awful trouble. She'd be furious if she knew."

Vachell remembered hearing about Dorobo people; they were a small bright-eyed race of hunters who belonged to the forest and lived on honey and game. In the old days they had been adepts at killing elephant and buffalo with poisoned arrows and at trapping smaller beasts in pits. Now the Government had forbidden such pursuits, especially the use of poisoned arrows, and the Dorobo had left the forest, for the most part, to live on farms by catching moles and scaring birds and performing other light tasks.

Roy and Theo had gone in search of pigeons that morning up behind the pyrethrum shed, where juniper and olive-trees stood among the park-like pastures. They were quite certain that they had caught no glimpse of their father, nor of any one else except one or two natives, whom they knew, going down towards the pyrethrum.

Vachell asked them to take him up there, and to show him where they had done their hunting that morning. They started out with enthusiasm, forgetting, with the resilience of childhood, the dreadful, half-comprehended things that had happened that day.

"We'd better take the bow and arrows," Roy suggested with transparent innocence, "if you want to see exactly what we did. I can show you which trees the pigeons we shot at were in."

The weapons were kept concealed in the mash-room behind a bin of kibbled maize.

"Mr. Munson never comes—came in here," Anita Adams explained. "Mrs. Munson does occasionally—she's got a key —but we didn't think she'd be likely to move the bin. It wasn't safe to keep the weapons anywhere in the house." All three had the air of conspirators; the secret drew them to-gether with a bond of enmity against a hostile world. Miss Adams looked into the incubators to see that the lamps were burning properly and Vachell noticed that the surfaces of the eggs were bare of crosses; they had been turned since he had seen them on the previous day.

"I've got to mix some more mash for the chickens," she said. "Roy, you and Theo show him where you went."

Beyond the drying-shed Roy took Vachell over the ground he and his sister had covered early that morning, picking out the trees where he had fired at birds. His bow was long and only slightly bent, and the arrows, instead of being sharp and pointed, had thick ends shaped like trumpets, about two inches across. The bird, if hit, would be knocked off its perch and stunned by a blunt instrument instead of being pierced by a barbed tip. It was a new idea to Vachell, and he asked Roy to give a demonstration. A fat, pink-breasted dove cooing in the branches of an olive-tree was marked down as a quarry, and an elaborate stalk conducted until the hunter was within a few yards of the tree. Then Roy put his blunted arrow to the bow, drew back the string, and let go. He had fired many shots before, and this time the law of averages was ready with a reward. The trumpet-ended arrow caught the bird on its side and knocked it spinning to the ground. Roy dropped the bow with a loud squeal of delight and darted forward with an excitement that no big-game hunter confronted with the corpse of a record lion could exceed.

But the dove was not dead. As soon as he picked it up it started to flap its wings. He swung it by the legs and hit its head against the ground, but without effect; it flapped more than ever in a last effort to escape. Roy seized its head between his first and second fingers and, with an expert jerk, snapped its neck. The jerk was practised, but too strong, for the head parted completely from the body, and the headless dove, hanging from its feet with a bleeding neck, danced convulsively in Roy's hand.

"Gosh," he exclaimed. "Look at it wriggling without a head!" He observed the phenomenon with great attention, oblivious of the blood that was spattering his bare legs. But his sister stared with open mouth and widening eyes, and then turned her back and burst into tears.

"That's the way brothers are," Vachell told her. "Don't pay any attention—he didn't hurt the bird. It didn't feel any pain."

But Theo was not to be comforted so easily. "It's like Miss Adams' pigeons," she sobbed. "I found them with no—no heads on. They had no heads." She went on crying and Vachell, holding on to a damp hand, led her back to the schoolroom as quickly as he could, glad to get out of sight of the dead dove. In some way he could not define the little incident was more horrible than the sight of Munson's dead body on the bed. At any rate, he thought, he'd found out what he wanted to know. Although the children had spent that vital half-hour, six-thirty to seven, within sight of the pyrethrum shed, their attention had been too closely held by other things to observe who had passed—if any one had done so—along the footpath leading from the Wests'.

CHAPTER 7: A STRANGER WAS WAITING AT THE Munson homestead when Vachell returned—a tall young man wearing, for some obscure reason, a very decrepit burberry over his crumpled khaki slacks and shirt, and sucking at an empty pipe. He was sitting on the rail of the living-room veranda, kicking his heels against the uprights and apparently lost in thought. A bare head revealed a thatch of curly fair hair. He had a concave, upturned nose that looked like a button in a broad, good-humoured face. When he became conscious of Vachell's presence he jumped off the rail and came forward with a long, outstretched arm and a friendly grin.

"Hello, hello," he said. "My name's Parrot. The police in possession, I see. Can't find any one else about at all." He waved an arm in a vague all-embracing gesture which made his burberry flap against his knees. "Where is every one— Mrs. Munson, Corcoran, the kids? They haven't got Munson lying in state by any chance, have they?"

"No," Vachell replied. "How did you hear the news?"

"Oh, it's about everywhere, you know—news travels like billy-o in this part of the world. True, false, and wish-fulfilment, all the same. We always hear about the next war a week before it doesn't start. Last week there were a thousand tanks camouflaged as a herd of wilde-beest coming over the Abyssinian border, and the week before all the railway bridges had been blown up by Italian spies disguised as Franciscan missionaries. The boys have practically declared a public holiday on my place, so I came up here to see if there was anything I could do. Neighbourly, you know, and that sort of thing."

"I didn't know the good-neighbour policy operated so well in this neck of the woods," Vachell observed.

Parrot laughed, crinkling up his face in a whole-hearted way. He looked young, but on closer inspection Vachell decided he was older than he looked. There were lines under his round, rather childlike blue eyes. He wore a small moustache, so fair and clipped so short that you overlooked it at first glance.

"There's not much love lost between Munson and the rest of us," he admitted. "But after all, the fellow's dead. I came up to see if there was anything I could do. Sudden deaths are apt to leave things a bit up a gum-tree, if you know what I mean."

"Mrs. Munson's in her room," Vachell observed. "I don't know where Corcoran is. Quite a crowd coming up to pay their respects to the widow. I guess Munson was more popular than he knew."

"Oh, aren't I the first?" Parrot made a grimace of disappointment. "I hoped old Mother Munson might be so softened by the gesture she'd keep her cows to herself in future—they're hers now, presumably. But I suppose Dennis West had the same bright idea."

"No. Wendtland," Vachell said briefly. He was watching Parrot with veiled but keen attention. All Munson's neigh-

bours seemed to have good reason to dislike him, and he wondered a little that one of them should hurry so promptly to
the scene, full of consolation for the widow. Corcoran, after
all, was there to take care of the farm.

"Oh, him." Parrot rubbed the bowl of his pipe with a
thumb and grinned again. Vachell noticed that his hands were
seldom still. "Well, he can stay Mother Munson with
swastikas and comfort her with the sayings of the Führer
better than I can. I'll just go and show my face through the
door and push on, then. What's the idea about Munson, by
the way? Heart attack, or something?"

"There'll be an autopsy. Until then it isn't possible to say.
Do you raise pyrethrum, Mr. Parrot?"

Parrot looked mildly surprised. He gave the impression of
a man who would never be more than mildly moved by any
emotion. "Well, a little, in the early stages—I've just begun.
I'm a new hand at this game, you know—been here less than
a year."

"Do you have a drying-shed?"

"I've just built one, of sorts. Why?"

"There's a possibility Munson was overcome by fumes
from the charcoal brazier. How does that strike you, as a
pyrethrum grower?"

Parrot shook his head. "I haven't enough experience to
give an opinion. Can't say I've felt like passing out myself
yet, but then it's early days to say. Perhaps some one was
plotting against his life and introduced a poison gas into the
shed to mingle with the charcoal fumes. I say, that would be
a neat trick, wouldn't it?"

"Sure," Vachell agreed. Parrot's friendly but facetious manner was getting a little on his nerves. "I guess you've hit on it, Mr. Parrot. Fact is, Munson was a Nazi spy, but he double-crossed his outfit so the Nazis fixed a pipe in the drying-shed and put through a deadly, colourless, odourless gas, hitherto unknown to science. The other end of the pipe comes up at Berchtesgaden."

Parrot nodded gravely. "A device worthy of their devilish ingenuity," he observed. "But you're wrong about the gas. They just got Hitler to talk down the pipe about the will to peace of the German nation and that did the trick."

He dropped his pipe into the pocket of his quite superfluous old burberry, grinned good-bye to Vachell, and strode off, the coat flapping against his legs, towards the Munsons' bedroom.

Vachell felt vaguely unsatisfied about Parrot. He seemed to be an amiable, good-natured sort of Englishman without too many brains, but he was quick-witted enough, and hardly the type to gravitate towards the scene of a sudden death out of morbid curiosity. Still, he might feel that neighbours were neighbours, even if they didn't always get along, and after all it wasn't every day that sudden death overtook a robust farmer next door.

Prettyman had found no sign, however faint, to suggest that the louvres of the drying-shed might have been blocked. They drove back to Karuna together, Prettyman silent for once, finding his audience unsympathetic. His theory was that some one had slipped some poison into Munson's tea. Vachell said shortly it was probably heart-failure, and relapsed into his thoughts. Two points puzzled him most: why Munson had gone into the drying-shed on his morning for grooming prize bulls, and why he had put on his old shoes. He wished, too, that he'd understood what Wendtland had said.

The doctor's report would not be ready until late; so he filled in the time with a visit to Munson's solicitor. He was surprised to learn that Munson had employed a woman, until he learnt that her fees were slightly lower than those of her rival in the town. It was said that Munson brought enough cases, mainly against natives, to keep Mrs. Innocent for the rest of her life—if she had ever got paid. As it was, he paid her just enough to keep her in a state of hope, so that she didn't refuse his work altogether. She was said to be clever, but her brisk manner alarmed the more conservative farmers, so they got their own back by shaking their heads and saying darkly that she sailed a bit too close to the wind.

Clara Innocent's office was in a new stone building over a boot-shop in the main street of the small but active farmers' town. She greeted Vachell cordially, and with undisguised interest; the news of Munson's death had already created a local sensation. She was a plump, active-looking woman with a freckled face, a fuzz of auburn hair and large, broad hands. A pair of horn-rimmed spectacles gave her a look of wisdom which Vachell assumed she cultivated as much as she could, but from the lively expression in her brown eyes and the humorous lines at the corners of a rather large mouth he imagined that her legal studies had not smothered her ability to see a joke. She wore a severely cut grey flannel suit with a white stripe and a crêpe de Chine blouse in apple green.

She got up when Vachell entered and shook hands with a firm grip across a big table covered with documents and a huge typewriter, which took up more than its share of space. He judged her to be a woman of forty to forty-five, good-looking when young, before she let her figure go. She had a hearty, forthright manner that might be disconcerting socially, but made her easy to deal with on strictly business lines.

"Well, is it murder or natural causes, Mr. Vachell?" she asked at once.

Vachell explained that so far he didn't know.

"Our minds are made up here," Clara Innocent continued. "Every one's saying: 'I told you so. It was only a question of time.' They all think some native did him in, of course, and Heaven knows there are plenty with a grievance; I've seen some sent down myself on evidence as phony as a Red Sea mermaid. You'll be wanting to know about his will, I suppose?"

"I've no right to demand the information," Vachell said cautiously. "Of course, if Munson died from natural causes it's no concern of ours. Just the same, if you reckon there'd be no harm in giving me a line on it in confidence, I'd be in your debt."

"Lord, no, I don't mind in the least," Mrs. Innocent said heartily. "As long as you don't let on to Mother Munson; I expect she'll be popping round here any moment now. She disapproves of me, anyway, and after what I've got to tell her I'll be lucky if I come out alive. It's rather interesting about this will. Munson altered it not long ago, and now it's rather a curious document. And it's going to make the old girl hopping mad."

She reached for a folded document on her desk and spread it open. Vachell was surprised to find her making quite such short work of professional etiquette. Then he remembered that most of the police work in Karuna at present went to her rival, who had less experience but was preferred on account of his sex.

"Here it is," Mrs. Innocent added. "The old will left everything to Munson's wife, and after her to their son. That was made just after Roy was born. About six months ago he came in and said he wanted to draw up a new will, but the provisions were to be kept absolutely secret. As you'll see, he left the farm, stock, and all equipment—the whole bag of tricks—to his nephew, Edward Corcoran, until his son Roy comes of age, when he, the son that is, takes over a half share. And there's a proviso that Corcoran can buy Roy out, if he wants to, at a price to be determined by the Land Bank Board."

"That's a hell of a will," Vachell observed. "Where does Mother Munson come in?"

"That's the curious part. She gets no capital or property at all. But Corcoran has to pay her an annual sum, as a first charge on the estate, based on the mean price of butter-fat for the year. If butter-fat is ninety cents a pound or over she gets five hundred a year. If it goes down to seventy-five she only gets three hundred, and if it drops to sixty or under he only has to pay her one hundred a year. It's a fantastic idea and I did my best to dissaude him, but he insisted, and I couldn't refuse pointblank; I don't find anything against it in law."

"He had originality," Vachell said reflectively. "Did Mrs. Munson know about this?"

"Not unless she found out just recently. Mother Munson had him pretty well where she wanted him, you know. She was the stronger character of the two. He was terrified she'd find out about this will, and the very last time I saw him he mentioned it again. 'Don't say a word about it,' he said. 'My life wouldn't be worth living if it got round to a certain quarter—you know.' So I'm pretty sure he never gave it away."

"Any idea why he changed his will?"

Mrs. Innocent smiled and shook her head. "For a lawyer I'm inclined to be indiscreet, I'm afraid. Some of my male colleagues keep up a pretence of guarding secrets only known to themselves, their client, and God. I can't do that, I'm afraid, but I do draw the line somewhere. Frankly, I can make a guess, but that isn't evidence. Anyway, as a policeman, your guess ought to be better than mine."

Vachell read the will through. A small amount of German property was left to a brother in Hamburg, but there were no other minor bequests. Mrs. Innocent and one of the Land Bank directors were appointed trustees. There was no provision at all for Munson's daughter, and nothing beyond a half-share in the farm at the age of twenty-one for his son.

"How much did Corcoran know about this?" he asked.

Mrs. Innocent shrugged her shoulders and looked out of the window at the heavy clouds piling up over the lake. "I haven't any idea. Perhaps nothing at all. Perhaps, on the other hand . . ."

She did not finish the sentence, and Vachell read the will through again. The butter-fat provisions were very shrewd. They adjusted the burden on the farm to its capacity to pay. In good years it would pay the full amount, in bad years much less. If all interest charges and mortgages and loans were on that basis, he thought, modern farming would be another story. It was altogether a fairer deal than squeezing the farmer for a fixed sum to meet interest in years when he received a quarter as much as usual for his output.

He could think of only two reasons for the drastic change in Munson's will: a violent quarrel with his wife, or a very successful piece of blackmail on the part of the new heir.

Mrs. Innocent walked with him down the stairs and shook hands at the door leading into the street. He noticed with appreciation that she had not succumbed to the large woman's tendency to flop; her clothes and her hair were under good discipline.

"You know," she remarked, as a parting shot, "if you want to find out more about the causes that led up to the change in Munson's will, I understand that you're well placed at present for some first-hand research."

Vachell looked away down the broad sun-flooded street and made no reply. The shiny bodies of parked cars reflected the sunrays like mirrors, and the glare made him screw up his eyes. Natives in every variety of costume, from smart young bloods in double-breasted suits and pipe-clayed sun-helmets to bewildered old men in blankets come to see a daughter in the native hospital, ambled up and down the black-paved street. Two people stepped out of the grocer's across the way: a short, dumpy figure in khaki drill, and a taller, more slender attendant, carrying the parcels, in brown corduroys, slacks and a windbreaker jacket. Vachell shook hands and said good-bye quickly, and walked away. A little later he looked back and saw Mrs. Munson and Edward Corcoran disappear into the doorway leading to Mrs. Innocent's office. A solution to the problem of Wendtland's message flashed into his mind. It was a hunch; he had them sometimes, and they were seldom wrong. He pulled at the lobe of one ear and cursed to himself. Mrs. Innocent was a shrewd woman, Wendtland a smart young man. Right, or wrong, there was nothing he could do.

CHAPTER 8: THE AUTOPSY REPORT, WHEN THE doctor brought it round to the police office that evening, was long and technical, but it boiled down to something quite simple: Dr. Lawson had been unable to establish the cause of Munson's death. All the organs, so far as he could see, were in a perfectly healthy state. He had found no sign of disease or inflammation in the region of the heart. The lungs had been subjected to a careful examination, but no damage from toxic gases could be detected. It was true, Dr. Lawson said, that if a person died from excessive concentration of carbon dioxide there need be no specific symptoms, since the cause of death would be simple suffocation; but the state of the lungs did not suggest that suffocation had in fact occurred.

No trace of poison had been found in the alimentary tract, stomach or liver, but the doctor refused to commit himself on the subject of poisoning. The common toxins such as arsenic, strychnine, hydrocyanic acid or compounds of the barbituric group could, he believed, be ruled out, but laboratory tests of a more elaborate nature than he could apply might reveal traces of less obvious poisons, such as members of the alkaloid group. Prettyman, therefore, was dispatched at once for Marula, with a cargo of sealed jars in the back of the car, and instructions to return immediately and check up on Wendtland's movements for the last few days. The Government pathologist promised, on the telephone, to get to work on the specimens first thing next morning.

"About all I can tell you," the doctor said disgustedly, "is that the fellow died from cessation of the action of the heart."

Vachell took the report of the autopsy to read it carefully through. Munson seemed to have been in excellent health. The spleen was enlarged, but that was due, presumably, to malarial infection in the past; in the war he fought in the East African campaign. The report mentioned an old fracture of the knee; two deep lacerations on the right forearm, sealed now with scar tissue, such as might have been caused by the claws of a leopard or lion; a fresh puncture on the instep of the right foot; and a small cut on the chin.

An unsatisfactory report, Vachell thought; until the cause of death was established an investigation was like firing bullets into the dark. And unnecessary, too, very likely; the man might have died of natural causes after all. No one seemed to think so, from Mrs. Munson to the native boys, who—according to the police corporal he had left out at the farm—believed that some disgruntled ex-employee had done the job in revenge. But there was nothing to go on, nothing definite and clear. Prettyman had even drawn a blank in the shed where the body had been found. In his childhood Vachell had believed the truth of a pious saying to the effect that even the longest river flowed somewhere to the sea. Africa had taught him that this conclusion was entirely false. Only the exceptional river, in Africa, flowed as far as the sea; most of them petered out in swamps or sand-banks on the way. It was the same, he reflected, with this Munson tangle. Everything seemed to peter out in a swamp of irrelevance or a sand-bank of blank ignorance and lack of clues.

The Wests' house seemed peaceful and secure, after the

jagged atmosphere of the Munson farm, when he arrived back just after dark. Red setters swarmed over him in ecstasies of welcome, and Bullseye, who had apparently made herself quite at home, almost broke her lower jaw with smiling, and lay on her back and waved her legs in the air. A wood fire was blazing on the big stone hearth and bottles winked invitingly from a sidetable. The Wests greeted him solicitously, and Norman Parrot emerged from the depths of a chair whose sagging springs made it seem even larger than it was. He waved his pipe in a friendly greeting, and subsided again.

"Come and give us the lowdown," he said. "We're discussing Munson, of course. Did one of his Nazi rivals spray the pyrethrum flowers with cyanide gas? Or did Mother Munson let loose a deadly tarantula? Or did Corcoran pay the boys' wages on time, and the poor old boy just pass out from shock? We're all agog to hear the official theory, to be enshrined in the Secretariat files and dispatched to Downing Street for consideration by the assistant deputy Under-Secretary of State, who is unfortunately away visiting the Gonococcus Islands just at present, but will deal with it on his return."

"Don't pay any attention to him," Janice said. The excitement with which Vachell looked at her changed to surprise; there was something different about her face. Her eyes were laughing, almost dancing, to-night. She looked younger, more vivacious, as though a heavy care had released her mind from its oppression. "Now you've come we can talk about something else, so as not to break all those rules you have about not speaking of cases until they're over and no one is interested any more."

"Oh, we don't worry about rules like that in Chania," Parrot said cheerfully. "There was a case the other day when they didn't discover till it was all over that the prisoner's brother-in-law was on the jury. He was the only one who insisted on a guilty verdict, and he talked the others round till he got it, too. I was just saying, my theory is that Munson was done in by one of these native poisons. There's half-a-dozen growing round here that would kill us all in two shakes of a lamb's tail if the cook choose to put a leaf in the salad. The only thing that surprises me is that they haven't done it before."

"Rot, Norman," West said. "Half this native poison business is hot air, in my opinion. Most of them are perfectly ordinary herbs, but by the time some witch-doctor's muttered a lot of spells over them, the natives think they're as deadly as hell."

"You're wrong about that, old boy," Parrot insisted. "If you don't believe me ask neighbour Jolyot Anstey. He's a tremendous dab at them—he's analysed them all and tried them out on frogs and God knows what. The other day we were playing golf at the club and I sliced into a patch of thick stuff at the sixth. There was a sort of bush with a mauve flower there and Anstey said: 'See that bush over there? One leaf chopped up would kill five men.' He said that the Wahuba used it a lot in the old days, and wasn't it tragic how all the old native arts were dying out. I said, yes, we ought to have a stall for native poisoners at the next Arts and Crafts Society Show with demonstrations at eleven and three, and the old boy wasn't at all pleased."

"There you are," West said to Vachell. "We've found your murderer for you. Look for a Wahuba of not less than sixty, who has a down on Munson and a relation who caddies at the club, and you've got your man."

Vachell sipped his drink, leaning against the mantel-piece, his eyes fixed on the crackling logs in the fire. He had to make an effort to keep them away from Janice. She sat in silence, stroking a dog, her face still and yet alive and happy, half shadowed by the soft light. "I'd like to see this Jolyot Anstey," he remarked. "He sounds to be quite a guy."

"He's a priceless old bird," Parrot said. "Used to be a surgeon, one of the Harley Street bigwigs with a knighthood and a good 'Citadel' racket, before he came out here. Now he lives on top of a mountain and broods. He's got a perfectly good, or at least a perfectly cock-eyed, theory about practically everything on earth, from what diseases the inhabitants of Chania died of in ten thousand B.C.—he digs up bones all over his farm—to the causes of rust resistance in wheat in nineteen thirty-nine. Most people think he's a crank, but I must say I rather like the old boy."

"He has a perfectly lovely daughter," Janice said.

Parrot glanced across at her over his glass and Vachell, watching him, was conscious of a look of admiration mixed with a sort of wistfulness in the other man's rather comic, snub-nosed face. Parrot's eyes were round as buttons, and a very bright blue.

"Her neck's too long," he said. "I don't like long necks. They remind me of a tame swan I kept on the Bosphorus— one of the Abbotsbury swans. She came to a very sad end.

I left her shut up in the bedroom of my lodgings one day—I always locked her up when I went away, for fear of Turkish grebes—and she was kidnapped by some cut-rate eiderdown manufacturers from Constantinople. I never heard of her again, and since then I can't stand people who remind me of swans. Besides, I wouldn't like to put our Ted out of the running."

Janice looked across at Vachell and smiled. "Just to bring you up to date on our local gossip, Sir Jolyot Anstey has a beautiful daughter ——"

"So-so," Parrot put in.

"—Daphne, and young Ted Corcoran fell for her in a big way. But Sir Jolyot would break in pieces if he knew his daughter was thinking of marrying into the Munson family, and I guess Karl Munson would have fed Teddy to the hogs if he'd thought the boy's mind was on anything but keeping smut out of the oats and couch out of the pyrethrum. Old Anstey was just rat-poison to him."

"It doesn't sound the sort of love-affair likely to burn up the town," Vachell remarked.

"I wouldn't be too certain," Parrot said. "You never know what may go on over the boundary fence. I've an idea . . ."

"Let's talk about something else," West broke in abruptly; and added in a mumble: "One gets sick of village gossip." He looked ill and nervy, Vachell thought, and the lines in his face seemed to have deepened.

Dinner quite unexpectedly took on a sort of festive nature. West, alone, was abstracted and out of the mood. As the meal went on Vachell got an impression, impossible to analyse or confirm, that some unspoken understanding existed between Norman Parrot and Janice West. They were both gay and full of laughter, as though they shared a common cause for celebration. It made Vachell uneasy; he had struck another current that wasn't on any chart.

Parrot talked, almost continuously, about odd corners of the world in which he claimed to have travelled, and strange experiences he had certainly never had. If he'd been in half the countries he talked about, Vachell reflected sourly, he'd need to be twice the age he looked and even more unsuccessful. No one would move around so much unless they couldn't hold down any job. He said he had been a surveyor, but even that was hardly a good enough excuse. He claimed to have discovered a gold-mine worked by the ancient Persians in Portuguese East Africa and a new species of deep-sea fish in the Antarctic, to have spent six months with an Arab sea-captain who smuggled slaves up the Persian Gulf and an unspecified period in a lamasery in Tibet. By the end of the meal Vachell had put him down as one of the three most prolific liars he had ever met.

CHAPTER 9: A LITTLE BEFORE TEN O'CLOCK
Parrot said good-night and rattled off down the road in an
eight-year-old Model A Ford, the wings fixed on with wire
and with very little body left. West took a lantern and went
out to make a last inspection of the stock, and Vachell could
no longer dodge a duty already too long postponed. It was
obvious that he couldn't go on staying under the Wests' roof
any more. He made his excuses as tactfully as he could.

"I've no right to persuade you," Janice said, "but all the
same I wish you didn't feel the way you do. I'm—well scared,
I guess. It sounds silly, I realize that. I'm worried about
Dennis, too. You know he was a prisoner in the World War,
and he gets terrible nervous attacks sometimes. Lately he's
been worse and now this . . . this accident to Rhode has
shaken him apart. I shouldn't say these things, it's my worry,
not yours. But it helps a lot to have some one to rely on here,
some one you can trust, from outside. . . ."

Vachell experienced a wave of irrational pleasure, accompanied by a dryness in the throat. He cursed himself inwardly
and walked to the door to recover composure.

"It's swell of you to say that, Mrs. West," he said evenly.
"But it isn't true. If I were more reliable maybe I'd be able
to stay."

She took a fresh cigarette out of a box and put it into the
holder without speaking. His hand was shaking a little when
he held the match.

"You see," he went on, "when a guy's working on a case he has to forget he's dealing with human beings. He has to act like a chess-player studying the pieces on the board. He can't decide to capture a knight because he hates the way it moves crabwise, or let a rook go free because he likes to root for rooks. And if he found he had to bring up his pieces to make an attack on the queen . . ." He shrugged his shoulders and left the sentence unfinished.

"It would be a social predicament to be her guest at the time," Janice concluded. "I won't say any more. Go ahead and bring up your pieces." He had killed the laughter in her eyes; they had gone cold. She tilted her head back and drew on her cigarette. Her attitude had changed insensibly; all the hardness had returned.

"I've had a swell visit," Vachell went on, "and now I have to pretend I'm a social columnist. That's no way to act, but I'm in a jam. This district raises fine crops of gossip, and even policemen get a little blown into their long, furry ears." He paused to kick a smouldering log back on to the fire. Janice said:

"I guess it irritates them so they get mad and take it out in beating around the bush. What you want to know is: did Karl Munson make a pass at me and if so what did I do about it, and what attitude did Dennis take up?"

Vachell drew a deep breath and said: "Thanks a lot. You ask all the questions while I sit back and make a note of the replies."

"There isn't much to say." Her voice was without warmth. She spoke a little briskly, as if she were reciting a lesson she had rehearsed before. "Karl Munson was—well, the Victorians had a word for it: he pursued me with his attentions. You saw him—not an attractive man. I was afraid that if I just walked out on him and left him cold it would make him so mad he'd jump the tracks. You know, he was a dangerous man. He hated Dennis anyway, but he didn't do anything about it because of me. I was scared he might let everything go if he got mad with me as well. So I stayed friendly, and all the time I had to stall. It wasn't very amusing, and I can't pretend I don't thank God it's over now."

"Thanks," Vachell said. "Did you often meet him alone, without other folks knowing, and where were meetings like that held?"

Janice smiled, but only with her lips; her eyes had gone hard as stones.

"If I had, I shouldn't tell you," she said. "But I didn't, because I didn't care for Munson and had no wish to see him alone. Do you expect women to give truthful answers to questions like that?"

"No," Vachell said. "No, I'm not that dumb. But I have to ask them, so the Commissioner can read about it and see how hard I work for my pay. Do you happen to know if Munson's wife was wise to the . . ."

West's step sounded on the veranda and he came in, walking heavily, three setters at his heels. He put down the lamp, and its light gleamed blackly on the barrel of a shot-gun that he held in his other hand.

Vachell looked at Janice and saw her dark eyes widen a

little as she caught sight of the gun. She put one hand, small and brown, up to her throat, and there was fear in her look.

"What are you going to do with that gun?" she asked.

"Use it," he said shortly, "if anything comes."

The moon was up behind the forest by the time they went to bed, silvering tree-trunks and grass, making bushes look like silent crouching monsters whispering among themselves. The night was full of subdued soft noises, shaken now and again by the shrill, drawn-out scream of a hyrax from the forest, one of the company of small furry tree-conies that hid from daylight down the snug hollows of trees. There was a sharp bite in the air, and a smell of dew, and a sort of expectancy that made Vachell sleepless and ill at ease.

He stood for a little by the open window, smoking a last cigarette and staring out over the grey lawn into the blackness of bush and valley beyond. A circle of lights, twinkling like stars far below him, marked the outline of Karuna, but nowhere else was there sight or sound of the works of man. The sky was heavy with stars; the hills and plains of Africa lay in unbroken expanse around him. He felt oppressed by the vastness of his surroundings, the weakness of man. His cigarette stub, flicked out of the window, glowed for a moment on the grass and vanished from sight. Restless, somehow apprehensive, he slipped his revolver into a pocket and stepped out on to the lawn, closing the door softly behind him. Bullseye snuffled at the barrier closed in her face and whined once or twice, but then accepted the inevitable and padded back to her basket.

The police askari was again on guard. Vachell exchanged a

few words with him and strolled along the path to Munson's farm. It wound through a big paddock, among scattered native trees whose twisted branches formed curious tortured shapes, and past clumps of bush that were rustling with hidden life. Once Vachell heard the sharp, startled whistle of an invisible reedbuck, and a little later a violent fluttering in the black foliage of a tree. He passed through a creaking home-made gate and out into the unpaddocked land, where the bush was thicker, and the grass knee-high. A little farther on the path dipped suddenly into a steep gully with a trickle of water at the bottom, and Vachell had to use his hands to clamber up among the rocks on the other side. That was the boundary, he supposed, between West's and Munson's land.

The tall pyrethrum shed loomed suddenly in front of him, so unexpectedly that he halted in his tracks and his hand went automatically to his revolver pocket. Then he smiled in the darkness at his own nervousness. He had come upon the shed abruptly around a bend of the path. It stood among the trees, black and faintly menacing, with its curious top-heavy outline. He walked on past it, and other buildings came into view. Indeterminate snuffling sounds, suggestive of cattle, emerged from some of them. The homestead buildings were black, formless shapes around the uneven lawn. In front of the living-room, moonlight fell on to the light roof of a box-body car, making it appear like a giant mushroom. Vachell walked up and peered inside. It was an oldish Plymouth that he did not recognize. The living-room was dark and silent; no one was there.

Light emerged in a thin streak between a gap in the curtains of Mrs. Munson's room, and lay in a narrow pencil over the grass. Vachell, treading noiselessly, reached the open window, and listened with pricked ears. A man was talking rapidly in German. Vachell expelled his breath slowly and cursed to himself. He needed a course at the Berlitz school to handle this case. He raised his head very slowly until his eyes were above the level of the sill. The curtains were flapping slightly in a light breeze, and he could see the whole scene within. Mrs. Munson sat at the table in the centre of the room, knitting something in brown wool. The table was littered with papers that looked as though they had been blown there by a high wind. Opposite sat Wendtland, his hands resting on his thick bare knees, leaning forward in an attitude of tense concentration. His naturally red face was flushed and shining with sweat, and he was talking with intense earnestness—not in anger, but as if he was trying to convince an obstinate listener of something of the first importance. Several times he thumped his knee with a clenched fist, and twice he mentioned Mrs. Innocent's name. Mrs. Munson sat like a basilisk, without replying. Once she shrugged her shoulders and made a brief remark in an indifferent voice.

Unexpectedly, Wendtland flung up his hands in a gesture of finality and rose to his feet. He was facing the window and for a moment his eyes seemed to rest full upon Vachell's. For a split second no one moved. Then Vachell ducked, leapt sideways with a crabwise motion, slid around the angle of the building and waited, flattened against the wall. He heard sounds from the room, footsteps, and something that might have been the curtains being drawn back. Then came a long silence, unbroken in Vachell's ears save for the thumping of his own heart.

He did not know how long he waited, but it seemed an hour. He could hear no sound, now, from the room. Moving cautiously, he edged back around the corner to the window. It was shut, and the curtains closely drawn. There was still no sound from within. He moved on along the back of the building to the other end, past the closed window of Munson's bedroom. As he drew abreast of the window his ears caught a new sound: a sort of scraping, as though something were being dragged across the floor. He froze in his tracks, straining every nerve to catch the sound. It stopped, and through the thin curtains came a faint gleam that moved and then suddenly disappeared.

Vachell let out his breath very slowly and felt a prickling in the small of his back. A flashlight had been switched on and off. There was some one in Munson's room.

He moved silently around the end of the building to the bedroom door, and paused with his fingers on the knob. He had only two hands to open the door, switch on his flashlight and handle the gun. With the gun in his right hand and the flashlight tucked under his right armpit he flung open the door with his left, stepped forward, drew the flashlight from under the armpit with the free hand and slid over the switch. The room sprang harshly into life. The bed had been pulled out from the wall and lay across the room at an angle, and a chair stood on the bed. The beam raked the walls swiftly, lighting up bureau, cupboard, other chairs. The silence was unbroken. There was no one in the room.

The other door, the one that led through a bathroom to Mrs. Munson's room, stared back at Vachell blankly from the wall on his left. The flashlight and the gun monopolized both hands. He tucked the flashlight under his armpit again, strode over to the door and tried to pull it open. Nothing gave; it was locked.

Something warned him of danger, but too late. He heard a sound behind him and at the same instant a violent blow on the point of the elbow crippled his right arm. Gun and flashlight crashed together to the ground. As he flung himself around to grapple, something hard encircled his neck and jerked his head back into his shoulders, and he felt, amid the agony of choking, a hand pressing up his chin. The arm, thrashing wildly, seemed to get entangled with something soft and yielding that felt like cloth. He struggled frantically for breath, his eyes and temples bursting. His knees gave way and he crashed to the ground, feeling hands on his throat. There was a blinding crash, a stab of pain, and then oblivion.

CHAPTER 10: It took some time, after con-
sciousness began to seep back, for Vachell to realize that he
was still alive. He was lying in pitch blackness on a hard floor,
and everything was aching at once—his head, his chest, his
arms. Red-hot needles jabbed him whenever he tried to move.
He sat up gradually, and bumped his head against something
hard and sharp. When he had recovered he stretched out a
hand to investigate. The thing he had bumped against was
smooth and cold. After further investigation he decided that
it was the edge of a bath.

He sat up then, and felt his ribs, arms and neck tentatively.
There seemed to be nothing seriously wrong. A groping hand
came on something familiar on the floor by his side; his own
flashlight. He switched it on, wonderingly. By its side lay the
revolver, within reach of his hand. He gazed at it half com-
prehendingly, and pulled himself up unsteadily by the edge
of the bath. It all seemed screwy, but his mind was too hazy
to think. The tap worked, however, and when he had bathed
his head in cold water and drunk what he could out of a
cupped hand he felt much better. Perhaps, he thought, this
unusually solicitous assailant had not only laid out his flashlight and gun by his side but had dragged him to the bathroom in order that he should come round conveniently close
to the tap.

The door leading to Munson's bedroom was no longer

locked. Vachell pushed his way in, too bruised and sore for caution, and found the switch near the door. Light flooded the room, and once again he found it empty. The bed had been pushed back against the wall, and the chair was once more in its proper place. A tidy-minded burglar, evidently, who liked to put things back as he'd found them.

In one corner of the room a square of the celotex sheeting that formed the ceiling was torn and gaping. It was the corner where, on his previous examination of the room, Vachell had observed a discoloration of the ceiling due to a leak in the roof. The damp had made the sheeting sag, and some one, by the looks of it, had put a fist through, or in some other way had torn a hole. That explained the pulled-out bed, and the chair on top of it. Some one, evidently, had known where to look for what he'd come to find. The space between the celotex and the iron roof was big enough to hold anything from a matchbox to a corpse. Now there was nothing up there but the droppings of rats.

It was painful to stoop, but Vachell managed to examine the room with a fair semblance of thoroughness. He was afraid that the burglar was too tidy-minded to have left any trace. The search of Munson's bedroom was without result. But in the bathroom, lying in shadow under the tub, he was rewarded by a find. A small one, certainly, but a tangible relic of the intruder: part of a pipe-stem, black and well used. The bit had been broken off at the end nearest the bowl. It might have been lying there, of course, for some time, if the boys were careless about the way they swept; it might have nothing to do with the case. Or it might have got caught up somehow in Vachell's clothes as the intruder had dragged his unconscious body through the bathroom door. In that case it was the first and only clue he'd found. With a sigh of hope he wrapped the fragment of vulcanite in his handkerchief and stowed it in a pocket. Funny, Wendtland didn't smoke a pipe—or at least he'd been smoking a small cigar when he'd come to call on Mrs. Munson that morning. Vachell's watch had got broken in his fall and stopped, so he did not know the time.

As he walked across the lawn, moving unsteadily as if he was drunk, he saw that Wendtland's car had gone. The window of Mrs. Munson's room was blank. Everything lay in silence, and the moon was high overhead.

He slept late next morning, and awoke sore, but more or less recovered, although he still had a headache and his bruised temple hurt him badly. As he shaved he observed that his throat, also, was black with bruises, which gave him the depressing appearance of having a dirty neck. A blue-and-white polka-dot handkerchief wound around it like a muffler gave him a rather rakish look. He frowned at his reflection in the glass, wondering which was better, to look as if he didn't wash his neck, or as if he was trying to imitate a tourist imitating a settler from the open spaces. In the end he left the handkerchief on.

He was late for breakfast, and the boy said that West was out on the farm. Janice, also, was nowhere to be seen. The sun was already hot, and the birds accompanied his breakfast with song and the flashing of brilliant wings on the lawn. It was too lovely a morning for even the thought that Janice might be avoiding him, that anyway he ought to leave, to depress him. The incident of the night had put new heart into him. For the first time something definite had happened that didn't melt into a mist of uncertainty and vagueness when you examined it. An undoubted person had hit him on the head with a very tangible blunt instrument, and that was a crime, whether Munson had been murdered or not.

But once again, when he reached the Munson place in his car after breakfast, the line seemed to peter out. He used the insufflator on every likely looking surface he could see in Munson's bedroom, but got no promising results. The surfaces were all rough, and seemed to have been wiped over. Mrs. Munson and Corcoran had gone into Karuna to the inquest, which was being held that morning. It would be purely formal, conducted by the District Commissioner, and there was no need for Vachell to attend. Prettyman would handle the police end of it, and an open verdict was the only possible one that could be returned. The funeral would be held immediately the inquiry closed.

A police corporal had been left at Munson's to make inquiries among the native boys and to keep an eye on the Europeans as well. Vachell found the askari in the kitchen, drinking tea. All had been quiet yesterday afternoon, the native reported. Corcoran and Mrs. Munson had gone away in the car about three o'clock and returned at five. Corcoran had ridden out to the farm on a pony until dark, and later, after supper, he had taken the car and disappeared until late. The corporal did not know the exact time he had returned, but it must have been after midnight.

Another bwana (that must be Wendtland) had come in a car at nine o'clock and stayed until about half-past ten. The corporal had heard the car go, that was how he knew the time. No, he had not seen the bwana leave himself, he was in bed then; he had not received orders to report the movements of people who had come to visit the farm. He had heard no other visitors, or strange noises, witnessed no intruders or unusual incidents, in the night.

Vachell dismissed the corporal in a reflective mood, and then called him back.

"There is a man here who catches moles," he instructed. "A Dorobo whose name is Arawak. I wish to talk with him; see that he is here when I return."

The corporal saluted, and Vachell climbed thoughtfully into his car. There was nothing much to be done until reports came in from the Marula labs and from Prettyman. A feeling of curiosity about Sir Jolyot Anstey, the Harley Street surgeon who had retired to the top of an African mountain to farm and brood, recurred in his mind. Anstey had a grudge against Munson, and a knowledge of native poisons. He was worth a visit, it seemed.

The road to Anstey's farm mounted a series of precipices through dense green forest; the rough surface would clearly become quite impassable in the rains. Few of the tree-stumps had been removed and jagged protrusions struck the underneath of the car with repeated whangs. Somehow the car staggered uphill like a drunken traveller, on second mostly, but sometimes on first. Three stops had to be made to fill the radiator, which boiled protestingly, unused to such ordeals.

Huge rib-trunked cedars rose up into the sky on either side, and lesser trees with graceful foliage stood between. The ground was thickly covered with a deep green waist-high plant, and creepers with brilliant orange flowers entwined themselves among the lower bushes. Here and there, where the road curved, the eye could catch a view of the blue valley below, sun-flooded and immense.

He must have climbed, he reckoned, at least fifteen hundred feet before he came out of the forest and saw the first cultivation, a field of young wheat. Anstey's farm lay on windswept heights above the forest, in the cold open glades. It was a wild piece of country, with a feeling of being on top of the world, of having nothing between the tree-tops and the depths of the sky. He supposed that the altitude must be between eight and nine thousand feet.

The homestead was built of cedar posts with a shingle roof, like a large log cabin; it was strange to a Canadian to encounter such a familiar yet now unaccustomed sight. Near at hand was the usual growth of sheds and shanties run wild, and a number of tractors and farm implements stood scattered around. He passed some rough-coated Hereford steers in a paddock, and a small mill by the side of a swift-running mountain stream.

The door of the house was open, and Vachell walked in. He found himself in a big barn of a room with no ceiling, so that he looked up into a forest of beams. In the centre stood a fine old refectory table of English oak, covered with a welter of papers and books. Copies of *Nature* were stacked high between the *Journal of Experimental Psychology* and

Farming in South Africa. Cases crammed with books lined the walls on either side of the fireplace. The remaining three walls, of bare logs, were incongruously hung with ancestral portraits of the blackest and most varnished kind. Vachell wondered what the Elizabethan gentlefolk in ruffs, doublets and heavy brocade would think of their strange environment, a log cabin on top of an African mountain, and of their descendant, clad in old khaki slacks, stained with tractor grease, who sat at a big roll-top desk in front of a window at one side of the room.

Sir Jolyot Anstey did not look up; but he heard the footstep, and shouted in a high-pitched energetic voice:

"Come in, come in! Who is it and what do you want?"

Vachell took off his hat and gave his name.

"I'm from Marula," he added. "I'd like to talk with you if you can spare a few moments."

Anstey got up abruptly and crossed the room with quick jerky strides. He was a shortish man of slight build, with pink cheeks, very blue eyes, and a shock of thick white hair. Everything about him seemed decisive; there was nothing indeterminate in either his manner or his looks.

"My name is Anstey," he said. "You're welcome to talk to me about anything you like so long as it isn't local politics or farm machinery, because I'm not going to buy any more. Sit down, sit down, and have a cigar. You're not a Labour Inspector, are you—or from the Agricultural Department?" A gleam came into his eye. "Because if you are, I'd like a word with you about your latest so-called rust-resistant wheat."

Vachell felt already a little guilty about belonging to anything so prosaic as the police. He explained his business briefly, whilst Anstey waved him to a chair and took one himself on the other side of the fireplace.

"Certainly I'll help you if I can," he promised, "although I considered Munson to be a despicable creature and a menace to the future of Chania, and I cannot be other than delighted that he is dead. I have reached an age, sir, when I no longer feel it necessary to pretend distress when those whom I consider to be influences for evil in the world are removed. I understand that Munson collapsed in his pyrethrum-drying shed and died immediately. Are you satisfied as to the cause of death?"

"No, that's why I'm here." Vachell explained about the autopsy and the lack of post-mortem symptoms, and added:

"I've heard that you're an authority on native poisons, sir. There's an idea that some native who had it in for Munson —there seem to be plenty around—slipped a shot of some such poison into his early morning tea. Do you know any native poisons a guy could swallow without knowing it, that would kill quickly and be hard to detect after death?"

"I know of six or eight," Anstey replied. "At least three exceedingly deadly poisons grow within ten miles of this house, any one of which would kill a man within twenty-four hours—probably in much less—giving rise to no symptoms likely to be recognizable by any one but a native practitioner, who would be of course familiar with them all."

"Can these be detected in an autopsy?" Vachell persisted.

"That depends, my dear young man, on who conducts it.

They can be, yes, by a skilled pathologist who knows what he is looking for, and how to look for it. But the toxic principle is in most cases chemically unstable, and very hard to trace."

Vachell nodded; Anstey was telling him what he had expected to hear. This was a hell of a case, he thought for the fiftieth time; every step took him deeper into the fog. How could you get anywhere when you couldn't even depend on doctors to tell you the cause of death?

His mind on poisons, he fired a question almost at random. "How about these arrow-poisons the natives used to brew for hunting animals, and for warfare too, I guess?"

"They use them still, extensively," Anstey said. "That is, arrow-poisons are used by most of the tribes that eat meat. I made a special study of them some years ago. The subject is much neglected, but one of great scientific interest. How much do you want to hear? You're young enough to know that you're on dangerous ground. It's much harder to stop an elderly bore than a charging buffalo."

Vachell smiled and lit a cigarette. "I don't know any chemistry to speak of," he said. "I'd just like a kind of concentrated essence of the facts I'd be likely to understand."

Sir Jolyot Anstey leant back in his chair, crossed his knees, and inspected the sole of the very old pair of plaid slippers that clothed his feet. "There are many arrow-poisons," he began, "but by far the most common are those derived from the Acocanthera species. So far as I know there are five common species normally used in East Africa, but in Chania *Acocanthera schimperii* and *Acocanthera longiflora* are the two sources most generally employed. To get the poison you boil down the leaves and bark of the tree in water till you get a black glutinous mass; and there you have your poison. It's the simplest thing in the world. I did it myself, most successfully, in an old petrol tin.

"The toxic principle is ouabain, a cardiac glucoside of the same group as strophanthin and digitalin. When heated with acid it splits up into a sugar and a glucose, a substance closely related to the sex hormones—but I don't suppose you'd be interested in that. According to Raymond, the Government analyst in Tanganyika, who has done some very valuable work on arrow-poisons, about three to five grains of the toxin are normally found in the coating applied to a native arrow-head. Since as little as two milligrams may be a fatal dose, the poison found on a single arrow-head would be capable of killing two hundred and fifty men. The toxin must, of course, be introduced directly into the bloodstream. When taken by the mouth the worst it can do is to induce a mild attack of dysentery. Is that what you wanted to know?"

"That's fine," Vachell said. "How long does it take to kill the victim? And what sort of symptoms does it have?"

"The answer to your first question depends on where the man is hit," Anstey replied. "Introduced near the heart, the poison may kill in as little as two or three minutes; thirty would probably be about the limit. Introduced in an extremity, say the hand or foot, it might take an hour, or at the most two, to kill. I have never heard of its taking longer than that. When it is used for its legitimate purpose of hunting, the natives say that an animal rarely goes more than a hundred yards. As regards your second question, the action of the poison is to paralyse the nerves that control the muscles of the heart. The symptoms are nothing more nor less than a cessation of the action of the heart."

"By God, sir, I believe you've got it!" Vachell exclaimed excitedly, sitting forward in his chair. "That's exactly what the doctor said—you used his very words. How about post-mortem symptoms?"

"As a rule there are virtually none. Ouabain can of course be identified—a test with metadinitrobenzene, for instance, gives a characteristic blue reaction—but only if the test is applied immediately and with great accuracy; in other words, only if you know what you expect to find."

"Say, that fits in from every angle," Vachell said. He was still excited, and crushed his cigarette into a brass tray. "This looks like the first real break I've had."

CHAPTER 11: ANSTEY RAISED HIS BUSHY WHITE brows a little and looked at his visitor in amused surprise. His vivid blue eyes were as bright as those of a squirrel.

"Don't tell me some one's been shooting off poisoned arrows at Munson," he observed.

"It's something a good deal more cagy than that. But thanks to you, sir, I believe we can get the wrappings off. I wonder how—say, what became of the poison you said you prepared? I suppose you threw it out when you'd finished?"

"I used some of it for my frog experiments," Anstey replied, wrinkling his forehead. "I can't remember what happened to the rest. If you like we'll go and see."

He led the way through a door at one end of the long room into what seemed to be a cross between a laboratory, a study, a tool-house and a junk-shop. A long bench covered with bottles in racks and a certain amount of simple laboratory equipment ran the whole length of one wall, and a big paper-littered desk stood beneath a window opposite. Various strange-looking cabinets and contraptions, at whose uses Vachell could scarcely guess, occupied the remaining space. One wall, he observed with mild astonishment, was covered with charts showing the movement of the stars.

Anstey glanced up and saw his visitor's eyes fixed wonderingly on the charts.

"Have you any knowledge of the chemical influence of the

stars on plant growth?" he inquired. "No, perhaps it is hardly a subject likely to be studied by the police. I assure you, though, it's a matter of absorbing interest and vast possibilities —far too vast, in fact, for us to realize at our present stage of intellectual complacency, social chaos and spiritual infancy. (The average native elder, whom we affect to despise as a savage, could teach me a great deal about medicine or agriculture, and you, certainly, a lot about law enforcement and detection of crime.) Are you aware, to begin with, that the chemical composition of various types of star has been determined by spectro-analysis?"

"No, I guess not," Vachell said.

"The spectra of stars in group O and B in the Harvard classification, for instance," Anstey continued, waving in the air a pair of secateurs that he had picked up, "show a preponderance of helium and hydrogen. In type A the helium has disappeared altogether and the metal lines are prominent; by the time you reach type F you find little hydrogen, but a preponderance of calcium; and the spectra of groups B, K and M betray the presence of many metals and of hydrocarbons in various forms. Thus, you see, the light sent out through space from one star is different from that emanating from another; everything depends on the chemistry of the star. Since, as we know, the phenomenon of plant growth is controlled by light, may we not suggest that the *quality* of that light can affect the growth of plants in ways which we do not yet understand? And to go a step further, mightn't we postulate that when stars of a certain type are in the ascendant, let us say those in whose molten mass calcium abounds, then the calcium-influence, as we might term it, will be predominant, and will stimulate some plants and retard others—will even, perhaps, affect the animal life of the planet? Mark my words, young man, one day the true chemical basis of astrology will be revealed."

"I guess you're right, at that," Vachell hazarded.

"It's a most extraordinary thing about this Acocanthera extract," Anstey remarked. "I could have sworn I saw it among these tins here only a few weeks ago. I know I haven't moved it myself."

"Don't you keep this room locked up?"

"Good gracious, no. I dislike locks, just as I dislike firearms; both indicate a distrust of one's fellow men which they then feel impelled to justify. I have never had anything stolen, so far as I am aware."

Vachell smiled and remarked: "If your method worked more often I could put in more time fishing. Dangerous stuff, though, to keep lying about. I guess you made enough to kill an army."

"Probably," Anstey agreed, "provided you had enough arrows."

At last he gave a triumphant grunt and pulled a tin from behind a pile of books on the bench.

"Here it is," he said. "I knew it was here somewhere." He handed it over to Vachell, who looked curiously inside. A black sticky substance, so glutinous as to be almost solid, occupied half the tin.

Anstey rubbed his chin, a puzzled look on his face. "It is a funny thing," he repeated. "I must ask my daughter about it when she gets back—at the moment she's away. She's my farm manager, you know. I'm certain that tin has been moved. I saw it myself over on that shelf about three weeks ago, the day the Wests were here for tea."

Vachell looked up from the tin with a jerk of the head.

"Yes—delightful woman that, delightful. We were talking about this arrow-poison, as a matter of fact, and Mrs. West wanted to see what it looked like, so I fetched the tin. But I'm sure I put it back. However, here it is now."

"And here, with your permission, sir, it stays," Vachell said. "I'm taking charge of this until the local population of thugs and maniacs is materially reduced."

Anstey was standing by the desk, gazing abstractedly out of the window at the rolling glade and forest that stretched away to merge into the blue valley far below. Now his manner underwent a subtle change. He brought his thoughts back from regions of theory and speculation with an obvious jerk, and looked at Vachell as if he were seeing him for the first time.

"You believe that this poison was used to bring about Munson's death?" he asked abruptly, in suddenly crisp tones.

"Maybe—maybe not. I can't tell, yet."

"You are right to be cautious." Anstey searched his visitor's face with his keen eyes, as if uncertain how much he could say. Then he added: "When my boy told me of Munson's death I asked his opinion and he answered: 'God has helped us, because this was a bad man.' I can almost believe he was right. We are told that God moves in a mysterious way to work His will. A student of the Bible, a Fundamentalist, might say that Munson's sins have found him out. Are you certain that you are wise to question the judgment that has come upon him at last? Many innocent people have suffered injustice and ill-treatment at his hands. Must others suffer, after his death—must even his dead body have the power to bring down misery?"

Vachell looked at him curiously, and silence fell on the room. The ex-surgeon's face was ruddy and healthy-looking as a child's, but his eyes shone with some hidden inward fire. A breeze that stole in through the open window rustled the papers on the desk, and Vachell answered:

"You're advising me to let sleeping dogs lie?"

Anstey nodded; his white hair was like a mane. "There are times when that is the wisest thing to do."

"Maybe, Sir Jolyot," Vachell agreed. "But I don't believe these dogs are fast asleep."

He drove down the hill, absorbed in a train of thought, missing several trees by inches and doing no good to the springs of the car. His mind was on Sir Jolyot Anstey, an enigma; a fascinating talker, a brilliant intellect, once a famous surgeon, now an experimental philosopher, perhaps; a man to whom ideas were more real than persons, a mind built of scientific precepts in whose corridors the elusive ghosts of religious belief walked and dwelt.

As soon as he got off Anstey's land he stopped the car on the edge of a glade, jumped out, and took a suitcase out of the back. He extracted a brown paper parcel, sat down with it on the running-board, and untied the string. Behind the car the heavy green shade of the forest ended abruptly; the high noon sun streamed over him, warming his shoulders and his bare head. A scarlet-winged turaco screeched in a falling cadence from the concealment of a tree. Vachell felt the excitement of the hunt as he fumbled at the string. He had a theory, and now he was going to see if it worked.

The parcel fell open and revealed a pair of heavy brown shoes, shaped like Indian moccasins, with thick leather soles. They were Munson's, the ones he had worn on the morning he died. Vachell turned them over and examined both soles with great care, letting the sunlight fall on them and screwing up his eyes in the glare. On the sole of the right shoe he found what he was looking for. Taking a magnifying glass from his pocket he inspected it closely, and then ran his finger along the inside of the shoe. He felt like shouting, but instead he whistled a bar of an old tune, tossed his magnifying glass into the air and caught it, and returned it to a pocket of his coat. A glance at the autopsy report confirmed his theory, which had blossomed, now, like a full-blown rose in his mind.

In the sole of the right shoe was a small hole, almost invisible to the naked eye, where something had been driven through the leather. And the doctor, fortunately thorough, had noted a small, fresh puncture in the sole of Munson's right foot. Now, Vachell thought, things would begin to move. Now he had proof that Munson was murdered, and he knew how the murder had been done.

CHAPTER 12: PRETTYMAN WAS WAITING AT THE Munson farm to report progress. The inquest was over, and an open verdict entered by the District Commissioner; no juries were called to inquests in Chania.

"Well, Munson's underground," Prettyman added. "I left the whole family having a good tuck-in at Grant's café—pork pies and strawberries and cream. Mother Munson's paying. It's created quite a sensation in Karuna already."

"How was the funeral?" Vachell inquired. "Did it draw the town?"

"Not exactly, but about a dozen people turned up, and there was quite a Nazi atmosphere in a small way. Wendtland and a couple of his boy-friends were pall-bearers, all dressed up in their Bund breeches, which are much too baggy round the knees. (They start ballooning too low.) The fourth was Corcoran, of course. He looked a bit down about it all, I thought. I don't think he's altogether happy about being a sort of honorary Nazi, if you ask me."

"I'd like to know where he was last night," Vachell observed.

Prettyman's eyes rested on his chief's bruised temple and gaily decorated neck. He smoothed his moustache with one forefinger and inquired solicitously:

"Did you have a bit of a bust-up, sir? Nothing wrong, I hope?"

Vachell shook his head. "A guy crowned me with a blunt instrument. He was burgling Munson's room."

Prettyman raised his eyebrows and smoothed down his hair. "After Munson's papers, I suppose. I don't understand why Mother Munson and Corcoran are so thick with this Wendtland bloke. Munson loathed him, if my information's correct, and was out to spike his guns. Naturally, Wendtland would try to get hold of whatever dirt it was that Munson had on him as soon as he could, so I suppose he ——"

"Burgled Munson's bedroom and cracked me on the head when I interrupted," Vachell concluded. "That would be a swell idea except that Wendtland and Mother Munson seem to be good friends, so why stage a hush-hush burglary in the dark? Why not just walk in and take over the papers, so long as he knew where they were? There wasn't any need to put me out, either. The papers were Mother Munson's property, the police couldn't take them over, not without breaking fifteen international conventions and scads of laws directly descended from King John. Did you find out what Wendtland did with his time yesterday, by the way?"

"I haven't had time to go out to his farm and check up with his boys, sir, but I've caught him in one lie already. I asked him to give an account of his movements, and he said he was busy on the farm till soon after nine, when he went into Karuna to get a drum of cattle dip and have a part of a plough repaired. He told me that he heard the news about Munson's death in Karuna. That struck me as being unlikely, and it occurred to me, sir, that Corcoran might have phoned him, as soon as he—Corcoran—got to Karuna, and before he came to see me."

Prettyman glanced at Vachell to see if the point had gone home. He hoped that the C.I.D. chief was a man who appreciated initiative in a rising young officer, and would put in a fair report so that credit would be given where credit was due.

"I managed to check this with the exchange before I came out here, sir," he went on. "The supervisor got a move on, for once, and found that a call to Wendtland's house was put through from the public call-box in the post office at approximately nine-forty yesterday morning. Corcoran got to my office at about a quarter to. That just about fits, doesn't it, sir?"

Vachell nodded. "Good work. No way we can be certain the call was Corcoran's, but it looks like it. Then Wendtland hot-footed it out here to see if he could pick up the papers he knew Munson had, but found we'd got here first."

"It begins to look as though Mother Munson and Corcoran were double-crossing Uncle Karl, don't you think, sir?"

"Wendtland gave Corcoran a message in German," Vachell went on, speaking his thoughts aloud, "probably about the papers, and came back here at nine o'clock the same night. Maybe he came to collect the papers then. Well, he wouldn't need to burgle them, if Mother Munson was in on his racket, so that leaves us with X and a broken pipe-stem. . . ."

A native came up with a note held in an extended hand. He wore a white house-boys' kanzu, and Vachell recognized Mwogi, Munson's personal boy.

"This letter has come to you from Bwana West's," he said.

Vachell tore it open with a slight contraction in the chest and a quickening of the pulse. There were only two lines, in a sloping, sprawling hand. "This came for you by to-day's post," it ran. "Hope it will catch you at Munson's. We expect you back to-night."

A typewritten envelope of a cheap brand, bearing a local postmark, was enclosed. Inside was a piece of common ruled note-paper with a few typed lines. It ran:

"If you want to know the murderer of Karl Munson, find out who he was going to meet in the pyrethrum shed, and ask Dr. Lawson who went to him last month and what he prescribed."

Prettyman read it through twice, his lips pursed in a whistle. "By God, sir, this is interesting," he exclaimed. "You know, that's just what I've been thinking: if we could only find out what made Munson go into that drying-shed I believe we'd get at the truth. I've been thinking about that ever since yesterday morning. It seems to me there's only one thing likely to have taken Munson there."

The young policeman paused dramatically, hoping for an eager prompt. But his superior did not even glance up. He was unfolding a second note that he had taken from his pocket.

"Only one thing," Prettyman repeated, raising his voice a little. "And that is—an appointment with some one he very much wanted to see—secretly. A lady, in fact."

Again he paused, but again no encouragement came. The superintendent was staring intently at the two notes, one in each hand, comparing the writing.

"Don't you agree, sir?" Prettyman said desperately. "We know which lady he was interested in. And the pyrethrum shed is right on the path that leads to their farm. Supposing, now, Mrs. West had made an appointment to meet him there, not meaning to keep it, of course, but knowing that if she didn't turn up he'd wait for her until the fumes of the charcoal braziers took effect and he died. . . ."

At last his chief seemed to take in what he had been saying. Vachell looked up, and a grin spread across his face. "Keep going, and you'll finish up in the Big Four," he said. "You got an idea there. Take a look at these two chits, will you?"

Prettyman took them in his hand and examined them carefully. One was Janice West's covering letter; the other the unsigned note Vachell had found among the loose papers in Munson's room.

"D. is being difficult," he read aloud. "I'm afraid he'll suspect. Don't want him upset now. Be at same place tomorrow, same time, will get there if I can. You understand, don't you? It's all so difficult. Love."

"Would you say they were written by the same hand?" Vachell asked.

"Definitely not. They're absolutely different. I don't think one could possibly be the other in disguise. You mean . . . this looks as though Munson had some other woman in tow?"

"I don't reckon Munson had any woman in tow," Vachell said. "There's things to be done in Karuna. Come on, let's go."

Prettyman followed behind, feeling resentful. These blokes from headquarters are always as stuck-up as hell, he thought; they don't believe any one else is capable of having ideas. But the handwriting on the note Vachell had found seemed, somehow, familiar. He was certain he had seen it before. The problem buzzed in his head, troublesome as a mosquito, while Vachell gave instructions to the corporal and questioned Mwogi further about Munson's boots. As they reached the cars he swallowed his resentment and said:

"That handwriting in the note you found among Munson's things, sir—I'm sure I've seen it before, and in the last month or so, too. I have an idea it's at the station, in a letter some one wrote about a complaint. In that case I'll be able to find it on the files."

"Fine. Check it when you get back," Vachell said. "Want to make a bet?"

Prettyman looked doubtful. "Not if you know the answer already, sir."

Vachell tore a leaf out of his note-book and scribbled two words. He folded the paper twice and handed it over to his assistant.

"A bottle of Scotch if I'm wrong," he said.

"What—you give me?"

"Sure."

"Done," Prettyman said. "If I may say so, sir, you're giving a neat performance this morning of the Master Mind."

"It all comes from the stars," Vachell explained. "They send down mineral emanations—strictly according to the Harvard classification, of course."

Prettyman looked at him pityingly, and not without a trace of alarm. He hoped, as he got into his car, that the crack on the head had not affected the C.I.D. chief's mind.

Vachell spent the afternoon in the distasteful job of writing a report. It was waste of time, but in accordance with the first principle of colonial government: that at all costs the yawning maw of the registry, the gaping mouths of files, must be fed. The Commissioner, Major Armitage, was a great report reader, and if a particular sample didn't come up to standard his choleric temper was apt to erupt. Vachell appended a request for a résumé of all information in the hands of the police about the Nazi Bund, including an outline of their last plan, so far as it was known, for organized sabotage in the event of war.

At four o'clock he rang up the Marula labs. The Government analyst reported that he had been working on the specimens all day, but had found no traces of any of the recognized toxins or irritants in the stomach, liver, spleen or intestines. "Of course, you realize that this is a long job," the analyst said. "And, frankly, there are certain tests too delicate to be applied with the apparatus I've got here. Besides, there's the rapid rate of deterioration found in the tropics to be taken into account."

"Okay," Vachell said. "Make the analysis as thorough as you can. There may be a question of eliminating all possibilities but one in court."

In the rush of events the mystery of the maniac who had killed Dennis West's dog and Miss Adams' pigeons had receded into the background; but it was unwise, Vachell reflected, to let it recede too far. Munson's murder—if murder it was, and the arrow-poison theory was right—might or might not be connected with internecine warfare in the Nazi Bund; in the meantime, so far as was known, a dangerous maniac with some kind of pathological blood-cravings was still at large. So far birds and dogs had supplied the blood. It might be humans next time.

What was wanted, Vachell decided, as he rattled along the dusty road to the Wests' in his car, was a psychiatrist's advice. Most likely an expert in abnormal psychology could dope it all out after five minutes' conversation with the person whose twisted mind drove him to this midnight prowling with a knife. There would certainly be some psychological explanation of the whole thing. The trouble was that no expert in abnormal psychology lived in Chania, so far as he knew, unless Sir Jolyot Anstey included an acquaintance with psychiatry in his store of esoteric knowledge. But somehow he did not feel like consulting Anstey about it. A man who saw in murder a manifestation of the judgment of God was hardly dependable from the standpoint of the police.

It was because of the maniac that Vachell was going back to the Wests' farm. He knew that he ought to leave, to have left already in fact; but he had a feeling that there was more to come. For some reason the Wests' place seemed to be the centre of the maniac's orbit. He or she—it—had been around there twice at least: when the dog Rhode was attacked, and before that, when Janice's delphiniums had been senselessly, maliciously destroyed. It might come there again. And Janice West had asked for protection. A couple of native askaris were insufficient to provide that. Besides, at the Wests' he could keep right in the centre of things. He could reach the Munsons' on foot in fifteen minutes, and without advertising his arrival, as he couldn't fail to do whenever he went there in a car.

There were plenty of good excuses, he thought ruefully, as his car bumped over the Wests' lawn, for staying on where he had no right to be.

CHAPTER 13: ALL THROUGH THE EVENING

Janice West was affable and polite, but some elusive change in her manner made Vachell feel shut out and lonely, ill at ease. She had trusted him before—in subtle ways she had shown that she thought him her friend. Now the trust was gone, and a blank wall stood in his path.

There was nothing he could do. He fell back on an impersonal manner, too; a police superintendent spending the evening with strangers on the road. He talked about some of his cases, they discussed local politics and the increase in native crime, and listened to the news on the Empire broadcast.

The news was depressing, too. West puffed at his pipe and said little. He looked harassed and rather ill. One of his cows had slipped a calf; he was afraid an epidemic of contagious abortion might be on the way. The only one of the party who seemed to feel entirely at home was Bullseye. She had settled down on excellent terms with the setters, and spent the evening curled up at Vachell's feet in front of the fire.

Her master took her for a bedtime walk over the misty lawn, and let her bark fiercely at the deep shadows of trees and bush which began where the garden ended. The moon was rising, low over the forest, and black formless clouds drifted across the sky. A rustle in the bush beyond the split-bamboo fence that bounded the garden made Vachell strain his eyes. He saw nothing, but diagnosed a duiker disturbed in its evening meal. From the forest behind the house a hyrax screamed suddenly, and the noise subsided into a long-drawn mixture of rattle and croak. The valley below was like a vast black chasm, and in it, as the cloud passed over, gleamed the silver-white of water lit up by the moon.

The askari on guard was leaning against a tree at the bottom of the garden. He stood to attention and reported that no one had passed that way along the path leading to Munson's farm.

It was half-past ten when Vachell got back to his room. He drew the curtains to let in the moonlight, and opened the windows wide. A smell of honeysuckle drifted in. The lawn lay white outside, and peaceful. The small grey figure of a duiker picked its way across. Beyond lay the bush, a dense black cloak that hid a predatory world of bloodshed and cruelty, a sleepless world where eternal vigilance was the price of life. After a little he picked a light novel from his dressing-table and read himself to sleep.

He awoke, it seemed, an instant later. There had been some sound, and Bullseye heard it too. She barked sharply and ran whining to the door. There was a moment of deep silence and then everything seemed to happen at once. A shout sounded from the garden, a shot cracked through the air and Bullseye sprang like a steeplechaser out of the open window and raced, a white streak, across the lawn. Vachell leapt out of bed, seized his police revolver from the table, rammed his feet into a pair of shoes and followed. There was nothing to be seen. He sprinted after Bullseye and when he reached the bottom of the lawn he saw a movement in the bushes. A moment later the askari, panting loudly appeared.

"There was a thing . . ." he gasped, his voice hoarse; and then stopped abruptly.

Away to the right, in a patch of bush, came a sudden bark and then a sharp yelp of fright. The yelp turned into a sort of shriek and then died away in a whine of pain. Vachell plunged off towards it, forcing his way through the bush, whistling and calling to Bullseye all the time. He tried to keep the direction but knew it was hopeless unless the dog could answer. No more sounds came, and when he got to the place where he thought the yelp must have originated he stood still and called. His voice sounded empty and futile in the vast darkness. The moon was hidden by clouds, and the disturbance had silenced all the normal noises of the night.

Then he heard a rustle in the bushes to the left, and a white figure came crawling low on the ground. He knelt down and stretched out his hands, and felt something warm and sticky. There was enough light to see that the dog had a bleeding cut across the face, and that an ear was nearly severed from the head. Vachell swore softly. The askari, who had followed behind, gave an exclamation of horror.

"It was the thing that struck him!" he exclaimed. "The thing that ran away!" The native was still panting from his chase.

"Give me the story," Vachell said.

"I was patrolling as you had told me," he began. "I had reached to over there beyond the bwana's house, near the cow-houses. I heard a noise like a chicken crying. I went towards it and then I saw a thing in front of me, a bad thing, bwana, I do not know its name. It was crouching down on the ground like this." The askari bent double and moved a few paces in a crouch, like a baboon. His voice was uneven, the whites of his eyes showing from fear. "It walked so that I did not know if it was a hyena or a monkey, or a madman. And then it jumped."

"It came from where?"

"I do not know. It came from near the cow-houses, but suddenly I saw it there, like a hyena, like a spirit! Then it sprang to one side and ran towards the house. I shouted, "Stand, stand!" but it ran and I followed. But it ran upright, bwana, like a man. When it got near to the house it swerved over the grass and then into the bushes beyond the flowers. There was something shining in its hand. I could see that it would escape so I fired, as you told me, bwana, at its legs. But it jumped the fence, like an antelope, and my bullet went beneath. I came to the fence a moment later, I was close behind, but it had vanished completely. It had gone.

The askari looked nervously around as though expecting to see the nameless thing crouching in the shadow of a bush.

"Bwana, it was something very bad," he added.

"What kind of a thing was it?" Vachell asked. "Was it large or small?"

The askari shook his head. "Bwana, I could not see well, the moon was hidden and the night was dark. It ran like a man, yet what man walks doubled up like a hyena? It was a short thing, not tall, short like a spirit. But the walk, that was like a frog. I think it was a spirit, bwana, an evil spirit sent to bring great harm."

"Spirits do not strike dogs with knives," Vachell said. Bullseye was whimpering softly at his feet, stiff with fright and pain. Vachell lifted her gently and carried her back over the low fence and across the lawn. The fence would be an easy jump for a running person. And there had been no rain; the ground was hard and dry. No chance of footprints on the lawn.

There was a light on the veranda and both the Wests were there. The Commander was fully dressed, in slacks and an old tweed coat, and breathing heavily. Janice had thrown her black silk dressing-gown over red pyjamas, and her eyes were wide with fear. In the lamplight her face looked white as a magnolia flower, and her rumpled hair was a dark halo. She was shivering slightly, with her arms crossed over her chest and her hands tucked under the sleeves of her dressing-gown.

"What's happened?" West asked. His voice was sharp and harsh, the gun was in his hand. Then he caught sight of Bullseye and exclaimed: "Good God, another one! Is she alive? You'll want permanganate and hot water. Did you get him? What was the shot?"

"Yes. No. The askari fired at something but it got away."

"Something? What?"

"I don't know."

The lights went on in the sitting-room and a house-boy

appeared, his eyes blurry with sleep. West told him to bring hot water and permanganate of potash at once.

"Where were you when you heard the shot?" Vachell asked.

"In here."

"The sitting-room? You didn't go to bed?"

West shook his head.

"One of my new Friesian heifers was going to calve. She's almost pure-bred, and this is her first calf, so I thought I'd see her through. After you and Janice went off I read for a bit and went out soon after eleven to see if she'd begun. She hadn't, so I came back here. I'd been reading for about twenty minutes when I heard the shot. I dashed out, but I saw you just ahead, so I left you to it and went to see if Janice was all right. It was a bit of a shock, I can tell you. We don't often get midnight man-hunts on a quiet dairy farm."

Somehow the last sentence seemed to strike a false note. West looked ghastly: it was not the moment Vachell would have expected even a feeble effort at the facetious. Bullseye lay shivering violently on the couch, still bleeding a little. Janice was sitting on a chair with her eyes on her husband's face, her legs crossed, and her hands clasped in her lap. She had gone over to look at Bullseye when Vachell first brought the dog in, but now she sat away from him, averting her eyes, as though she was going to be sick. She had blood on her hands.

"You found Mrs. West in her room?" Vachell asked.

"Of course," West answered shortly.

"I was in bed when I heard the shot," Janice said quickly.

"I saw some one running down by the fence out of the window, and a few moments later Dennis rushed in. Then we came across here to see if the dogs were all right."

"You came direct from your bedroom to this veranda?" Vachell asked.

"Yes."

"Give me your right slipper, please."

She looked at him as though he had gone crazy. He repeated the sentence; his voice was expressionless and hard. West made an uneasy movement by the door.

Without answering she pulled off the mule and handed it over, her eyes on his face. He put his palm over the sole for a moment and handed it back. There was fresh mud on it, packed under the heel, and the sole was wet. He said nothing at all. A covered way with a cement floor led from her bedroom to the veranda, and the lawn was dry.

Neither of the Wests spoke. The house-boy came with a basin of warm water, some cotton, and a bottle of permanganate tablets. West held the lamp while Vachell went to work on Bullseye's wound. It was a deep knife-slash that had just missed the eye and ran down from ear to cheek. The dog squealed in pain as the permanganate stung. Vachell held her still by the muzzle and discovered that the underpart of the jaw was bruised and tender. It was easy to see what had happened. Bullseye had overtaken the quarry and got a blow on the jaw. She had sprung again and the knife had slashed out at her throat, just missing. Luckily the shock had made her give up: she was only eight months old. The next knife-thrust would have been the last.

"Both askaris will be on duty the rest of the night," Vachell said, when the first-aid job was done. "One outside your door and the other over by the farm buildings. Has the heifer calved yet, Commander West?"

"No. Not yet."

"If you have to go out to her, the askari will take you over."

"My God," West said, "are you trying to put me under arrest?"

Vachell stood up and wiped his hands. "No, sir. I'm trying to secure your safety. I don't want any more accidents to-night."

"I can look after myself, thanks," West said shortly. "*And* my wife."

"The askaris will be there just the same," Vachell replied.

He put Bullseye to bed under a blanket in his room, locked the door, and posted the two askaris. It was still only half-past twelve. He slipped a torch into his pocket and went out to the farm buildings. The cows slept out in the paddocks, but in the loose boxes he found two animals lying down in the straw. They gazed at him in placid indifference, their velvet eyes soft in the darkness. He played the torch over their sleek forms, wishing he knew more about farming. To his inexperienced eye both were fat-bellied but he could not tell which of the two was on the verge of calving. Their jaws moved with the deliberate motion of a liner in an even swell. He left them, feeling at a loss, and found his way to a small duck-pond he had noticed that morning among the farm buildings. It was a shallow depression roughly lined with concrete, fed by the overflow from a big corrugated iron receiving tank into which the ram pumped its constant flow. The working oxen came there to drink when they were out-spanned, and for the rest it was available to chickens and ducks. Around the concrete's edge was a trampled, muddy border pitted with the footmarks of many animals. Vachell bent down to study the story written in mud, flashlight in hand. Oxen had come there to drink the evening before. He found the record of a naked human foot, and then, just on the edge of the pond, he saw the mark of a small-heeled shoe. It was not a clear impression, but it was fresh. He drew a small steel measure from his pocket, took the dimensions as well as he could, and noted them down. Only the heel-mark was clear; the toe was blurred. He could tell no more about it than that the foot was small.

Grass stretched around him like a rough grey carpet; the buildings squatted like hunched beasts in their own shadows. The moon had come out now; it made the tin roofs into shining pools. He played his torch over the grass. The questing beam flickered past a darker patch, returned, and held the discovery pinned down by a shaft of light. Vachell held the beam steady but he caught his breath and small cold prickles rippled up his spine. There was a dark stain on the moonlit grass. He walked up to it slowly, bent down, and touched it with his hand. Hair rose slowly with a thrill of horror on the back of his scalp, and he rubbed together fingers glutinous with blood.

A little way off something lay like a limp discarded parcel

in the shadow of a hen-house. He walked towards it, forcing forward his reluctant legs at every step.

He reached the object and turned it over with his foot. It was the lifeless body of a duck. The head had been wrenched off and one wing half torn from the body. A dribble of blood from the mangled neck and head stained the ground. A second duck, headless also and mutilated, sprawled on the grass close by. The door of the wooden coop was open, and a piece of wire which had secured the fastening gleamed in the moonlight on the ground.

CHAPTER 14: THE FIRST THING VACHELL SAW in the morning was a fly-catcher with a white-rimmed eye sitting perkily on the window-sill, and beyond that a deep red rose swaying in a light breeze. In the clean freshness of morning it was almost impossible to believe in the events of the night, to think without incredulity of that crouching monster in the cow-house shadows craving the warm, thick feel of blood as a dipsomaniac craves for alcohol; of headless ducks bleeding on to moonlit grass; of a slashing knife-thrust in a bull-terrier puppy's face. Blood-lust and roses, the obscenity of madness and a purple waxbill swaying on a twig— such discordant elements could not be made to blend. But Bullseye's bandaged head, the revolver on a table, bloodstains over Vachell's dressing-gown, furnished proof that it was not a nightmare, and quelled, in doing so, a little of the brilliance of the sun.

By breakfast-time Vachell and the two askaris had searched every square yard of bush below the garden, the bush that had swallowed the crouching figure as completely as a lake swallows a stone. They had found nothing at all. The askari who had seen the figure remained convinced, though he would no longer admit his belief, that a spirit had attacked the ducks. The ground was hard, and there was no sign of footprints. The marauding figure had left no trace, beyond its bloody signature of headless ducks, and Bullseye's wound.

137

At breakfast both the Wests looked as though they had not slept at all. Janice's pale smooth-skinned face showed nothing of her feelings, but her eyes looked tired and for the first time he noticed little crowsfeet scarring their corners. West's hand shook as he lifted his coffee-cup, his eyes looked haunted; Vachell wondered how long he would resist a breakdown.

"Your heifer calve all right?" he inquired.

The Commander shook his head. "Not yet."

After Vachell had dressed Bullseye's wound and packed his bag he said good-bye to Janice. The time had come when no excuse could justify his staying on. His eyes avoided her face, but he could not help his senses responding, as the ear to music or the blood to rhythm, when he held her hand in his own.

"I'm sorry we had to meet like this." He could think of nothing better to say.

"You must come again to visit us when all this . . . when this nightmare is over. Maybe it will be different then," she replied.

"I'm sending a couple more askaris over to-day," he added. "There'll be two on duty all night. If they're any good they'll see that nothing like last night's performance happens here again."

West looked greyer than ever, and his face twitched a little as he came to see his guest off the farm.

"It's a ghastly business," he said. "It's so . . . so, well, indecent. I wish . . . I suppose you couldn't . . ." His voice tailed off.

"Let the whole investigation drop?"

West looked startled and then nodded his head. "Well, I was going to say something like that. Look here, you don't know, do you, that Munson didn't die from the fumes in the pyrethrum shed? That's what it looks like. Doctor couldn't find any other cause of death. Isn't that good enough? You know what sort of man he was. Far better out of the way. Couldn't it be left at that?"

"How about Rhode," Vachell asked slowly, "and what happened last night?"

"How do you know there's any connexion? Very likely there's some native in the district who's gone crazy and prowls about at night, but he'll soon be brought in. His family will take him along to the native hospital, I expect. Naturally we're upset about Rhode and the . . . last night, but I don't want to lodge a complaint. . . ."

His voice tailed off again as he gave Vachell the sort of look a dog who'd stolen a bun off the tea-table might give its master, hoping against hope that the matter would be overlooked.

Vachell got into his car and pressed a thumb on the self-starter.

"Cops can't listen to fairy stories all day," he said. "It's nice, but they have to work sometimes, to keep up appearances."

"The Mail Must Go Through," West said, with a ghost of a smile. "I'm afraid some one may get run over."

Vachell slipped in the gear lever but kept the clutch pedal down. He glanced up at West's face.

"You don't have any ideas, I suppose?" he asked.

West hesitated and Vachell could see that some sort of struggle was going on in his mind. At last he shook his head.

"No," he said, "I haven't. It's beyond me."

Vachell waited, but no more came.

"If you develop any, take some advice; don't talk to any one but a policeman," he said.

As he drove down the hill he could see, in his mirror, the Commander standing bare-headed on the lawn, staring at his feet. He looked somehow defeated and forlorn. Afterwards the picture came back very clearly to Vachell's mind, and he reflected often on the irony of events, that this last message should have been an unregarded warning.

In Karuna he found that a preliminary report from the labs had come in, but it was negative, as he'd known it would be. Prettyman had checked on Wendtland's movements and found several of his natives who were ready to swear that their employer had been on his own farm the morning of Munson's death, until after nine o'clock. But Wendtland had dined the night before, as Vachell knew, at Munson's place. The Dorobo hunter Arawak could not be found; Vachell had a general call put out for him by telegraph to all the police-stations and district headquarters in the colony. Since Dorobo could live for years in the forest on honey and the produce of their traps and boys he did not entertain very rosy hopes of the effectiveness of the appeal. He tried to see Mrs. Innocent again, but she was pleading all morning in court and couldn't be called out.

After an early lunch he drove back to the Munsons' farm, leaving Prettyman to catch up on ordinary routine. He could tell that something was wrong as soon as he drove up; the homestead looked deserted, and in the distance he could see a native running, in itself a sign of something unusual. Before he could get out of the car the children came tearing out of the schoolroom, excited and apparently alone.

"There's a fire!" Roy called out. "A big one, with huge flames, it's coming this way." He halted, panting, beside the car. "Oh, you're the man we told about Arawak's bow and arrows. Look, will you please take me to the fire? I can help just as well as the others. You'll take me, won't you, please?"

Theodora, standing beside her brother, said: "Oh, yes, *please*! We'll be awfully good, really, we won't get in the way or anything."

"I can't do that," Vachell said. "I'm sorry, but your mother would bawl me out and I guess Miss Adams would get mad with us all. Listen, where is this fire?"

Both children looked downcast and disappointed. Vachell knew his stock had fallen with a bump.

"I *do* think you might take us," Roy said. "We'll jolly well come anyway, though. I'm not going to miss all the fun. It's up by the edge of the forest, I think. You can see it, over there."

A thick cloud of smoke stood up in the sky above the forest, towards Anstey's land. There were vultures wheeling about in it, black specks in a dense grey pall.

Vachell started up the car and steered for the smoke, jolting along farm tracks that skirted the paddock fences all over the farm. As he drew closer the sharp acrid smell of burning filled the air. A steady wind was blowing, enough to fan the flames and carry the vicious red snake of fire into the forest and up the side of the mountain, or perhaps across towards the buildings and the stock.

The car rounded a corner and he saw the fire ahead, creeping low over the knee-high grass towards a wall of forest. The foliage of scattered trees was blazing and shrivelling visibly, and black smoke arose in angry swirls. Kites and cranes were circling overhead, darting at intervals into the smoke to seize mice, frogs, and insects as they scurried and hopped in panic before the running flames. There was something very ugly about a big fire.

Through the smoke, on the far side of the flames, figures darted and called, beating at the fire with sticks and damp sacks. The bark of axes sounded from the forest beyond. Evidently Corcoran was trying to clear a lane in the fire's line of advance. It was going up the hill and into the forest, away from the Munson homestead; but if it went far enough in that direction it would encounter Anstey's house and buildings in its path.

On the right the fire had been checked by the gully dividing Munson's land from West's. Vachell clambered up the gully, got behind the line of flames, and ran along to join Corcoran and his gang of boys, who were chopping undergrowth and small trees against time to clear an open barrier. Corcoran's face was as black as his men's and his hands were scratched and bleeding.

"Lend a hand, there's a good chap," he shouted. "Anita's got a gang trying to hold the flames back—no chance of putting them out now. Take some of her boys and have a shot at heading it off from the other end. Once it gets a real hold in this forest we're sunk. West should be along any minute.

"Know how it started?" Vachell shouted. The crackle of advancing flames half drowned their voices.

"God knows. It's the devil, anyway." Corcoran, swinging an axe, went back to his job, and Vachell ran on to where Anita Adams, blackened with ash and with eyes red and streaming from smoke, was beating viciously at a spitting line of fire amid a row of natives. He picked out four who had brought their long iron-bladed weeding knives and ran on to the far extremity of the fire. It was eating its way rapidly up the slope towards the forest's edge. He shouted instructions to the natives, and they began to hack and clear and beat with frantic energy.

It was a race against time, and the fire had a big start. At intervals the report of bursting timber shocked the ears like rifle shots. The natives worked silently, save for coughs and grunts as they hacked and beat at bush and smouldering grass. They could feel the fire gaining on them all the time. In two minutes Vachell's hands were slippery with sweat, his eyes and throat smarting from billowing clouds of smoke. A little later he heard a shout behind him and looked round to see that West had arrived, axe in hand, with Norman Parrot and another gang of natives at his heels. They were all strung out now, in a long line, from Corcoran's end to Vachell's, but the smoke was so dense no one could see more than a few yards. Vachell's gang was holding back the tip of the tongue of flame, but the fire was gaining ground farther along and the whole line was being pushed back steadily into the forest.

All sense of time left Vachell's mind. Soon he was panting for breath, unconscious of legs and arms bleeding from scratches. He was in the forest now, with brambles and undergrowth tearing at his back. The air became hotter, and filled with noises of alarm. A sudden crash behind made him turn to see a heavy, dark form plunging away through the green waist-high undergrowth.

"Wild pig," West shouted. He was working next in line. "The fire must have got round behind us. We'll have to watch our step. I'm going to see if Janice is all right."

"Where is she?" Vachell shouted back.

"Farther along, with Corcoran, I think. The fire's getting away a bit now. Careful you don't get cut off. They move like hell sometimes."

He was gone in an instant, swallowed by the underbrush. The fire had caught the branches now, and was crackling like a demon. There seemed to be a new note in its roar; it was getting its head.

Another crash in the bushes made him turn to see a bushbuck doe leaping through the shadows, her chestnut coat flecked with white. Behind her hopped a small bushbuck calf, scared out of its wits. Too bewildered to see where it was going, it almost hit Vachell's legs; and then, paralysed by a new horror, it stood dead still in its tracks, trembling like a blade of grass. Vachell put out a hand and touched its soft warm coat. As if electrified, it crouched to the ground and leapt forward like a red bullet. It went back towards the fire, away from its mother, hopelessly lost.

The boys had moved out of sight down the line, summoned by shouts from Parrot. Something seemed to be going on down that way. Vachell began to wonder if Janice West was all right. It seemed hopeless, now, to try to stop the fire; it was about time to get out. He turned back, meaning to go around the end of the line of flames and get behind them. But a tongue of fire that had crept around unnoticed and sprung up without warning inside the forest stopped him abruptly. He could see the glow of the devouring flames through a dense grey wall of smoke. The wind blew aside the smoky curtain for a moment and the red glare became visible beyond. It was uncanny to see fire overhead, in the tree-tops. The noise was a searing sound, like the perpetual tearing of calico amplified a hundred times. Heat came at him as if it meant to get him personally. No hope of getting through that way. He turned back and headed in the other direction, towards where West and Parrot had gone.

Keeping the fire on his right, he worked his way down through clinging undergrowth and the tangled mossy branches of trees. Parrot and the boys seemed to have cleared out, leaving the fire in undisputed possession. He called once or twice, but the roar of the flames drowned his voice. There was no sound, now, of shouts or the hacking of bushes. He crossed a little game-path, the heat strong on his right cheek, and saw something lying there, black in the shadow. It was the bushbuck calf—or another just like it—that had collided with his legs a little while before. Wondering if it had got caught by the fire he turned it over with his foot, and the toe of his shoe came away dark with blood. Surprised, he bent over it, and then felt a sudden shock of horror. The animal had not been killed by fire. Its throat had been cut from ear to ear.

He examined the small, limp body with nervous hands, half alarmed and half incredulous. To find amid this display of Nature's ruthlessness a footnote, as it were, on the wanton cruelty of man had a nightmarish quality. One of his companions had found the lust for blood unsatisfied by the fire's destruction, had found time to kill a fear-crazed animal in the midst of fighting the flames.

The fire was crackling close upon him now, driving gusts of smoke and hot air into his face. He looked around quickly, for what he could not say: and saw the gleam of metal between the tangled arms of a bramble. He picked out a woodman's hatchet, and ran on gripping it in his hand. He had seen that hatchet, or its double, half an hour before.

An ominous crackling and roaring just ahead brought him up dead in his tracks. Immediately in front smoke stood up like a wall in the sky. Fear of another kind swept over him now. Fire was ahead and behind; there was no way to get around.

There wasn't time to think anything out. The pace of the advancing flames seemed to have doubled. Vachell pulled out his handkerchief and tied it over his mouth and nose. He rammed his thick felt hat down over his eyes, grasped the hatchet, and ran at top speed towards the line of flames.

Fallen logs, clinging brambles, twining creepers held him

back. The heat grew more intense, the roaring louder. He glanced up and saw, beneath the brim of his hat, a wall of fire coming at him with a sort of gloating fury. He took a deep gulp of air and smoke through the stifling handkerchief, put his head down, and charged into the flames. A wave of white heat enveloped him and violent pain seared his arms and face. Something seemed to seize his foot; he stumbled, and flung out his arms. A scorching pain swept over his flesh, and his lungs were choking. Just as he seemed about to drown in a black, burning sea he felt a cold blast of air in his face, and collapsed on the ground in a paroxysm of coughing. The bare, black earth was hot, but not burning. He drew deep gulps of cold air into his lungs. Still coughing, he staggered farther out of the danger zone, scattering birds who were searching for the scorched bodies of insects. Beyond, the sun flooded a smokeless landscape; he was safe.

CHAPTER 15: THREE CARS WERE PARKED TO-
gether on the blackened pasture where the fire had passed.
Vachell walked unsteadily towards them, still grasping the
axe. His tongue and mouth felt dry and swollen and his heart
bumped unevenly, but that was not only because of his escape.
His eyes searched the group from a long way off for the figure
he dreaded not to see. There was some one missing, but it
wasn't Janice West. She was there, her pale face smudged with
smuts like the rest of them, laughing over the blisters on her
hands. Anita Adams, with considerable presence of mind, had
brought a pocket first-aid kit, and was sticking elastoplast over
broken blisters. Parrot, still in his old burberry, was assisting,
and Corcoran was discussing the next move with two of the
Natives. They were all relieved to see Vachell appear.

"We were getting rather anxious," Corcoran said. "I was
afraid you'd be cut off. The fire's going uphill now like a bat
out of hell. You look as if it damned nearly got you."

"I had to buck it," Vachell said. "I needed my eyebrows
singed."

Every one was startled when a voice from one of the parked
cars said, with acid vehemence: "There's a native cattle-track
about a mile back, leading straight to Anstey's farm. You
could perfectly well have followed that." It was Mrs. Munson, sitting behind the wheel of the farm car as though she
had been bedded out there.

148

"Thanks a lot," Vachell said politely. "I'll use it next time I get mixed up in a fire. Where's Commander West?"

"He went back," Janice answered. "He said he wanted to make sure all the boys had got out of the forest safely. Norman, there are none missing, are there?"

"No, they're all present and correct," Parrot said. "At least, my bodyguard is, and I think I see all yours. This is where they come into their own, being black to start with. Self-colour's so much smarter than this mottled effect, I think."

"I wish Dennis would come," Janice said. Then, for the first time, she caught sight of the axe. She put one hand to her throat, a gesture he remembered as if he had seen her do it a hundred times. "Where did you get that?" she asked. Her voice was low and flat.

"I found it, in there. I guess your husband dropped it, Mrs. West."

Janice made no comment. He could not see her eyes— they were fixed on the axe; but he could sense the uneasiness in her mind.

"Did any one see West after he went back?" Vachell inquired.

There was a short silence. Anita Adams, her first-aid job completed, looked up from the step of the car where she was sitting, elbows resting on her knees.

"I was just behind Janice and him," she said. "I saw Commander West turn back, and he passed me. He shouted something about it being all right for Janice that way, he was going to make sure the boys didn't try the other direction, as it wasn't safe."

"What did you do?"

"Me? I caught Janice up, and we came back together."

Vachell looked at Corcoran. "What about you? Did you see Commander West?"

Corcoran shook his head, and ran a hand through his ruffled brown hair. He had a gash down one cheek and his shirt was torn.

"No. I didn't see him at all, after he first turned up, I mean. I asked him to go along down the line to your end of the fire, I thought there was more hope of stopping it at that end. Parrot was with him then."

The eyes of every one turned to Parrot. He was standing close to Janice, lounging against the side of a car. His fair hair lay in close curls all over his head, making him look much younger than he was; but his voice was anxious.

"I didn't see him after he went back to look for Janice," Parrot said. "I went on beating and hacking till it looked quite hopeless, and then I thought I'd better get every one out while the going was good, just in case things got out of hand. I found Janice here, but no sign of Dennis. I suppose he . . ."

The harsh voice from the Munson car startled them all again. Every one had forgotten about the figure behind the wheel.

"Talk, talk, talk," it said. "West can perfectly well look after himself, I've no doubt. But if you all think something's happened to him, why don't you go and look?"

A dead silence followed her remark. It was too logical to

dispute. Vachell put on his hat and leant the axe against the wing of a car.

"A guy has to draw breath between fires," he said. "Did you see the Commander during the fire-fighting operations, Mrs. Munson?"

"No, I didn't."

"Did you come up here right at the start of the fire?"

"Mind your own business."

"For God's sake don't let's start quarrelling now," Corcoran said, with unexpected force. "We've got to find West first. He's sure to be all right, he probably got driven back into the forest a little way, but we'd better make certain before we all go home."

He walked over the blackened pasture by Vachell's side. The short tufty stubble scrunched beneath their feet and a little cloud of ashes kicked up behind each footstep.

"I'm afraid my aunt's not in a very good temper," he explained, half apologetically. "She had a bit of a knock over my uncle's will. There's going to be a hell of a row about it, but if I know Uncle Karl he'll have got it all sewn up tighter than a bale of wool. Look here, what's the idea? We can't possibly find West, you know, even if something *has* gone wrong."

"We can look. Maybe he made that cattle track Mrs. Munson spoke of. He knew about it, I guess?"

"Oh, Lord, yes, every one does; the natives use it a lot. He'd be quite safe, you see; he'd only have to strike the track and follow it up to Anstey's place. The fire hasn't got as far as that yet."

They walked on in silence over the fire-scorched ground. The earth was still warm under their feet, and quite lifeless. Every blade of grass and leaf of bush, every grasshopper and spider had perished; all about them was black and forlorn. Several crested cranes with brightly coloured plumage, gobbling fried insects, rose unhurriedly and flapped away, trailing their long legs behind.

"I don't see what we can do," Corcoran repeated. "If West didn't get round the fire in time we can't reach him now." His voice betrayed his uneasiness; Vachell said nothing. He was walking very fast, almost at a run. On the edge of the forest the big trees were still burning; some of them would go on smouldering for days. The heat was intense, the air thick and stifling with smoke.

Corcoran halted on the edge of the devastated area, and asked: "What next?" He was clearly reluctant to go on.

"West had trouble with his lungs," Vachell invented. "I didn't want to say this in front of his wife, but I'm scared the smoke may have choked him. I reckon we're about opposite where I found his axe. I'm going in to search. It's easy behind the fire; all of the cover's burnt out."

"West's no fool," Corcoran protested. "He's had experience of bush fires. He'd turn back if he felt the smoke getting too thick for his health."

"If he was able," Vachell said, and walked on. Corcoran started to say something, checked himself, and shrugged his shoulders. Then he, too, began to search, taking a zigzag path through the burnt-over woods. Now and again a branch fell from a burning tree with a crash and a shower of sparks.

A chip off a smouldering log that fell just behind him flew into his shoe and burnt his heel severely. He cursed loudly and limped on with increased reluctance. Vachell was well ahead, quartering the ground like a bloodhound. He seemed quite determined that something had gone wrong.

A few moments later Corcoran stopped abruptly, and stared at the ground by his feet. Out of some straggling brambles that had been singed but not destroyed protruded something stiff and black. Corcoran leant down very slowly, to make certain, and then raised his head and tried to shout. The sound emerged from his throat as a sort of hollow croak.

Vachell heard it, and came racing back. He pulled aside the half-charred brambles with a vicious tug; burnt at the roots, they snapped off easily. A faint smell of burning feathers was in the air. Corcoran's eyes were fixed on the end of a black, shrivelled-up leg, bearing the remnants of what had once been a shoe.

CHAPTER 16: PRETTYMAN'S COOK HAD PRE-
pared a large tea, for he understood that the bwana from
Marula was an important Government officer who had eaten
no lunch. He was surprised, therefore, when the tray reap-
peared in the kitchen with the food almost untasted on the
plate.

"Europeans are wasteful like chiefs whose wives are so
numerous they do not know which is which," he remarked.
"Why do I make cakes, when they are rejected as if they
were stones? Why am I not left alone to sleep, if food is
cooked for weevils?"

"It is the way of Europeans," the house-boy said philo-
sophically. "I think this European is ill—he pushed the food
away and his appearance is that of a man whose head aches
severely. What does it matter? He has left plenty of tea in
the pot for us, and there is sugar in the bowl."

"It is true," the cook agreed, "that there is always a medi-
cine-man ready to profit by another's sores."

In Prettyman's bare, tin-roofed veranda Vachell smoked
one cigarette after another while the sun went down in a blaze
of crimson over the hills. His eyes were tired and there was
something dispirited in the way he sat, forearms resting on
thighs, hands dangling down between his knees. Even Prettyman, leaning on the rail chewing a pipe, knew there was something seriously wrong. The superintendent had returned late,

still black as a stoker, insisting on a bath before tea; and then he had eaten next to nothing, and kept silent as a giraffe. Prettyman could understand that he'd feel upset; West had been his host, and no man would want to break the news to Janice. Still, policemen had to learn to take it, Prettyman reflected; a man so senior ought to be used to anything by now.

"It's a darned funny thing, if you come to think of it," he ventured, "that *two* fellers should get overcome by smoke, ostensibly, and go west in the same week. Of course, there's no doubt this is all open and above-board, I suppose? I mean, no one could have poked West into the fire, or any hanky-panky of that sort?"

The superintendent threw his cigarette-end over the veranda railings and watched its parabola through the air. He took so long to reply that Prettyman thought: huh, so you won't talk; but then Vachell leant back in the wicker chair, stretched out his long legs, and said:

"On the surface everything looks tidy as a convict's cell. West went back to see if all the boys had come out safely; he got cut off, tried to buck the flames, and the fire got him. It's happened lots of times before. It may have happened like that to-day, and we'll never prove it didn't; but I just don't believe it, that's all."

"You think he was done in, too," Prettyman exclaimed. This was worth waiting for. "But how? He was a strong man and if any one tried any monkey business . . ."

"If you'd decided to buck a line of flames, and you had an axe in your hand, would you drop the axe before you ran?"

"No, I don't think so—no, I'd swing it in my hand, to clear brambles and things out of the light."

"So would I. I found West's axe just sixty yards from where his body was lying. Beside it, on the ground, was the body of a bushbuck calf, with its throat slit from ear to ear. It was lying in a pool of blood, but there wasn't any blood on the head of the axe. Does that tell a story to you?"

Prettyman scratched the back of his neck in bewilderment, and said: "Definitely not. I suppose you mean that West found this blood-lust maniac butchering the bushbuck, and got done in himself. But he was a great hefty feller, axe in hand, and you'd think he'd be a match for any one. Instead of which apparently he just dropped the axe and ran straight into the fire. Why?"

Vachell shrugged his shoulders. The obvious explanation was not an easy one to talk about. "Maybe he decided on safety first, justice second. There wasn't time to start an argument."

"I don't see how it could have happened while every one was dashing about fighting the fire. Can all the people concerned account for their movements?"

"Parrot was close to me, next in line, but I reckon I didn't see him clearly enough to be sure he was there all the time the fire lasted. You couldn't see a thing in all that smoke. The boys farther along the flame-line said they kept Miss Adams in sight, but evidence like that isn't worth a cent. Several boys said they were with Corcoran all the time, but when I grilled them a little it was pretty clear they were too mixed up in the smoke and too busy on the job to know whether he was in among them or a mile away. Old Mother

Munson was keeping company with the kites on the edge, snooping around for something to gobble up, I guess. It's a hell of a spot. You can't check on people's movements in a forest fire."

"It does seem rather a mess," Prettyman agreed. "Where was Mrs. West all the time?"

"Fire-fighting, like the others."

"Did any one see her at it?"

"No more than the rest."

It occurred to Prettyman that questions on this theme were not welcomed by the superintendent, so he said no more. Vachell was trying not to think of the last part of the afternoon, how he had broken the news to Janice and carried in, on a piece of sacking, all that was left of Dennis West. He had managed to stop her seeing it, but that had been hard. After that, Norman Parrot had unobtrusively taken her in charge. Shorn of his facetious manner he had seemed at a loss for words, but he had put her into a car and driven her back to her home, and arranged for the native boys to carry on with the work of the farm. Janice had refused to go to a neighbour, or to let any one come to stop with her at home.

The two askaris were still on duty there, but Vachell wasn't satisfied. He'd always played his hunches, and now that the hunch was bad he couldn't pretend it wasn't there. It was very bad, and very much there. Things that had long been hidden, festering in the dark, were bursting out, like pus from a rotten sore too long bandaged up. Once the boil had burst there was no retreat. The evil had to come out, but who would be corrupted by its poison none could say.

When it had grown dark enough to see the red glow of a cigarette across the narrow veranda, Prettyman broke in on his thoughts. From the living-room came a tinkle of glasses and bottles; the sun had gone down, and the house-boy had not forgotten to observe the European ceremony connected with that daily event.

"Would you like me to make my report now, sir?" he inquired. "It's past office hours, but I thought that possibly in a murder case . . ."

Vachell relaxed in his chair and laughed. "Murderers do get careless about Government hours," he said. "It doesn't show a proper spirit in this time of national emergency, but since it's too late to stop the rot I guess you'd better go ahead."

"I followed out your instructions," Prettyman began. "First of all, about the anonymous note. You know, 'If you want to find the murderer of Karl Munson, ask Dr. Lawson who went to him last month and what he prescribed.' I haven't been able to trace the typewriter it was written on yet. It isn't Munson's own machine, I got a sample of that and the type's different. West and Parrot say they don't possess one. Wendtland does, I believe, but I haven't been able to get its fingerprints yet. It may be a long job. There are probably dozens of typewriters in the district and if I have to check up on them all . . ."

"It won't be necessary," Vachell said. "Did you see Dr. Lawson?"

"Yes. I saw him first thing, but he couldn't help much. I asked him whether any one connected with the Munson household had been to see him recently, and he said neither

Uncle Karl or Mother Munson ever went near him. He said Ma Munson would much rather bleed to death than pay for a suture. The only person connected with them who had been to see him lately was Anita Adams."

"Why, what was the matter with her—malnutrition?"

"Well, yes, in a way—at least it was some sort of digestive trouble, I gathered, only Dr. Lawson said it was because she was run down. He told her she ought to go away for a rest, but she said she couldn't afford it and wouldn't leave the children anyway, so he gave her an ordinary tonic and she hasn't been back since. I don't see what we can get out of that, do you, sir?"

"It doesn't seem to fit," Vachell agreed.

"Then there was the second point," Prettyman went on. "So far I've had no luck. I couldn't find a soul on the place who saw any one go into Munson's bedroom between the time he went out to the cowsheds, on the day he died, and the time his boy started to do out his room."

Vachell nodded in the darkness. "I didn't expect you would. But some one walked into Munson's bedroom, just the same. The guy who killed him did."

The house-boy appeared with a tray of drinks and put it down on a table. He came back a second time with a gasolene lamp, ready pumped and lit. Prettyman poured out two whiskies, handed one to his guest, and took a small, black note-book out of his pocket.

"I've got everything I collected in here," he went on. "Actually, I don't think any one could have got into Munson's room unobserved for the best part of half an hour after he left, which was about six-fifteen a.m. One of the poultry-boys, by the name of Mbegu, was sweeping the paths round about the sort of shed the Munsons sleep in, at the time Munson went out. He says he saw the bwana leave his room, and that for some time after that he was sweeping under the windows and round about the front of the rooms; and he's absolutely positive that no one else went in or out. Of course, you know how unreliable that sort of evidence is, sir; but this boy does seem awfully positive, and says he does the same job every day and he'd be sure to notice if anything so unusual happened as some one sneaking into Munson's room."

"He needn't have sneaked."

"No, I mean gone in, in any manner. Of course, we can't be certain how long this boy was there. He says till seven, but seven is just a nice round hour, and we can't rely on that. But Mrs. Munson says that she came out of her room at about a quarter to seven and he was still on the job. So we can knock out the time between, say, six-fifteen and six-forty-five, so far as the person we're trying to find is concerned. After six-forty-five there doesn't seem to have been any one about until Munson's boy Mwogi went in to make the bed and sweep his bwana's room a little after a quarter past seven. I think we can be fairly sure of that time, because Mwogi said he started on the bedroom directly after he'd taken the children's breakfast across to the schoolroom, and I gather that's held punctually at seven-fifteen. So this burglar chap's best bet for getting unobserved into Munson's bedroom seems to have been some time between a quarter to seven and a quarter past."

"How about the window in back?"

"In my opinion we can rule that out. Luckily, it looks slap on to the kitchen and the boys' quarters, and you know what a kitchen's like at that hour. People of all sorts coming and going, three-quarters of them having nothing to do with the household staff but just drifting in for a chat. The chances would be a hundred to one you'd be spotted if you tried to climb in by the window. Besides, if you *were* seen, obviously your actions would arouse a good deal of interest, to say the least. But the door of Munson's room isn't in sight of anything, except the side windows of the sitting-room, and if by any chance you were seen walking in, no native would think twice about it—that is, if you were some one belonging to, or in some way connected with, the Munson family, as I gather you're assuming."

"Okay, check on that," Vachell said. "It makes sense, though it's not conclusive. But you've overlooked one thing."

"I'm sorry, sir," Prettyman said, a little stiffly. "If I may say so, it would be easier to make an efficient inquiry if I were to be given some indication of what the person I'm trying to trace intended to do."

"He did it, he didn't intend. I have to tighten up a few bolts on the theory before I put it on the road."

"I'm sure you know best, sir. May I ask what it is I overlooked?"

"The third way into Munson's room."

Prettyman poured out two more drinks, squirted the soda into them, and said, a little defensively: "You mean the door that leads into the bathroom, and then into Mrs. Munson's room. Yes, but the poultry-boy swears that no one went into either room, Munson's or his wife's."

"No one who wasn't already there."

"Yes, I see," Prettyman said slowly. "You mean, before Mrs. Munson went out she could have simply walked through. Yes, I suppose she could. There's no method of proving it one way or the other, I'm afraid."

"None," Vachell agreed. "Go ahead with the rest of the story."

"I tried to get every one's movements for that half-hour straightened out, but it's a hell of a job, sir; you can't get any native to be accurate about times. Wendtland seems to have a cast-iron alibi; he was thirty miles away, on his farm. So was Parrot, according to his headman, though I haven't had time to check that yet with his other boys. Mrs. Munson emerged at a quarter to seven, as I told you, and went to the store, where she issued weeding knives to natives working on the pyrethrum and made out labour tickets until Munson was discovered at eight. By the way, sir, there's one small point there—I can't see any connexion, but it might be worth noting."

"Yes?"

"There's a big drum of cattle-dip in the Munsons' store. It's open, any one can get at it, and, of course, it's full of arsenic. I wondered if it was quite safe, seeing how things are."

"Things aren't safe just at present, however else they are. Would there be a farm in the district that didn't have a drum of arsenical cattle-dip lying around?"

"No, I suppose not," Prettyman admitted. "You can get

hold of it anywhere. I just thought it might be rather a tempta-
tion. Well, to get on with the story: Miss Adams was coping
with the chickens at the specified time, apparently that was
her usual morning job, and Corcoran was out on a pony setting
the task for some boys who were seeding and harrowing a field
of oats. That's as far as I got. I didn't have time to do the
Wests, sir—besides, I thought you'd probably got them
taped."

"I haven't anything taped yet," Vachell said. "I guess you
got all this from native boys?"

"Every bit of it, sir. They all seemed quite definite, I must
say, and, of course, natives can be observant enough, but it's
no good pretending they've got the least sense of time."

"I often wondered how a spider would feel if it got tight
and had trouble on all eight legs, with three knees to a leg,"
Vachell remarked. "Well, I guess this is it—fixing times of
people working on a farm in Africa, with native witnesses who
don't use clocks. If I ever decide to rub out a guy I'll pick a
quiet dairy proposition for a background. One moment you're
milking a cow, next you're bumping off a neighbour, and
then you're back again feeding the pigs. There's one thing,
though." He knocked away a flying beetle that was hitting
the lamp like a simple-minded bull.

"Yes?" Prettyman inquired.

"We have a hidden witness who may give us a line."

"A hidden witness?" Prettyman inquired. "I don't quite
understand."

"A way of checking on the alibis," Vachell said. "It's a
shot in the dark, but it's worth a try."

CHAPTER 17: CLARA INNOCENT WAS NOT ALTO-
gether at ease. Her manner was as hearty as ever, but she
fingered the papers on her desk a little too frequently, adjusted her shoulder straps a couple of times, and kept her eyes
on the activities of the street below. Shops were opening up
and down the main street of the little town, and natives with
big baskets in their hands were setting out on marketing ex-
peditions before the rush began.

"You start work early, Mr. Vachell," she said conversationally. She put on her spectacles, and fingered the wave at
the back of her head. "There's plenty to be done, no doubt.
It's a shocking business about Commander West—terrible for
her, poor thing. She's such a nice woman. One can only hope
it will bring home to the Forest Department the necessity of
doing something really effective to check these grass and
forest fires. It always takes a dreadful accident of this sort to
get any action out of a Government department, I'm afraid.
Always excepting the police, of course."

"Thanks," Vachell said. "The fire wasn't pleasant, but I've
come to you for information about a client."

"I'll do anything I can, of course, as I told you before. But
you'll realize, I know, that one comes up against certain
standards of professional ethics, and so on. . . ."

"I don't believe they cover what I want to know, Mrs.
Innocent. Mrs. Munson came to see you here on the afternoon of her husband's death?"

"She did indeed. It wasn't an easy interview by any means, Mr. Vachell. I gave you an outline of Karl Munson's will. Well, you can imagine how Mrs. Munson felt about *that*!" She laughed heartily, and darted a quick sideways glance at her visitor from behind her horn-rimmed glasses.

"Badly, no doubt," Vachell said, without joining in. "When she called, did she or Corcoran leave any sort of a package here, with instructions for its delivery to a third party?"

Mrs. Innocent raised her eyebrows and said: "A package? No, not that I know of, Mr. Vachell."

"I'd advise you to think again, Mrs. Innocent. That package contained documents, and maybe the kind of documents it doesn't do for a loyal citizen to handle. As a lawyer I don't need to remind you of the position of a go-between in cases that involve information likely to endanger the safety of the public, or be of use to the King's enemies. . . ."

The shot went home. Mrs. Innocent looked extremely uncomfortable, and fidgeted with the papers on her desk.

"I really don't know what you mean," she said. "I don't know anything about information of that sort. Mrs. Munson is my client, you must remember, and if I execute a commission for her in good faith I hardly think it is a matter for police interference. . . ."

"Then you forget the extent of the police authority here," Vachell said. "Mrs. Munson is an alien. I guess you forget that too. Munson was a leader of the local branch of the Nazi party and Wendtland is an agent of the German Government. If I were you I'd check on your position as an intermediary before you decide to refuse assistance to the police."

Mrs. Innocent flushed angrily and pulled off her spectacles with a quick, agitated gesture. "You've got no right to say that!" she exclaimed. "It's a total misconception of my position. At no time have I been an intermediary, or in any way . . ." She leant back in her chair and gave a half-hearted smile. "You're entirely wrong, Mr. Vachell. I apologize, I lost my temper for a moment, but it's not very soothing to be accused of what amounts to being a traitor to my country, I'm sure you'll agree. I have no information to give you, I'm afraid."

"Maybe I can refresh your memory again," Vachell said slowly. His face was hard and without expression, but there was a wary look in his eyes. Dealing with a lawyer, he was venturing a long way on to the enemy's ground. And a woman at that. He wished this job didn't involve bullying women so much.

"Under our constitution here, the Governor-in-Council can cause to be revoked licences issued to solicitors to practise law or to plead in Court," he went on. "This power is very rarely exercised, but in the case of persons believed to be rendering assistance to the agents of a foreign political organization working against the security of the colony, it might be found necessary to bring the provision into force."

Mrs. Innocent stared for a few moments at her visitor without replying. She kept her temper this time.

"I see your extensive knowledge of Nazi organization has made you an admirer of what I believe is the Gestapo technique," she said at last, her voice edged with anger and heavy with sarcasm. "I didn't expect to learn blackmail methods from the police. What do you want to know?"

"What you did with the package Mrs. Munson left with you two days ago."

"I am, or rather was, Munson's solicitor," Mrs. Innocent explained carefully, choosing her words. Anger made her voice shake a little, but it was under control. "I acted for him on various occasions. I did all his legal work. Naturally I knew he was connected with the local Nazis, that was common gossip, but it was nothing whatever to do with me. Any more than it would be my affair, Mr. Vachell, if General Goering was your uncle, or if your wife was a lion-tamer, or if all your children had webbed toes."

"You paint a pleasing picture, but I'm not married, Mrs. Innocent. Shall we return to the package Mrs. Munson left here the afternoon of her husband's death?"

"She left a package, I admit. She asked me to say nothing of this, and to oblige a client I gave her my word. This you have forced me to break by, if I may say so, illegal and unscrupulous means."

"You have the package now?"

Mrs. Innocent shook her head. "It was called for within an hour of her leaving it in my office."

"By Wendtland?"

"Yes."

"And, knowing Wendtland's position here, you still think you did nothing to aid and abet the King's enemies?

Mrs. Innocent laughed; she'd had time to think the position over, and now she was sure of her ground. "Mr. Vachell, you really shouldn't take me for a child. Lawyers are rather too hard-boiled to fall a victim to spy mania, you know. The position is that a client of mine left a package in my office to be called for by a friend. She might equally well have left it at the grocer's or the chemist's or the bank. I haven't the slightest idea what was in the package, I didn't ask, and to be honest I don't care. I should say that it contained documents of some kind. If you can find anything irregular in that you're welcome to it, and I shall be the first to congratulate you." She pushed back her chair with a gesture of finality, and got up.

"It's what wasn't in the package that interests me," Vachell remarked thoughtfully. "Forgive me if I offer some advice. Next time Mrs. Munson uses your office as a mail-box, call me up and I'll see to the special delivery."

From Karuna he drove out to the Munson farm. The wide, dust-sheeted road was growing so familiar now that he dodged the worst bumps automatically. The fields of maize he passed on either side were restfully green, the plants already tall and sturdy.

That morning he developed a sudden interest in the technique of farming, and Mrs. Munson was called upon to satisfy it. Her pallid face went pink with irritation when he plied her with questions about poultry-raising, the keeping of labour sheets, the system of issuing tools and native rations, the repairs done two days ago to the corn-crib roof. He inspected the labour sheets and the boys' monthly tickets, watched the weeding of the pyrethrum, and even insisted on seeing her prize white turkeys that had been imported from Holland, as eggs, by air.

"So this is what we pay the police for!" she exclaimed. "So

that they can badger with questions a person whose husband has been dead two days! So that they can ask how to mark a boy's ticket or weed pyrethrum while a murderer stays at large a mile away—while naked sin flaunts itself unpunished in their faces. That is why we pay taxes to keep up the police!"

"There's no proof yet that your husband was murdered," Vachell suggested mildly. "I'm sorry, we can't go to work on that till the report from Marula comes in."

"Proof! Can't go to work!" she snorted. "Red tape, putting off, nothing to be done, always the same story! What proof do you want besides the evidence of your senses? Are you blind? You are all the same, because a woman has a painted face and a willing body. . . ." She broke off, her face red, to berate a native who had appeared at the heels of an escaping calf, which galloped at full speed across the lawn. When this was over she outlined briefly but forcibly her views on the increase in native crime and the inefficiency of the police. Not until the native took his leave did she return to the subject, and then she was more cautious; he got the impression that she felt she'd said too much.

"I hope you are satisfied that you have done everything to protect my two children and myself," she said. "My husband is murdered, yesterday there is a fire over my land and another death, and the same person stays close at hand and unmolested, a mile away from my house. The murderer is not caught, and you leave me here with only two black apes of askaris. I am saying nothing, it is hopeless, but if there is more trouble it is you who will be to blame. Perhaps there will be questions even in Marula, if more than two people are murdered in one week, by the same hand."

"We'll do all we can to protect you," Vachell said. "If you'd like Inspector Prettyman to come out here for a while . . ."

"Prettyman! That little squirt!" Mrs. Munson snorted savagely. "He'd be the first to have his head turned, to be taken in by the false smile and the lying tongue. . . ."

Vachell found her strange mixture of blunt colloquialism and Calvinistic mock-biblical disconcerting.

"Okay, we'll leave Prettyman out," he said. "But tell Corcoran he should carry a gun, and don't stray out of sight of him or the askaris after dark."

At the mention of Corcoran he could see her stiffen, and the high colour left her face. Her lips set in a tight scar across her pudgy face.

"Corcoran," she spoke the name slowly. "I shall have a lot to tell him, one day soon."

Vachell shot a question at her quickly.

"Does he smoke a pipe?"

"A pipe, Edward? No." She answered as he had hoped, without thinking, and then frowned and asked sharply: "Why?"

"I need to borrow some tobacco," Vachell replied.

The askaris gave their brief reports before he left. The only piece of information they had for him was negative: after diligent inquiry (according to instructions) they could not find any one who knew of a note delivered to Munson the day before he died. It was just possible, the corporal admitted, that a man bringing a note might have delivered it to Munson out on the farm without being noticed by any other native; but if the chit had been brought first to the house, which was the invariable custom, one of the house-boys would certainly know of the matter. All had been tackled, and all were positive that no note had come.

This news interested Vachell a great deal. He thought about it in the car as he bumped over a farm track to Norman Parrot's; and by the time he arrived it had given him a new and very startling idea.

The boundaries of Parrot's farm marched with Munson's on the other side from West's; Anstey's land lay above, a much bigger block, having a common boundary with Parrot's, Munson's and West's. Parrot's homestead was one of the least pretentious that Vachell had seen. It consisted of a ram-shackle mud-and-rubble two-roomed cabin with a wooden veranda and a corrugated iron roof. Two big water-tanks flanked the corners and a rough kitchen surrounded by two or three native huts stood out at the back. On almost any other continent the place would have looked mean and sordid; but in the African sunlight, with green grass all around, two beds of antirrhinums in front and a bougainvillæa beginning to climb up a veranda post, it was cheerful and thoroughly at home.

Everything looked new and unfinished, and as yet no gar-den had been made out of the bush. Parrot had been settled there less than a year, Vachell recalled. He was a new-comer to the colony as well as to the district; Prettyman, the foun-tain-head of gossip, had said his reputation was that of a good fellow but a bit of an ass, with not enough practical knowledge of farming and too many damn-fool ideas.

This time Vachell drew a blank; Norman Parrot was not at home. He was not on the farm either, his house-boy said; he had taken the car early that morning and driven down to the station, but he had not yet come back. Very likely he had gone on to Karuna, the boy added; perhaps the bwana would like to leave a note. He showed Vachell into the living-room, and waved a hand at a table covered with a litter of bills, catalogues, letters, pipes, magazines and other miscellaneous things.

The rest of the furniture had barely got past the crate stage. There was one comfortable arm-chair, but evidently Parrot sat on a Tate's sugar crate to eat meals off a couple of planks laid across two Shell gasolene cases. A big stone fireplace rather incongruously occupied most of one wall.

The books, stacked on rough shelves, were a mixed bag, mainly technical volumes on agriculture and stock-raising—Parrot evidently took his farming seriously—and accounts of travel. There were well-thumbed German and Italian dictionaries; some detective novels, and one or two tomes on international law. A couple of framed school-group photographs leant against a wall, and on the desk was a picture of a group taken on a houseboat in what looked like the mountains of Kashmir. Parrot was one of the party; so some of his stories of travel in foreign parts, Vachell reflected, were true. Propped up on the mantel-shelf was a picture of a very attractive brunette, taken by a San Francisco studio.

West's funeral was being held that morning in Karuna, and

most likely Parrot had gone in to attend it. Vachell had no desire to write a note, but instead he took a quick look around. The pipes on the desk attracted his attention. They were old, well worn and undistinguished, like the rest of Parrot's possessions, from his burberry to his books. There were three of them, all in use and all intact.

Vachell looked them over and walked to the door. The house-boy, with the usual faith in, or indifference to, European actions, had retreated to his own quarters and left the bwana alone. He had better look into the bedroom, Vachell supposed. It was a box of a room, only big enough to hold a camp-bed, a chest of drawers, table and a trouser press. The press lay open, as if a pair of pants had recently been taken out. There was a photograph propped up against a bottle of Eno's on top of the chest of drawers. He crossed the little room to look at it, and found himself gazing, with a shock of surprise, at Janice West. She looked younger, in a subtle, indefinite way. The shape of her face, perhaps, was less mature. But the same dark vital eyes, the familiar high cheekbones and fine pointed chin stared back at him. The picture had been taken in London, he judged some years before, and bore no inscription.

He put it down roughly and turned to go, but as he did so an object half hidden by some loose papers caught his eye. It was the bowl of another pipe. He picked it up, casually, then felt the muscles of his stomach contract a little and his pulses quicken with the familiar excitement of a find. The light from the window fell on the bowl and he turned it over and over in his hand. It was well used, smooth and black with nicotine, but the pipe was useless, for the stem had been snapped in two.

CHAPTER 18: THE FIRE HAD GONE HIGH INTO
the fountains, and from Anstey's road Vachell could see a
thick, grey-yellow cloud hanging over the trees above the
bamboos, mingling with the true clouds above the crest.
A faint haze blunted the sharp outlines of distant hills and
imparted an unusual sort of blurred, North European look
to the wide view. Anstey's farm had escaped damage,
Vachell found; the fire had swept up the mountains to the
right and gone around behind his land.

He found Sir Jolyot Anstey down by the farm buildings,
supervising some boys who were repairing the wall of a shed.

"We had a tragedy here last night," he told his visitor. "In
a sense, I imagine, a result of the fire."

"Some one get hurt?"

Anstey shook his head. He was hatless, and his thick, white
hair shone like silver in the bright sun. "No, but two calves
met a very unpleasant end. Look at that." He pointed to the
damaged wall of the shed.

The building, a calf-house, was made of heavy, unshaped
cedar posts driven into the ground and set shoulder to shoulder, with strong wire-netting nailed across them on the outside. But two of the posts had been loosened by digging down
to their feet, and then pushed apart so as to permit the passage
between them of something as big as a medium-sized dog.

"That space isn't big enough to let in a man," Vachell
observed.

"It wasn't a man. Look over there." He pointed to one side, and lying in the shade of a grain-store Vachell saw the mangled body of a dead calf. Its neck was torn wide open and it was caked with dried blood. Along its flanks were deep lacerations, as though a rake with knife-sharp prongs had been drawn over it.

"A leopard," Anstey explained. "Evidently it was driven from its usual haunts by the fire, and came here in search of food. We've had them before, of course, but not for some time, I'm glad to say."

Vachell examined the hole by the calf-shed wall with close attention. "It hardly seems possible a leopard could figure all this out, and force a way in," he remarked.

"Leopards are the most cunning of all the beasts of prey," Anstey said. "They are also by far the most bold. There's no doubt it's a leopard, you can rest assured of that—we found the pad-marks this morning, and the other calf had been almost entirely devoured. It killed the second from sheer lust for blood, I imagine, since one calf has hardly been touched." He glanced shrewdly at Vachell and added: "I believe I can hazard a guess at what was in your mind. I have heard strange rumours lately about some unpleasant atrocities alleged to have been committed in the district—dogs attacked, ducks decapitated, and things of that nature. How much truth is there in them, if I may ask?"

"Too much," Vachell said.

Anstey nodded. "Would you do me the honour of coming up to the house? It is time for the mid-morning cup of tea, an admirable habit—at any rate in countries where it is customary to rise early and get much of the best work of the day done before eleven o'clock. Those rumours sounded too circumstantial to be invented, I thought. You realize, of course, that such actions are very likely manifestations of a recognized, if fortunately rare, form of insanity?"

"A kind of homicidal mania," Vachell suggested, "applied to animals, instead of to men?"

"It's something that in the old days would have been put down as a form of sorcery or witchcraft, and probably caused the death of a number of innocent suspects at the stake. To-day psychologists could, no doubt, provide a number of convincing, but in fact little more illuminating, explanations. One might, for instance, put it down (let us say) to a frustrated power-complex, a perversion of that universal urge to dominate others, to be acknowledged as a personage by one's fellows, finding an outlet in a mentally weak individual forced by circumstances to remain a person of no account."

"It seems a far cry from an urge for power to the mutilation of dogs and birds."

"Quite so, but a close acquaintance with the speculations of modern psychology would leave you dumbfounded at the distance a psychologist's cry can carry," Anstey remarked dryly. "Personally, I distrust purely psychological explanations of conduct—or, shall I say, I find them incomplete. The abnormality perhaps has its origin in some condition of the ductless glands. A colleague of mine, for instance, once treated a patient who displayed the most inordinate and insatiable appetite. She would eat a whole shoulder of lamb at a sitting and still rise hungry from the table. The children of one of her employers (she was a domestic servant) kept white mice, and one day she was detected pulling off their legs and tails. Mentally she was undoubtedly a victim of arrested development, and one might point here to the parallel of the small boy in Struwelpeter who was in the habit of pulling off the wings of flies. Undoubtedly she had some glandular abnormality. In the later stages it was associated with obesity and a craving for sleep, and in due course she was certified as insane."

"An unpleasant story," Vachell remarked. They reached the house and a native servant brought a tray of tea and fruit cake, and set it on the table.

"Very likely you are up against something of the same nature in this case," Anstey went on. "In its early stages, the physical symptoms of the glandular state are often not apparent. Weak or strong?"

"As it comes," Vachell said. "It's possible for a person with this glandular defect to conceal his abnormality when it isn't, you might say, in possession—to appear quite normal in between bouts?"

"Oh, certainly, yes. In the earlier stages the impulse would only attack him at intervals, very likely when he was subjected to some emotional strain. In between whiles he would not only appear normal but *be* normal; in fact, he might even be oblivious of the actions he performed while under the compulsion of his craving. Blood, you know, has a peculiar effect on many people. It frequently repels. You would be surprised at the number of people who feel sick even at the mention of the word. Every sensation probably has its perversions, and a craving for blood, though fortunately rare, is no doubt the perversion of the more normal sensation of repulsion. Here, no doubt, is the true foundation for the very ancient and remarkably widespread legend of the vampire."

"Vampires in modern dress," Vachell remarked.

"You will find, I believe, that every persistent myth, one that has come down to us in many forms through the ages, has some foundation in one of the diverse aspects of human activity. Even werewolves probably have a prototype somewhere. Unfortunately modern science is much less efficient than mythology. It may demonstrate the reality of the vampire, but it will fail to supply us with a sprig of garlic to put over our doors."

Vachell caught a glint in his companion's frosty blue eyes that made him wonder if he was being taken for a ride.

"I guess the police provide the garlic," he said. "We didn't get an anti-vampire precautions course in our training, but just the same we reckon the protection of the citizen against vampire depradations as part of our job. No thanks, I don't care for a second cup. Sir Jolyot, where is your daughter stopping at present?"

Anstey paused with the teapot half-way to his cup and glanced sharply at Vachell's face.

"My daughter? She's spending a holiday with some friends. It's fortunate that she should have chosen this time to be away. Although my daughter is a very competent farm manager, Mr. Vachell, she is still very young, and I am exceedingly glad that she was not here during the last few days. She was very fond of the Wests, and I'm afraid she'll be most upset at the tragedy of yesterday's fire. A bad business, that. Dennis West will be a great loss, poor fellow, and I don't know what Mrs. West will do."

Vachell lit a cigarette reflectively and killed the match in the dregs of his tea. "Are you sure," he asked slowly, "that it was, in fact, your daughter's choice to go away?"

Anstey put down his cup and looked across at his guest. His expression was set and hostile, and Vachell could almost feel the impact of his eyes. His was the sort of gaze, Vachell reflected, that registered like a physical touch, that a stranger couldn't fail to feel if it was turned on to him in a crowded room. Anstey got up before replying, took a small cigar out of a box, lit it, and stood with his back to the fireplace.

"My daughter's actions, you understand, are entirely her own affair, and to some extent mine," he said at last. "They are nothing whatsoever to do with you. I could perfectly well tell you to mind your own business and go to the devil. On the other hand I observe that you are a shrewd young man, and as I think I can see the paths along which your mind is working I shall answer that question as directly as it was put. The fact that my daughter has gone away was not her own choice. I insisted on her going, for some weeks at least, for a reason of which I think you are perfectly well aware."

"To get her mind off Corcoran for a while."

"Exactly. Daphne is only nineteen. She lives a life for which I believe she would sacrifice almost anything rather than change, but it is, nevertheless, unusually solitary for a girl. She sees few young men, or at least she sees them only from time to time; she has had no opportunity, as yet, of developing powers of sound judgment and discrimination. I am not, I hope, a specimen of the old-fashioned father who drives his daughter's suitors from the door, but nor am I willing to stand aside and see an unscrupulous young man with bad heredity and worse environment, unfortunately the possessor of an easy superficial charm, take advantage of my daughter's ignorance to talk her into marriage before she has had a chance to develop her own character and to know her own mind. I trust I make myself clear?"

"Perfectly, sir. You believe that Corcoran and your daughter had got so far as to talk of marriage?"

"I am certain of it."

"I believe that Munson objected, on his side, to his nephew's plans."

"I have no knowledge whatever of Munson's views, and no interest in them," Anstey said coldly.

"Munson was sore as hell at you, sir—on account of the legal action you brought against him, I guess, and also the ideological differences between you. He wouldn't have let Corcoran marry your daughter, and unless Corcoran quit the country altogether he couldn't have married without his uncle's consent. He had no capital to start on his own. You realize that Munson's death removes the major obstacle to marriage with your daughter, from Corcoran's point of view?"

"No, I do not," Anstey said shortly. He was staring intently at the glowing end of his cigar. "I have no knowledge, naturally, of Corcoran's plans, but I cannot see that his prospects will be affected in any way. Mrs. Munson, I believe, was always the more rabid and least generous of the two."

"Mrs. Munson doesn't inherit the farm."

Anstey raised his bushy eyebrows and said: "Really? You over-estimate my interest in the Munsons' affairs, Mr. Vachell."

"Corcoran gets it," Vachell went on. "He can do what he likes. He'll be the boss now."

This time Anstey did not pretend to be indifferent. He glanced up over his cigar, frowning, and snapped:

"What do you mean? Munson has a son."

"The son gets a half share when he's twenty-one, if Corcoran doesn't choose to buy him out at Land Bank valuation."

"But that's iniquitous!" Anstey exclaimed. For the first time Vachell saw him really moved. "A man has no right to disinherit his wife and son! Under French law that would not be allowed. And now, after all, Corcoran . . ."

He turned his back and leant against the big stone fireplace, his forehead resting on a forearm, his head bowed. Vachell thought that the ex-surgeon didn't want his expression to be seen. When he turned around, flicking away his half-smoked cigar, he was perfectly composed.

"So Corcoran gets his uncle's farm and gets rid of the major obstacle in the way of his matrimonial plans, at one stroke," he observed. "No doubt the implications have not escaped you."

"They have not," Vachell agreed.

"There is, however, another obstacle in the way," Anstey added, with a trace of grimness. "I can see that I shall have to do without a farm manager for some time."

A little way below the homestead, on his way back, Vachell stopped the car at the junction of the road (a courtesy title, as in the case of most Chania thoroughfares) with a track leading off into the forest to the left. It was overgrown with weeds, grass and creepers, but the trampling of cattle had evidently kept it from reverting to forest, and it was clear of trees or fallen logs. Vachell walked a little way along and decided that a car could use it without too much difficulty in dry weather, though not in wet. He couldn't see any signs of a car's recent passage, but there had been no rain for over a week and the ground was hard. A pony, of course, could get along it any time.

He found Prettyman at the Karuna police office, catching up on routine.

"I went along to the funeral to keep an eye on things," he reported. "There was quite a crowd. Every one liked West, and the news was on the wireless last night, so a lot of people turned up. Mrs. West looked terribly cut up. Natural, of course. I must say it's lucky they pop people into coffins to put them underground, it all looked very decent, nothing to tell they were only burying a lot of roasted bones."

"Was Parrot there?"

"Yes, looking frightfully respectable in a gent's lounge suiting, without that old raincoat of his, for once. He looked as though it had got him down, too. Of course, he was very friendly with the Wests. He brought her, I think—anyway he was standing with her all the time and sort of helping her out. He's got it badly, if you ask me. Shouldn't wonder if he didn't step into West's shoes one of these days, when things have blown over a bit."

"You'll find it nice to go to weddings for a change," Vachell remarked. "You know, you're wasted in the police. If the *Evening Standard* heard about you they'd fire Corisande and sign you up."

Prettyman sighed, and measured the prospective of the desk across the room with a pencil held upright in his hand. "I know you think I listen to gossip too much, sir," he said, "but, after all, in a district like this it's half the job—among the Europeans, I mean. I wanted to be an artist, as a matter of fact. However, I've traced something I hope you'll think useful—more worthy of a policeman, so to speak."

He took his wallet from an inner pocket of his khaki coat and pulled out a small slip of paper, folded over several times.

"Shoot," Vachell said.

"It may mean a bottle of whisky for me."

"You remembered whose handwriting was on the note I found in Munson's room?"

"Better still, I've traced a letter in the file written in the same fist. We'll make absolutely sure. Have you got the original note, sir?"

Vachell ran through the papers in his pocket-book until he found it—the scrawled, hastily written note cancelling a date because some one called D. was getting suspicious, the note of a person having a flirtation or an affair.

"That's it," Prettyman said. "Now, here's the letter on the file." He drew towards him a sheet of note-paper covered with handwriting in the same loose scrawl. "Dear Sir," it began, "I wish to report the theft of a high-grade Hereford heifer belonging to this farm which was last seen . . ."

"Check on that," Vachell said. "They're the same."

"Now we'll see about this bottle of whisky; I'm counting on it, because no one could possibly guess." He started to unravel the slip of paper on which Vachell had written a name. "I must say, the last thing in the world I'd ever have believed is that a girl like that, with quite a decent cove already eating out of her hand, would look twice at a nasty piece of work like Munson. He's at least . . . well, I'll be damned!"

Prettyman stared incredulously at the piece of paper in his hand and then at his superior. Vachell grinned.

"No whisky," he said.

"By God, no," Prettyman agreed. "Well, congratulations, sir. I had too pure a mind. Fancy a damned nice girl like Daphne Anstey carrying on with a stiff-necked old Boche twice her age. . . . Well, it just shows, you simply can't tell what any woman will do next."

"Check on that, too," Vachell said.

CHAPTER 19: AFTER LUNCH VACHELL DROVE a little way out of Karuna to an acacia wood on the edge of the big lake. It was shady there, and cool, and pleasant to hear pigeons calling and birds chirping overhead. He lay on his back in the shade and tried to get the facts sorted out in his mind. There were too many and yet not enough. Too many motives, too many lines crossing and re-crossing in a hopeless tangle. Yet, concerning Munson's murder, West's sudden death, there were almost no facts at all.

He went through the stories each person had given him, bit by bit, trying to find a flaw. Sooner or later all murderers were forced to lie about their movements, and he believed that with perseverance some little discrepancy of fact or statement could always be found. Sometimes the discrepancy was so insignificant that it was overlooked altogether; but always, he believed, it was there, a challenge to the investigator. Sometimes, even when found, it could be explained away; but at other times it couldn't, and that was the beginning of the end.

But although he sought all the afternoon, he had not sifted from the evidence the one fact that would satisfy him before, in the cool of the evening, long shadows from the acacias fell across the lake shore and it was time to return. People concerned in the case had lied, often enough. But the inexplicable lie, the lie without apparent point, eluded him.

He looked in to the police office on the way back and found

Prettyman still there, long after hours, catching up on routine.

"I wish people would stop stealing stock and brewing beer illegally and busting into houses while murder cases are on," he remarked. "One gets so awfully behindhand. They've no consideration. Oh, by the way, the lab rang up. The fellow gabbled off a lot of technical terms about Munson's innards, but what it all amounted to, as I understood it, is that they're stumped. Absolutely. Can't find anything, and they're mailing you a report to that effect to-night."

"That's what I expected," Vachell said.

"Well, sir, you won't have many disappointments in life if you keep that up. What do you think did him in—the evil eye?"

"*Acocanthera schimperü.*"

"Aco what?"

"Native arrow-poison. You can read all about it in there." He threw a copy of the *British Pharmaceutical Journal* on to the table. Anstey lent me that. There's an article on page one hundred and sixty-two."

Prettyman stared at the superintendent as if he were seeing things. "Sir, do I understand that you believe some one shot Munson with a bow and arrow?"

"If you'll forgive me for saying so, Prettyman, you are a little inclined to sail off into space in pursuit of conclusions. I didn't mention a bow, and the arrow only as an adjective."

"Oh," Prettyman said blankly.

"No one used arrows, so far as I know. On the sole of Munson's right foot Dr. Lawson found a small, fresh puncture. In the sole of his right shoe I found a small hole. Figure it out for yourself."

Prettyman thought for a little and suggested: "A nail."

"Right. A small nail, unless I miss my guess, hammered through the sole so the point stuck up enough to scratch Munson's foot when he rammed it into the shoe. He kicked the shoes into the wall opposite, pulled on an old pair, and made tracks for the farm without waiting to bawl out his boy. Does that suggest any further conclusions?"

"That he was in a hurry, or he'd have called in the boy to curse him, and to get the nail taken out."

"That's the way I figure it. It looks like he had an early appointment to keep. Between the time Mwogi cleaned Munson's shoes the night before, and six o'clock next morning, some one stuck this nail in Munson's shoe and doctored the tip. A touch of poison would do the job; Sir Jolyot told me there's sufficient on one arrowhead to rub out two hundred and fifty men. He said also it would take half an hour to two hours if it entered the bloodstream at a point far removed from the heart—for instance, a foot."

"Damned ingenious," Prettyman said. "You're sure of those medical facts, I suppose?"

Vachell tapped the journal lying on the table. "You can read about them here. Parts of the article are fine, exciting reading, packed with human interest. It tells of a native in Tanganyika who made successful passes at a neighbour's wife. Finally this guy decided to bump off the husband, so he got some fruits of the castor oil bush, round pods with big, strong prickles, dipped them in the arrow-poison, and scattered them around on the path this husband used to go to work. Sure enough, the husband trod on one and died. The pay-off was when the woman screeched because she saw her small son toddling along the path. So, you see, the method's been tested, and found reliable enough to win a Good Housekeeping seal."

"By God, sir, it looks as though you'd got hold of the method all right," Prettyman said excitedly. "By the way, could any one have seen the article with that story in it?"

"Any reader of the *British Pharmaceutical Journal*."

"Which boils down to Anstey; but, of course, the natives would know all about the way the poison behaves. It looks as though it must be some one who knows a good bit about native customs and so on—unless, of course, it's actually a native."

Vachell shook his head. "I reckon not. For one thing, I believe Munson had a date in that pyrethrum shed. That's the only way to explain his going in there at all, aside from his hurry when he got dressed."

"In that case the murderer's idea must have been to make it look as if Munson was choked by the fumes," Prettyman suggested.

"It looks that way. And then, there's Dennis West."

Prettyman raised his eybrows and chewed the end of a pencil, to help his concentration.

"You still think he was murdered, too, sir? By the same person, of course. It seems rather hard to find a motive to cover both."

"Self-defence, the second time. West had a hunch who it

was, all along, but he wouldn't talk. The way I figure it, he caught the killer red-handed with that little bush-buck calf. This paper of Anstey's says that if the poison hits the blood-stream near the heart, it will kill in two minutes. So all the killer has to do is to jab West somewhere in the chest with any sort of weapon—a sharp-pointed stick would do—smeared with a touch of poison, and his troubles are over. There isn't any antidote and poison's infallible. West couldn't make the rest of the party in two or three minutes. Along comes the fire to burn all the flesh off his body, and there's the perfect murder. So perfect, we couldn't get to first base trying to prove it was a murder at all, much less who did it. Our only chance is to get the Munson killer and then we'll have the guy who killed West, too."

Prettyman had been chewing his pencil hard. "This question of the nail in Munson's shoe," he said thoughtfully. "Did Munson's boy find it when he did out the room at seven-fifteen?"

"No. He looked Munson's shoes over carefully when he saw them strewn around the room, and he's positive as daylight there wasn't any nail, then, in the sole. If he's on the level that evidence is dependable, he couldn't miss a nail sticking up out of the sole. So you see what that gives us. Between six-fifteen and seven-fifteen that morning the murderer walked into Munson's room and swiped the nail, reckoning if we found no sign of any funny business, we'd write it off as death from misadventure, with a rider on the danger of charcoal fumes in pyrethrum-drying sheds. It darned nearly worked out."

"It would have, sir, if it hadn't been for your bright idea," Prettyman said dutifully. "Well, I'm glad I know now what the feller I was trying to find was supposed to have taken from Munson's room. That brings us back to the question, who was Munson going to meet in the pyrethrum shed? I'm afraid there *can* only be one answer to that, knowing Munson's little ways. But it does seem an extraordinary hour for a date, doesn't it, six-thirty in the morning? I simply can't imagine being romantic on an empty stomach like that, at any rate not in a pyrethrum shed. Although, according to some statistics in America I read the other day, the second most popular time was ten in the morning and apparently a canoe . . ."

A knock on the door interrupted his remarks, and the lanky figure of Dr. Lawson loomed in the doorway.

"Good Lord, you are late," he said. "How you fellows do work. The influence of the Big Four in One from Marula, I suppose." He came in and pulled the door to. "I hope I'm not intruding, but a small point occurred to me which I thought I'd better mention, since it's connected with the case I assume you're working on now."

Vachell pulled a chair out from the table and said: "Sit down, doctor, and give us the lowdown. It's good of you to come."

"Thanks, but it won't take a moment, and very likely it's a point of no importance in any case. It's about that question you asked me, Prettyman—whether one of the Munson family or their pals had consulted me professionally lately. It had something to do with an anonymous note, I believe."

"That's right," Prettyman said. "You told me about Anita Adams."

"Yes, and it puzzled me a bit, as there didn't seem to be any possible connexion between that and Munson's death. I was going through my books to-day to send out some bills, and I was reminded that I did see some one else about a month ago who, although not directly associated with the Munson family, is a neighbour, and has—er—been connected with them in a way. Only by gossip, of course, and there may have been nothing in it at all."

"Who was this, doctor?" Vachell asked.

"Perhaps I'd better tell you what I prescribed for first, and if you don't think it necessary I needn't give the name. I'm rather overstepping the mark, you know—professional confidence and all that, but I want to help you if I can. My patient complained principally of insomnia, and mentioned one or two other symptoms indicative of considerable nervous strain. I prescribed the usual things—rest, avoiding worry so far as possible, and a sleeping-draught."

"That contained a drug, of course."

"Yes, chloral hydrate, for which I gave a prescription that ought to have been renewed. I'm afraid the local chemist was a bit slack, they know every one so well, of course, in a small place like this, and I found to-day that three bottles have been made up."

"This is more like it," Prettyman exclaimed with enthusiasm. "This must have been what the anonymous note-writer was getting at. You could kill a person with this chloral stuff, couldn't you?"

"Well, if you made them drink enough of it you could," Dr. Lawson said.

Prettyman glanced across at his chief. "I think it's important to hear who it was, isn't it, sir? This anonymous bloke does seem to know something. He implied the person who'd been to see Dr. Lawson was the same as the person that Munson had a date with in the shed."

Vachell was pulling hard on a cigarette, staring out of the window at long shadows fading before the advance of night. He barely seemed to hear the other's comment, and his lean face was grave and set.

"Sure," he said at last, without turning his head. "Go ahead, doctor. We'd better have it straight."

Dr. Lawson polished his spectacles carefully before replying. "I don't like it," he said finally. "But I feel it's my duty to help. I'm afraid I rather let you down over that autopsy. . . . Well, all right, my patient was Mrs. West."

CHAPTER 20: "How on earth," Prettyman wondered, "did the writer of that anonymous note know about Mrs. West's sleeping-draught? That's what I can't make out. After all, people don't go about advertising things like that. It must have been some one who knew her jolly well."

Vachell sighed, and ground out his cigarette in an ashtray. He had been unresponsive to Prettyman's speculations since Dr. Lawson left. The young inspector looked at him quizzically, thinking: wonder if he's fallen for her too. He doesn't seem to like the way everything's working out. She certainly knows how to bowl 'em over.

"Munson wasn't killed with chloral hydrate," Vachell pointed out.

"No, this anonymous bloke slipped up there. He evidently knew about the chloral and jumped to the wrong conclusion that she'd used it on Munson. But he'd got the right idea about Munson going to keep a date in that shed. . . ."

"Do you have any letters from Mrs. Innocent on your file?" Vachell asked.

Prettyman looked surprised. "Cautious Clara? Yes, I expect so, sir."

"Fetch one along," Vachell said.

Prettyman went into the other room and rummaged about among the files. He came back with a letter in his hand, and switched on the light.

"Past gin-time and still at work," he remarked. "They ought to give us a bonus for this. Here's a letter about a boy who pinched the roof off old Hammond's house while he was away, and sold it to the railway. Mrs. Innocent defended him, and he got off on some legal point or other, as usual. That do?"

"Sure," Vachell said. He pulled out his wallet and extracted a flimsy sheet of typescript. "Here's the anonymous note. Look them over."

Prettyman walked to the light and held the two sheets of paper close to the naked bulb. He looked from one to the other, a frown on his fair-skinned, pink face.

"Gosh, sir, they *do* look alike," he exclaimed. "It's the same size type, bigger than a portable, and purple ribbon, and the a's and e's and o's want cleaning. . . . By God, you're right." He looked so astounded that Vachell grinned and said:

"For my next little experiment I shall require a gold watch, a solar topee and one thousand pounds sterling in single currency bills, and will some gentleman kindly put out the light. . . . It's easy when you know the trick."

Prettyman looked at his superior with a new respect. "You pulled a fast one that time, sir. I'd never have thought of Clara Innocent, if she'd been the last person on earth. But how on earth did she know so much about it? And why write a note? She could have told us just as well."

Vachell picked his hat off the table and walked to the door. "This case has long arid stretches," he observed. "You have things in common with this anonymous guy."

"Who, me? What?"

"Conclusion-jumping again."

"Oh," Prettyman said, dubiously. "Well, for God's sake let's go home and have a drink."

They dined in Prettyman's bungalow, late and tired. Vachell thought with a pang of his meals at the Wests'. The food at his new host's was poor, and badly cooked; no salads enticed him with their crispness, the vegetables were soggy and over-boiled. A young bachelor's household was the Mecca of lazy and dishonest cooks. Whisky after a long day went a little to Prettyman's head, and he told a long story about a girl he had met on the boat going home on his last leave, a bubble-dancer from a cabaret in Singapore.

They were still drinking coffee outside after the meal when twin beams of light suddenly flooded the short driveway and the wooden steps leading up to the veranda, and a car swung through the gate and came to a standstill in front of the house. A man got out, and a voice hailed them from the darkness. It was Edward Corcoran's drawl, but to-night it lacked the self-assurance that went with that sort of voice.

Vachell unfolded his long legs and emerged upright from the chair in the flick of a lizard's tail.

"Anything wrong?" he called. There was anxiety in his tone.

Corcoran switched off the headlamps, and came up the steps. He had on a white shirt that showed up against the starlit darkness.

"Not exactly," he answered. "I mean, nothing fresh."

"Have a drink," Prettyman invited. "Boy! Bring whisky-soda."

"Thanks," Corcoran said. "I hope I'm not butting in. As a matter of fact, I came to see you, Mr. Vachell. That is, I wondered if I could have a word with you. It's rather a—well, a confidential matter."

Prettyman took the hint. "I'll be in the dining-room if you want me, sir," he said. "I've got to catch up on some reports."

The house-boy brought the drinks and a lamp, and put them down. Corcoran was not at all at ease. His dark face, with its clear-cut, even features, was worried, and he kept running a nervous hand over his well-shaped chin. He was handsome as an extra, Vachell thought; finely built with a perfectly proportioned head, and a Clark Gable moustache.

"I've probably come on a hopeless errand," he began, cupping his glass with both hands. "I don't suppose you'll listen to me, sir, and I don't really know why you should. But at least it's worth a try."

"I'll listen anyway," Vachell said.

Corcoran laughed; he had an attractive, infectious smile.

"I'm afraid that was badly put. Well, sir, I don't suppose it's any use beating about the bush. You probably know what what I've come for, so I'll put it to you straight out. I know it's no good asking for them back, but would you agree to burn them, and forget about the whole thing?"

"Burn what?" Vachell inquired.

Corcoran laughed again. "I hoped you wouldn't take that line, sir. After all, it's no good either of us trying to pretend, is it—you that you didn't find them in the roof (God knows how you knew where he'd put them) or me that we weren't sick as mud when they disappeared."

Vachell did not reply until he had lit another cigarette. Then he said:

"Why do you want them burnt?"

"We want to let the whole thing drop," Corcoran said eagerly. "That is, my aunt does—it isn't my pigeon at all. It was all my uncle's idea. You know what he was like, obstinate as the devil, and when he got this idea into his head nothing would make him budge. But now that he's dead the whole thing's washed out, and I don't suppose you fellows are interested in the least. I told Wendtland as much, but he's in a hell of a stew, and won't be satisfied till he actually sees them go up in smoke."

"So it's Wendtland who wants the papers burnt."

Corcoran looked up at Vachell over his glass. The anxiety in his face had gone; his dark eyes were dancing with the amusement that seemed to come to him as readily as song to a bird's throat.

"Well, if you've read them, sir, I should think you'd understand. That sort of stuff is a bit embarrassing for any man to see on paper, I shouldn't like it myself; I'm glad no one has ever gone through my past with such a fine comb. But if, on top of all that, one's boss had such very strong ideas . . ." Corcoran shrugged his shoulders and drained his drink. "Well, it would cook his goose, of course."

"And why," Vachell inquired, "keeping this on a culinary basis, do you expect me to save his bacon?"

Corcoran grimaced, and helped himself to another shot of whisky. "You've hit on the weak point," he said, with candour. "To be quite frank, I can't think of any good reason. It's nothing to the Chania police what happens to Wendtland, and though of course the information isn't of any value to you, I suppose you like to put everything in a file. . . . In fact, there's only one bait I can think of."

"I'm still listening," Vachell said.

Corcoran hesitated, and swished his drink around in the glass. "You probably think my position is a bit, well, peculiar," he ventured, hesitation in his voice. "I'd rather like to explain. Technically I'm a British subject, but my mother's German and my father's Irish, and I was brought up largely among the South African Dutch, so I haven't got much loyalty to King and Empire running in my veins."

"I can imagine that," Vachell agreed.

"There's a lot of feeling against my uncle in the district, and I get the backwash. I don't give a damn what they think, I don't owe anything to the British and if their bloody empire doesn't go on paying ten per cent it's not my funeral. They can do their own dirty work."

"They generally do," Vachell remarked. "What is this, a political meeting?"

"The point I'm getting at is, I'm not a Nazi. I'm not anything. The whole lousy game means nothing to me, but if the Nazis want to have their little secrets, it isn't up to me to blab them all to the British."

"But you might be interested in a trade."

Corcoran looked up with a rather sheepish expression. "That's more or less the idea," he said. He laughed a little uncomfortably, and finished off his second drink.

"That sounds pretty dirty, doesn't it? The fact is, Wendtland's a friend of mine, and if I can help him get those lousy affidavits destroyed, I will. I don't know what you mean to do with them, but he'll go on sweating in his boots until he gets them. You can't be expected to hand them over without getting something in return, I realize that. All I've got to offer is information about the local Nazis' organization and so on here, but I think you'd find it useful. I've got pretty complete information about the set-up, and I don't really mind passing it on, because although I've got a lot of sympathy for the Nazis, I'd hate to see them taking over this country. That would mean the push for any one who isn't actually a German, including me."

Vachell smoked for a few moments in silence, considering this remarkable offer. Irish logic, he thought, would justify the horns off a bull.

"What makes you think I have the papers that Wendtland wants?" he asked at last.

"Well, of course you've got them," Corcoran said. "Who else could? By God, I cursed myself for a bloody halfwit for not thinking of that space above the ceiling in my uncle's room. How did you kow they were there?"

"Clairvoyance," Vachell answered. "You weren't around at the time they were found."

"No, I'd had a row with my aunt—my God, she dropped bombs all over me like a Vickers-Wellington with a belly-ache—and I went off to Karuna and got blind. When I came back she was in a tail-spin about the missing papers. As soon as she knew Uncle Karl was dead she'd collared all his papers—or so she thought—and left everything dealing with the Bund at Mrs. Innocent's office for Wendtland to pick up. She wanted to get shot of the whole Bund row. Of course she thought everything was there, but it wasn't, so poor old Wendtland rushed over to our place in a hell of a stew. He and my aunt looked everywhere, but drew blank. He'd no sooner gone than she found the hole in the ceiling and realized some one had pinched them from under her nose, more or less while she and Wendtland had been in committee about it next door. That made her wild, I can tell you. We talked it over, and realized that it must have been you. It was neat, if you'll allow me to say so."

"Easy when you know the trick," Vachell said modestly. "Help yourself to another. What was Mrs. Munson's position?"

"Oh, she'd been against my uncle in this from the start. He'd sweated blood to keep the organization going when it was nobody's baby, and then when Berlin sent out Wendtland to take over and make things hum, he was as jealous as a cat. I didn't blame him myself, but he couldn't realize that he'd shot his bolt. Even if he'd got Wendtland thrown out, *he'd* never have stood a chance of getting back in the saddle. My aunt saw that, and tried to stop him. She knew Berlin would never forget his part in getting Wendtland unstuck. They might have had to act on the information, but Wendtland was one of their blue-eyed boys, and they wouldn't have liked it one little bit."

"How did your uncle get the dope?" Vachell asked casually.

"Through my mother, mostly. She unearthed that Jo'-

burg—" Corcoran put down his glass abruptly and stared at Vachell. "Look here, what are you getting at? It's all in that letter she . . . You're not double-crossing me, are you? You can't—no, of course not, I'm going crazy." He rubbed a hand over his face. "Well, what about it? Are you going to play?"

He got up and looked across with a question in his eyes.

"I'll think it over," Vachell said. "The decision isn't in my hands."

Corcoran tilted back his head and laughed. "I'd forgotten you were a Government man," he said. "I've never heard one of 'em give any other answer. Do you have to refer this back to the Secretary of State?"

"I'll be out to-morrow. I'll give you an answer then."

"Okay," Corcoran said. "I'll have everything ready for a bonfire. You won't regret it if you agree."

Vachell leant against the veranda rail and watched the tail-light of the car recede out of the gate. For the time it took to smoke a cigarette he tried to roast Corcoran's story, driving out a steam of fiction to leave a residue of fact. There was a lot of solid matter left at the end. He wondered where the papers that Wendtland was so anxious to recover were spending the night. And what Wendtland would do if he discovered that a third party had cleared the board.

Later on he got out his note-book, and thumbed over the pages by the light of the petrol lamp. A sausage-beetle came and hurled itself repeatedly against the lampshade, hitting the glass with such force that it was a mystery why either the shade or the insect didn't break. It was a still, windless night, and the moon rose late. Prettyman came out to say good-night, but seeing that the superintendent had one of his silent fits he went off to bed without trying to start a conversation. Vachell sat on until the moon came up, deep in a chair, smoking and scribbling doodles on a loose page of his note-book, trying to get the tangled threads sorted out.

A little before midnight an idea clicked in his brain. It was like a movie of the collapse of a house of cards seen in re-verse: one basic card was put in position, and the whole struc-ture reared itself miraculously in the air. With a deepening excitement he ran through note-book and memory to check the foundations of the idea, and its implications. Everything fitted into a coherent whole. Motive was conjectural, but he had the rest—and, above all, the little discrepancy in one per-son's actions that had provided the key.

CHAPTER 21: THE COMMISSIONER WAS ALWAYS
difficult to understand on the telephone; he snorted like a
hippopotamus, and snapped: "What, what, what?" like a re-
peating rifle when he couldn't hear. But next morning, with
perseverance, Vachell made him understand that he intended
to make an arrest.

"Quite sure you're on solid ground?" Major Armitage
barked. "Can't have mistakes being made, y'know. International complications in this case, you realize that. German
Consul's been on at us this end, kicking up a hell of a row."

"It's a question of the public safety, sir," Vachell explained.
"I'm afraid we're not at the end of the road. There may be a
third murder in the next few days."

"A third murder!" the Commissioner's voice barked. "Can't
have that, wouldn't do at all. There's been enough comment as it is. I saw H.E. yesterday and he's quite concerned
about these incidents, quite concerned. You must see to it,
Vachell, you must see to it without fail."

"Yes, sir," Vachell agreed. He hung up, and sat for several
minutes staring at the phone. The lines on his long face had
deepened, and his eyes were tired. Prettyman noticed something dispirited about his movements, and wondered if he'd
had bad dreams, or a ticking-off from his boss.

"The hell of it is," Vachell said aloud, "unless there's a
third attempt, we haven't the proof to convict a bee of stealing

honey. And if there's a third attempt . . ." He left the sentence unfinished.

"We'll catch him in the act," Prettyman said cheerfully.

Vachell looked up with eyes that had lost their sparkle. The half-sceptical, half-amused expression habitual to his face had faded; he looked grave now, almost afraid.

"Catch a maniac who's got enough poison to rub out a hundred men," he queried, "a poison that you can leave around on a nail or a splinter or anything sharp that your victim's likely to handle, and kill him stone dead in five minutes when you're fifty miles away? A killer who's living so close to the next victim marked down for elimination, the job could be done any time in the twenty-four hours?"

"Put that way, it does sound a tall order," Prettyman agreed.

Vachell drummed on the office desk with his fingers for a little.

"Listen," he said suddenly. "Is there accommodation for women prisoners here?"

"*Women* prisoners?" Prettyman exclaimed, as if the superintendent had referred to green snow or eight-legged cows. "Well . . ."

"For God's sake, don't women in this district ever go wrong?"

"Well, there was Mrs. Shew," Prettyman said doubtfully. "She was a bit batty, and finally she had a row with her neighbour, a Seventh Day Adventist, and I must admit a tiresome sort of bloke, and jabbed him in the backside with a red-hot branding-iron. There isn't a woman warder or anything here, not for Europeans. My predecessor locked her into a room at the Black Buffalo and those swine at the Treasury knocked the hire of the room off his pay. Actually, the spare room in my bungalow would do, I suppose. . . ."

"Get it ready," Vachell ordered briefly. "And if there is an arrest, for Christ's sake don't talk."

"Hush-hush stuff?"

"For as long as possible."

"Okay," Prettyman said. "I'll have the sheets changed this morning."

But Vachell didn't make his arrest all day. He put it off a dozen times, reluctant to act, uncertain how to prevent a crime whose final shape, he knew, was growing hour by hour in a twisted, cunning mind. An almost unbearable feeling of expectancy tortured his nerves. He dreaded to see, at any minute, a figure coming running with urgent news, a car draw up with a squeal of brakes, to know that he must face the sight of the third victim, too late again to save a life.

He had the opening surprise of a long, nerve-racked, surprising day when he reached his first port of call that morning, Norman Parrot's farm.

"The bwana is not back," Parrot's house-boy said.

"Back from where?"

"From the burial of Bwana West."

"But Bwana West was buried yesterday morning."

"Yes, that is true. My bwana went to Karuna for the ceremony, and has not returned."

Vachell scratched his chin, taken aback. Parrot would hardly have stayed in Karuna all yesterday, kicking his heels. The only thing was to go back and pick up his trail. He spent the best part of a hot and aggravating morning trying to dig out news, but so far as he could make out Norman Parrot had vanished into thin air. He had been at the funeral all right, and soon after it was over he had been seen by the Indian bootmaker who repaired his shoes coming out of the doorway leading to Mrs. Innocent's office. But Clara Innocent herself denied emphatically that he had been to see her— she had never acted for him in any way, she said—and the Indian, on being pressed, admitted that he might have been mistaken, it might have been another doorway, or perhaps some one else, not Parrot at all. Telephone calls to Marula yielded no result. He had not checked in at any of the hotels there, or at the country club.

"Who are his pals?" Vachell inquired. "Maybe he took a fancy to go off on a visit."

"I don't know," Prettyman confessed. "He's a newcomer, you know, and I don't think he had any particular pals. He's friendly with most people, but no one more so than others, so far as I know, except the Wests. Funny his clearing off like that when she's left on her own. You'd think he'd stay and help her, now she's in a hole."

"We've got to find him," Vachell said. "This is no time for a guy to stage a disappearing act."

"I'll wire all the stations, if you like. After all, his car's gone too, so we ought to trace him by that. I'll get the licence number from the garage. Have you asked Mrs. West, sir? She'd be most likely to know what he's up to."

"Not yet," Vachell said.

He knew he ought to go up there, but he put it off again to go to Wendtland's farm. The young German was not there either. He had driven off that morning in his car, the boys said, after a telegram had come. Perhaps he had gone to Marula; they did not know; he often went away like that. In spite of its master's frequent absences the farm looked active and neat, with well laid-out paddocks, a chain of small conservation dams, and broad-base terraces on all the slopes. Quite a lot of money must have been spent on it; the British settlers were convinced this came from Nazi funds.

The askaris left on Munson's farm reported nothing unusual. Following Vachell's instructions, one had kept close to Mrs. Munson all day, and the other had searched all the buildings and sheds methodically for an empty gasolene can with a bottom blackened by fire. They had found two. Vachell inspected them carefully, using his magnifying glass, and then said: "All right, return them; and look again." The Europeans, they added, had not gone away, but the night before a leopard had tried to get into the bullpen, and Corcoran was building a trap on the lines he had learnt from the Dorobo, who were experts at the art.

It was dark before Vachell finally reached the Wests' farm. There was a light in the living-room and the dogs barked when they heard the car. He knocked and went in, feeling as if it were an operating-room and the anaesthetist were approaching with the mask.

Janice West was at the writing-desk, her forehead resting on one hand, wrestling with a water permit form requiring her to estimate the daily flow in cusecs of water over a dam. She looked up as he entered, and smiled.

"Come in," she said. "I've been hoping to see you all day." She got up and turned a setter off the sofa to make room. Her eyes looked enormous in a white tired face; her movements were jerky and he could see that her nerves were strained almost to breaking-point. She looked as though it was a long time since she had eaten or slept. "It's bad being without news," she added. "I haven't seen any one all day, but one hears endless rumours from the boys. Has anything fresh . . ."

Vachell shook his head, keeping his eyes on the pack of cigarettes in his hand.

"Not yet. I'm looking for Norman Parrot."

Her left hand went to her throat in the familiar gesture and rested there. "Norman . . . ? Nothing has happened to him?"

The question went unanswered.

"I need the information. Where has he gone?"

She shook her head. "I don't know. I didn't know he'd gone at all. When . . ."

"He was with you yesterday in Karuna?"

"Yes. He came to . . . to the funeral."

"Did he bring you back?"

She shook her head. "I came by myself. I wanted to. I haven't seen him since."

"Did he say where he was going?"

"No. I thought he was coming back directly to the farm. He never said anything about going away. I kind of expected to see him to-day; he said he'd come up. . . . Don't his boys know?"

Vachell shook his head. "Do you know of anywhere he'd be likely to go in a hurry, without so much as packing a grip?"

"No." She walked over to the sideboard and started to mix a drink, turning her back. "Gin-and-French or Scotch? I don't know him that well. I guess he's like that, he gets impulses. Maybe he's gone off for a few days fishing. He goes up to the Samaki river sometimes, to a little fishing-hut up there."

"In his best suit?"

Janice said nothing, but brought him over a drink. She did not meet his eyes. He knew that she was lying as certainly as he knew that he wanted to kiss her as much as he'd ever wanted anything in his life.

A sharp knock at the door made her start so much that some of her drink spilt over. She turned her head to watch the door with a frightened jerk. Her eyes were wide with apprehension.

Before she could speak the door opened to reveal a police askari, square-shouldered and erect. He brought his hand up smartly to the temple and the hand went on quivering like the surface of a gong after it has been struck.

"What is it?" Vachell asked.

"We have found a petrol tin, bwana."

Vachell nodded, and said: "Good. Where?" There was a sound like a breeze just stirring a tree's foliage as Janice expelled a deep gulp of air. Her muscles relaxed, and she walked across to the sofa and sat down.

"In a hut behind the kitchen, bwana. It is an old hut once used as store, perhaps, but now ready to fall down."

"Where was the tin?"

"In a corner, beneath an old sack and some boards."

"Bring it here."

The askari saluted again and vanished into the blackness outside. The setters, disturbed by the arrival of another stranger, roamed around the room and settled themselves afresh on the chairs. Neither of the people in the room spoke. The askari came back with an empty four-gallon Shell petrol tin held by the rim in one hand. He put it down on the floor and stood to attention.

Vachell turned it over and examined the bottom of the tin. There was a round black patch on the outside.

"This has been used to cook with," he observed. His voice was conversational, as though he was pointing out the features of a washing-machine or discussing the merits of a car. "You can see where the flames blackened the tinplate. Let's see what we can find inside." He held it up to the light and peered into its empty depths.

"I don't understand," Janice said. From the way she spoke he could tell that her mouth was dry.

"It's been recently cleaned," he went on, "but it's hard to clean thoroughly right in the corners. See that black deposit down there?" He held the tin so that she could see inside it. She pushed it aside and stood up, breathing fast.

"Do you have to put on this act?" she demanded. "Do you

think I'm impressed, do you believe it gets you anywhere? Why can't you say what you want to say, and go? Your askari has found an old gasolene can in an old hut. So what? What does it all mean?"

Vachell had produced a pocket-knife and was scraping out a corner of the tin. The blade came away with traces of a black sticky substance on the steel.

"It means that this is the utensil in which the arrow-poison that killed Munson—and your husband—was brewed," he said.

CHAPTER 22: IT WAS A LITTLE AFTER SEVEN when Vachell braked his car in front of the Munson living-room. Through the undraped windows he could see that the family had not yet begun the evening meal. Mrs. Munson, Corcoran and Anita Adams were sitting around an unlighted fire when he entered. He got the impression that he had interrupted a not too harmonious discussion. Corcoran's good-looking sunburnt face was flushed, and he was breathing quickly. Mrs. Munson, on the other hand, bore all the signs of having scored a good point. She was sitting four-square on the edge of a chair, her hands full of knitting.

"Excuse me for intruding," he said. "I don't want to break up anything. I just dropped in to see if everything was okay."

There was an awkward silence. Mrs. Munson broke it by saying, almost affably:

"We have been expecting to see you all day. Your two askaris are here making a nuisance of themselves to every one but doing no work whatever. Have you caught the murderer yet, may I ask?"

"There's been no arrest."

"I'm glad you've turned up at last," Corcoran said. "Now you've had a chance to consider it I hope you'll—" He broke off, glanced at Anita Adams, and frowned. "I hope you'll agree to what I said last night."

"Sorry," Vachell said. "I can't play ball."

212

Corcoran started to say something and checked himself sharply. He looked very annoyed.

"I can't see what use it can possibly be to you to have ——"

Mrs. Munson pulled him up with a gesture of a podgy hand.

"We can discuss that some other time," she said. "Mr. Vachell, will you have a drink? The whisky is finished, I believe, but we have some sherry here. Edward, will you get it from the cupboard over there?"

Corcoran raised his eyebrows in surprise. "Are we celebrating something?" he asked. "That's the first time I've ever heard any one offer a drink to a guest." He got up, crossed to a cupboard standing against the wall, pulled it open and extracted some glasses and a bottle of sherry, half full.

"I'm sure we should all benefit from a glass," Mrs. Munson said.

Vachell had never seen her like this before. She reminded him of the wolf in Red Riding Hood. "Sit down, Mr. Vachell," she went on. "You know, of course, that owing to the condition in which my husband's affairs were left my income in future is to depend on the price of butter-fat?"

"Is that so?" Vachell said, apparently much surprised. "You mean you were left shares in a creamery business?"

Mrs. Munson uncorked the bottle of sherry and poured out four glassfuls.

"You need not pretend that you knew nothing of this." Her voice had taken on some of its normal sharpness. "That Innocent woman admitted that she had talked to you about other people's affairs. I shall contest the will, and even in a country where justice is always twisted to suit the convenience of black pagan apes I shall get it upset. When my legal right to this farm is established I shall sell it, and take my children back to South Africa. In the Union there are decent people, respectable people fit for my children to grow up among. Not like the people here. Like women who brazenly enter houses where they should be ashamed to set foot, who come where they are not wanted, where they have wronged." She glared at Corcoran, and took a mouthful of sherry.

"I've told you already, Aunt—" Corcoran began, then he shrugged his shoulders and picked up his glass. "Oh, what's the use. Happy landings, and here's to the quickest way out of this bloody mess. Come on, Anita, drink it up. This is about the first free drink I've ever collected on this farm. Let's gather the rosebuds, even if they've got canker in the middle and black spot on the outside." He made a grimace at the sherry and put down the empty glass.

Anita said "Here's luck" and sipped hers without enjoyment. Vachell left his severely alone; bad sherry had no appeal.

"You had a visitor here?" he asked.

"My aunt says so," Corcoran answered. "I didn't see any one."

"Edward was not here. He was out to shoot a buck. Therefore he missed a visitor who was looking for him."

"I don't believe it," Corcoran said flatly.

Anita Adams got up and walked to the doorway with her long awkward stride, turned her head, and said abruptly: "I'm just going to see that the children are all right."

"Just a moment," Vachell said. "Did you see this unwelcome guest?"

"No. I was putting the children to bed." She opened the door and disappeared into the darkness outside.

"Suppose you tell the story," Vachell suggested to Mrs. Munson. His voice was soothing.

"There isn't a story. That West woman saw fit to come over here, to my own house, this evening. She asked to see my nephew. With my husband dead two days, she waited two days to start her poison on the next. . . . I found her sitting here alone, in this room. When I came in, and told her that Edward was not here, she left. That is all. I have no objection to the visits of decent people, although we're farmers here and don't spend all our time poodle-faking and drinking cocktails like some I could name, but this was too much. To come into my own home, two days after my husband's murder. . . ."

"Do you wish to make any accusation against Mrs. West?"

"I make no accusations against any one. I only tell what I know, the truth. I do my duty as a citizen, I hope."

"I can check on Mrs. West's movements at any hour of the night or day. If your story's a phony I can bust it wide open and leave you on the spot."

She looked at him with contempt in her small cold eyes. "You think I invented this?" She laughed a little, her shoulders shaking like a jelly. "What good would that do? You can ask my boy, Mwogi. He brought her in here to wait for me."

"Okay," Vachell said. "That's just what I'll do."

Corcoran went with him, out to the rough lawn where oxen grazed and hens and turkeys pecked by day. His annoyance seemed to have evaporated as quickly as dew before a hot sun; he spoke rapidly, forgetting his drawl.

"Look, there's something seriously wrong here," he began, as soon as they were out on the lawn.

"Even an Englishman," Vachell observed, "might concede a couple of murders indicated something a little wrong."

"No, I don't mean that. I mean since then—to-day. There's something queer going on."

"Yes?" Vachell prompted. "Shoot."

"There's nothing absolutely definite. To begin with, my aunt seems to be—well, the engine's snatching, if you know what I mean. Of course, Uncle Karl's death must have been a frightful shock, but it seems to me she's going bats."

"What's she done?"

"She hasn't exactly *done* anything. She's behaving oddly. For instance, when I got back from Karuna last night I thought I'd let her know how things had gone, and when I got to her room I heard a peculiar voice coming from inside. A sort of moaning, I thought at first, but then it sounded as if some one was talking very quickly in an odd kind of mutter. I don't know how to describe it. Then it stopped. I thought there must be some one in there besides my aunt, so I—well, I ——"

"You peeked through the window."

"Well, yes, I did. I couldn't make it out at all. No one else *was* there, only aunt in a dressing-gown. She was walking up and down the room as if she was an animal in a cage.

You know, prowling, sort of. It gave me quite a turn. I couldn't see all she did because I only had a crack in the curtains to look through, but after a bit she stopped prowling and went over to her big desk. When she came back into sight she was staring at something in her hand. At first I couldn't see what it was, she had her back to me. But then she put it down on a table and it looked like a small square of paper. She lit a match and burnt it up carefully, so that nothing was left. I know this doesn't sound much when I tell it like this, but there was something extraordinary about it when you saw it done. It was like a . . . well, more like some one going through a ritual than just burning an old letter."

"Was it a letter—could you see that?"

"No. I didn't get a clear view, but I didn't think it was one, somehow. It was too small, and it looked kind of stiff. And then, do you know what she did with the ash? She burnt the paper over an ashtray, and then she emptied it on to the floor! Doesn't that sound completely batty to you?"

"Your aunt is an unusual woman," Vachell observed.

"Oh, God, yes. There's one thing more." Corcoran spoke with hesitation, as if it was something distasteful that he had to say.

"Yes?"

"My room has been searched."

"When?"

"This evening. While I was out on the farm."

"Anything taken?"

"No, that's the odd part. If it was just another native

theft one wouldn't think anything of it. But nothing was taken, and God alone knows what they can have been after. I've got nothing worth pinching."

"Did you ask the house-boys if they'd seen any one hanging around?"

"Yes, of course. That's why I thought I'd better mention it, because you're going to question Mwogi. I may as well tell you he claims that he saw Mrs. West coming from the direction of my room, which is out behind the living-room. That was before she asked for me, and Mwogi took her to the living-room to wait. The whole thing simply doesn't make sense. Why should Janice West want to see me? And why the hell should she search my room? I don't believe it. I think Mwogi made it all up. Well, anyway, you can question him, but there's the story, and all I know is that my room *has* been searched."

Vachell sighed and lit a cigarette in the darkness. "This case is like a switch-yard with the signalmen drunk in the box," he remarked. "All the tracks cross and every one takes a hand at switching the points. Let's see how much Mwogi can add to the confusion." They walked towards the boys' quarters, behind the Munson block. A low hum of voices came from the kitchen, but that was the only sound.

"Listen," Corcoran said suddenly. From the forest came a sharp, low, grating sound, like the slash of a saw on wood. It ceased abruptly, and the silence was deeper than before. "That damned leopard. I built a trap to-day, quite close to the farm buildings. It tried to get into our calf-house last night."

The kitchen was hot and filled with smoke. Somewhere

amongst the crowd there was doubtless an oven and a meal cooking, but Vachell could only see a mass of black faces and long-legged forms draped around the small mud-walled room. A hurricane lamp stood on a table and a number of very old and dirty cards littered the floor. Huddled in the corner were some women, dressed in goatskins, their own soft skins well greased with castor oil. The long gourds of millet gruel which they had brought for their husbands stood beside them against the wall. A chipped teapot on the table competed with the old-fashioned drink.

Mwogi emerged from the smoke-filled gloom a moment after the door opened. He had shed his white robe and red tarboosh, and appeared in a pair of brown plus-fours, a green jacket, a football jersey and bare feet. "What is it you want, bwana?" he asked.

"You have a celebration when your master has died?" Vachell inquired.

"This is not a celebration. The cook is preparing a meal, but we are unhappy, and so we drink tea to bring strength to our hearts." Mwogi destroyed the effect of this by grinning broadly as he spoke.

Yes, he had seen Mrs. West, he said in response to questions; she had come on foot, he supposed, for he had heard no car, just as it was getting dark, about an hour ago. Perhaps she had been in Bwana Corcoran's room; he did not know. It was not his affair. She waited in the living-room alone while he went to fetch Mrs. Munson, and later on she went away. That was all he knew.

"All right," Vachell concluded. "One more thing. The

white man's beer that lives in the cupboard in the living-room. Has it been there long?"

"The sherry," Mwogi said, using the European word. "Yes, but it is always kept in my mistress's room. She does not like to offer it to strangers."

"Did you move it to the other room, where it is now?"

Mwogi shook his head. "No, it is not my affair."

"And the cupboard in the living-room," Vachell persisted. "Was it the custom to lock it, or to keep it unlocked?"

"It was always locked."

"What's the idea?" Corcoran asked.

Vachell did not reply at once. He was frowning in the darkness, trying to fit the sherry and the unlocked cupboard and Mwogi's story and Mrs. Munson's strange behaviour into a pattern that would make sense. Corcoran could see, in the shaft of light that emerged from the open kitchen door, that his face was stern and worried. Then, suddenly, the missing piece appeared in his mind, its outline stark and shocking: the open drum of cattle-dip Prettyman had seen in Mrs. Munson's office. The pattern fell neatly, and with finality, into place. Vachell came quickly to a decision.

"Listen," he said to Corcoran. "I have to get a message to Karuna urgently. It's very important. Will you take it in?"

"Right away?"

"Yes. And make it snappy."

"All right, I suppose so. But what's the sudden rush? I don't understand."

"You will," Vachell answered. His voice sounded full of meaning, and grim. He walked quickly back to his car, switched on the spotlight, and in the beam scribbled a message on a leaf of his note-book. He tore the note out, slipped it into an envelope and said:

"Take this to Prettyman, at his house. If he's gone out to the movies or somewhere chase him up, wherever he is. He's got to get that message. Even minutes may count."

"Good Lord, you *are* in a stew," Corcoran remarked. "Very Edgar Wallace, this is. All right, I'll deliver it. I feel I ought to wear a false beard, though, and go into Karuna in an invisible ray."

"Go in by car, and step on it," Vachell said briefly. "This isn't a joke."

Corcoran took the note without another word and made for the shed in which the Munson car was parked. Vachell stood still, his hands in his pockets, until he heard the motor start and the car back out and go. Then he walked over to the living-room, opened the door softly and stepped in. It was in darkness; Mrs. Munson had gone to her room, to prepare for the evening meal, perhaps. He tried the cupboard door and found it open. The bottle of sherry had been returned. He poured a very small quantity into a glass, sipped it, and made a wry face. The sherry was sweet and heavy, but beneath the sweetness was a harsh, gritty flavour. He put it back carefully, closed the cupboard and walked out of the room and across to the children's quarters. He rapped on the door of the room next to the schoolroom, that he judged would be a bedroom, and heard Anita Adams call out in Swahili: "Who is it? What do you want?"

"The police again. I'd like to speak with you a moment."

Anita Adams' voice sounded nervous when she called back: "All right. I'll come out." A moment later she appeared in the doorway, tall and angular, drying her hands on a towel.

"The children are asleep," she said. "Please don't talk too loud, we mustn't wake them. Theo hasn't been sleeping awfully well the last two or three days."

"I have some news that isn't pleasant, but it isn't so serious, either, as I guess it's going to sound," Vachell said. "I know you can take it, I'm depending on you for common sense."

She stared at him silently, standing very still. Her long face with its pallid skin looked grey in the starlight.

"What are you talking about?" she asked.

"A doctor will be here in about an hour. He's coming from Karuna."

"A doctor! Whatever for?"

"In a few hours' time you'll be attacked by a fit of vomiting, by cramps in the stomach and maybe dizziness, and tingling in the feet and hands. This will be a symptom of mild arsenical poisoning, but I believe it will pass off and there's no cause for alarm. You haven't taken a fatal dose. You ——"

A cross between a gasp and a groan came out of Anita Adams' throat. She stepped back a pace and put her hand on the doorpost for support.

"You're making this up!" she exclaimed. "You're playing some sort of joke."

"Jokes are out, just at present," Vachell said. "I'm giving you this warning so you won't get too excited when the sickness hits you. I reckon the doctor will be here by then, anyway."

"I don't understand," Anita said. Her voice was faint.

"Who's done this? How could I . . . you mean . . . in the sherry?"

"Yes."

"I thought it tasted funny." She was talking excitedly now, hurrying on, almost in a whisper. "It had a sort of bitter taste, but I thought that must be because it had been kept so long. But we all had it. Are they poisoned too—Ted Corcoran and Mrs. Munson?"

"Yes, they're poisoned too. But there isn't any danger. I'd go in and lie down. I reckon the doctor will be here before you start to feel anything, and he'll fix you up right away."

"Will it . . . hurt very much?"

Vachell shook his head. "Most likely the doctor will use a stomach-pump, but anyway it isn't bad."

She took her hand away from the doorpost and shivered a little in the sharp night air.

"The children," she said. "They're all right?"

"It was in the sherry."

"I've been thinking. I want to get them away. It's terrible for them here, they're scared to death. Besides, I'm frightened—it isn't safe. Every one here's been jittery for days, and now this. . . . Can I take them away from here? Will you back me up against Mrs. Munson, say they ought to go?"

"Sure. This isn't any sort of atmosphere for kids."

She sighed deeply, as if a great weight had slid off her mind. "Thank God. At last I'll be able to get them away. Have you told Mrs. Munson yet; about the arsenic, I mean?"

Vachell shook his head.

"Well, some one had better. Would you like me . . ."

"No," he said. "You needn't bother. I guess she knows."

CHAPTER 23: THE DOCTOR, WHO ARRIVED about midnight, found the arsenic poisoning case of great interest. Three people had taken, presumably, doses that were equal, or very nearly equal; yet the reactions were widely different.

"An excellent example of the dangers of dogmatism," he commented. "One doesn't often get what almost amounts to a controlled experiment, on humans. Look at the result. One guinea-pig nearly dies and another's only slightly affected. The third's midway between. You see? Now try to tell me the precise effect of x grains of arsenic on the human system! Like to have Sir Bernard Spilsbury here."

Corcoran was much the worst of the three. Vomiting and pains went on all through the night, and in the morning Dr. Lawson insisted on taking him to the hospital in Karuna. Anita Adams had a bad three or four hours, but by morning she had got the poison out of her system and fell into a refreshing sleep.

Mrs. Munson was affected least of all. It seemed as if her will-power could control her lumpy, ungainly body even to the length of resisting the ill-effects of poison. Vachell, watching her face harden with anger when the doctor entered her room, wondered if an intense, unreasoning distaste for having a doctor touch her, a pathological horror of the physical, might in some way have given her an armour against illness. At any rate, she was barely sick, and Dr. Lawson thought it very remarkable. There was no doubt, Vachell assured him, that she'd had her fair share of poisoned sherry.

It was the strangest dawn he could remember. He came out on to the lawn to watch it break in a long streak of red over the black hills beyond the valley. The grass was grey and sopping wet under his feet, and the air as cold as iron. He shivered uncomfortably, in spite of an old raincoat wrapped closely around him. The ashy sky flushed as he watched it, the birds twittered eagerly in the trees. Everything, the uneasy events of the night, the sick patients, the startled sullen natives, seemed nightmarish and unreal.

Mwogi, frightened into silence and work, brought breakfast for Dr. Lawson and Vachell in the living-room. The room looked sordid and unswept in the quickly strengthening sunlight. Soon afterwards Lawson took Corcoran away in the back of his car, done up in blankets and cushions. The young man's face was pale as paper and his eyes were full of fear. He had been retching and vomiting all night.

"He'll be all right," Lawson said. "No danger now, but he needs nursing. Besides"—the doctor looked around him in distaste, and made a small grimace—"this place seems to be about as healthy as the heart of the yellow fever belt. Hope those eggs weren't cooked in Coopers and seasoned with Woolman's salts. What was it—cattle dip?"

Vachell nodded. "Guess so. I never realized what dangerous lives farmers led. Poison lurks in every corner, it seems."

Dr. Lawson grunted. "Well, I hope you catch your murderer before he does any more harm. By the way . . ."

"Yes, doctor?"

"Those children. I don't think they ought to stay here. It's too—well, after all, there have been two sudden deaths and an attempted poisoning in the last three days. The Adams girl will be fit enough to move to-day. Tell her to get them away—anywhere will do. Can you bluff it through, do you suppose?"

Vachell nodded. "I guess so. I've no authority, but she wants to go herself."

For the first time since the trouble started the Munson farm was disorganized. The boys seemed to have lost their heads. The leopard had taken a calf out of the homestead of a native headsman; the man had heard it breathing through the cracks of the hut walls during the night. That seemed to frighten all the labour as much as, or more than, the extraordinary happenings among the whites. The leopard trap, erected in a game path running up into part of the forest that had escaped burning, would be ready for use that night.

Vachell strolled up to inspect it after breakfast, when Corcoran and the doctor had gone. It was made of big cedar logs hacked from the surrounding forest and sunk well into the ground to make a sort of cage. The headman explained the working with enthusiasm. The bait, a hunk of meat raw and preferably high, was tethered inside, and when the leopard came its weight would depress a stick which, in turn, would release a string that supported the heavy log door. Then the door would fall behind the leopard, penning it in, and next morning a European would come to shoot it with a rifle.

When Vachell reached the office, later in the morning, Prettyman reported no sign either of Parrot, who seemed to have vanished like a cloud, or of the mole-catcher Arawak, for whom a search was still being made. The young inspector observed at once that the C.I.D. chief was in a different mood. The lassitude he had noticed the day before was gone; now Vachell was brisk and decisive. He was unusually forth-coming, too.

"Well," he said conversationally. "I guess the case is in the bag. I'd like you to make an arrest to-day."

"Me?" Prettyman inquired.

"Sure. I have to go down to headquarters for a confer-ence with the Commissioner this afternoon. This case has some side issues that need to be cleared up. I'll be back this evening, but I want you to make the arrest at once."

"Okay, sir," Prettyman said. "May I ask whom I'm to drag off to the jug?"

"Mrs. West."

Prettyman looked at his superior with a mixed expression. He was not surprised, exactly, but he was upset, and the superintendent's convenient conference in Marula struck him as a dirty trick.

"You'll make out the warrant, sir, of course," he said, a little stiffly. "I'll execute it whenever you instruct me to. Malcolm, the magistrate here, is a bit of a tiger. I suppose, sir, you've got all the evidence taped?"

"No," Vachell replied. He tipped his chair back, put both

feet on the edge of the table and lit another cigarette. "The police case has as many holes in it as a mosquito net. I'm hoping she'll break down and give."

Prettyman raised his eyebrows, and rolled a pencil about on the desk. "Aren't you a little optimistic, sir? She'll see a lawyer at once, of course—Clara Innocent, I expect. Our Clara's hot stuff at tying everything up in legal knots."

"We can make a case. Then we'll go in and sew it up for the High Court. When we pull in Parrot and this mole-catching guy we can go to work."

"I suppose she did do it," Prettyman said doubtfully. "The motive doesn't seem very strong. She may have loathed Munson and got fed up with his making passes at her, but you wouldn't think she'd have to bump him off. And West—I suppose she wanted him out of the way. It seems a bit cold-blooded, I must say. Is she in with Parrot, do you think?"

"Sure, she had him on a string." Vachell tilted his head back to rest his neck against the back of one chair and stared fixedly at a corner of the ceiling. His face, leaner than ever with fatigue, looked as though it had been carved out of wood, and his light blue eyes were pin-points of concentration.

"She had enough of Munson," he went on. "Munson was only a fill-in—maybe a little different from the rest. When she wanted to give him the air, he kicked. Munson was no gentleman, most likely he threatened to go to West to shoot the works, anyway to raise hell all over the district if she didn't behave. He could have made things tough. So she decided to stop Munson in the only way she could be sure he'd stay stopped. She knew about the Acocanthera, Sir Jolyot Anstey explained it all one day, so she teamed up with this mole-catcher guy and stewed the poison and went over one evening to stick a nail through Munson's shoe."

"So far, sir, you've no proof."

"No, except that we found the gasolene can used to make the poison hidden in a shed on the Wests' place. I'm counting on this Arawak guy. Most likely he's been paid to scram to the mountains somewhere, it'll be tough to pull him in. Mrs. West has no alibi for the time when the nail was taken out of Munson's shoe. If you step on it you can make Munson's place from West's in ten minutes flat. The others have pretty good alibis for that half-hour—Mrs. Munson, Corcoran, Anita Adams, Wendtland and Norman Parrot. They were all working on their own jobs, in full view."

"You were staying at the Wests' then, sir. Didn't you see Mrs. West at all?"

Vachell shook his head. "Not until around eight-thirty. She was supposed to be taking care of the poultry, but there's no way to check that. She made a date to meet Munson in the pyrethrum shed, maybe at six-thirty or seven o'clock. Seems like a tough hour, but probably she told Munson she was having trouble in shaking West, but that was the time he had chores to do, so she could slip over with no questions asked. She never intended to keep the date. She figured his death would be put down to heart failure or asphyxiation or something, due to the charcoal fumes. That's where she slipped. If Munson had just dropped dead in a milking-bail or somewhere we'd never have been able to tie it up with

Mrs. West, but as it turned out, the fact that Munson entered the shed at all points directly to her."

"How about that note from Daphne Anstey you found in Munson's things?"

Vachell shook his head. "No dice. That was written to Corcoran. Munson intercepted it and kept it by him, meaning to raise hell with Corcoran. You missed a trick there."

"That's only an assumption . . ." Prettyman began, and checked himself. "Yes, sir. I'm sorry."

"All of this case is assumption. It's a hell of a set-up, we haven't even got medical proof that Munson died of arrow-poison or anything else. So far as the facts go, he's still alive, and West fell into the fire and got burnt to ashes. We won't get to first base that way."

"No, sir. But how about the dog-slashing and blood-letting and so forth? Do you blame that on Mrs. West, too?"

Vachell was silent for a little, leaning the back of his head against interlocked hands. His face was quite without expression when he spoke.

"There'd been no rain the night the Wests' ducks got their heads pulled off and Bullseye's throat was nearly slit. The Wests' bedroom is connected with the living-room by a concrete path. Mrs. West swore she hadn't been out of her room, but the soles of her mules were wet. There was an impression of her foot in the mud by the duck-pond, near where the bodies were found. The night the Wests' own setter was killed, Mrs. West was out of the room. All these incidents, except for some pigeons, took place around West's farm."

"And the bushbuck in the forest fire. She *could* have done that, of course."

"And West could have found her. He caught her bloody-handed, and so he was through. He had to go. I guess she'd been planning something like that, anyway. She's crazy for Parrot, and West stood in the way. A jab with a knife or a pointed stick near the heart, and he'd be out in a couple of minutes. Then Mrs. Munson got suspicious. She started to broadcast pretty obvious hints around, so her turn came next. We're up against a maniac, remember; not a sane individual at all. A shot of arsenic in the sherry, what does it matter if you get three dead bodies for the price of one. The quicker they come the better the sport, when you see 'em wriggle. Mrs. Munson is ready to testify she found Mrs. West alone in the living-room with the sherry in an unlocked cupboard, and the next thing she knew, three people who drank the liquor got a shot of arsenic in their stomachs. We have to pull her in. She's about as safe to leave around as a barrel of dynamite on top of a fire."

"Why didn't she carry on with the arrow-poison? It seemed to have worked like a charm. And there isn't a shred of proof. . . . I'm sorry, sir, it's not my business, I know. But there's one thing you've absolutely left out. You surely don't think it was Mrs. West who cracked you on the bean and pinched the papers out of Munson's room?"

Vachell withdrew his feet from the table, sat up, and ground out his cigarette. "No," he said. "No, I don't think that."

"Who was it, then?"

"That," Vachell answered, "is what I'm going to Marula to find out."

"And you really want me to make this arrest? You're certain it's wise?"

"Sure. I'll make out the warrant now." He drew a form towards him and signed his name. "Bring her in and keep her locked in your bungalow, and for Christ's sake don't let her sneak out of the window when the guard's looking the other way. And she's to see no visitors, understand—no one at all."

"Just as you say, sir. I can't stop her seeing Mrs. Innocent, if she insists."

Vachell looked at him thoughtfully for a moment. "No," he said. "No, I guess you can't. But watch her carefully as hell. I reckon two murders just about fills the quota for this district, this year."

CHAPTER 24: VACHELL WAS RUNNING AWAY,

and he knew it; but he had to get down to Marula to look at the C.I.D. files on the local Deutsche Bund, see the Commissioner, and, after that, put through a long-distance call to London. By a stroke of luck he found that it was the day for the bi-weekly air-mail service connecting Karuna with the London-Durban Imperial Airways service. He caught a plane from Karuna at eleven and was in his office in the capital by half-past twelve.

By now, he thought, Prettyman would have done the job. The young inspector hadn't liked it, and Vachell didn't blame him. It was a lousy job. Some women got hysterical and raved, and others cried or even fainted; but he didn't think that Janice West would do any of these things.

An hour in the office and ten minutes with Major Armitage was all he needed. He checked up his information about the Bund, and all that was available about the ramifications of the Landesgruppe Sudafrika in the Union, about the Deutsche Jugend für Sudafrika (a South African version of the Hitler Youth) and about the Deutsche Sudwest Bund in the South-West African mandated territory. After a short talk with the Commissioner he put in a call to London and spoke for five minutes to M.I.5. By two o'clock he was through in Marula, equipped with all the information he needed to tie up the loose ends of the case. But although he had got what he wanted he felt no satisfaction; he had to go back, the last and worst river was still to cross.

In unimportant ways his luck was in. He ran into an acquaintance, a mining engineer from the gold-fields, who was going back to his mine by way of Karuna that afternoon, and who offered him a ride. By five o'clock he was back again in the little town. The office was closed, and Prettyman's bungalow forbidden ground. He went into the Black Buffalo and ordered tea in a long, empty room with a radio in one corner tuned in to the Australian news bulletin, and one or two native servants drifting about as vaguely as clouds, dressed in long white kanzus with red sashes.

The tea-tray arrived and in its wake came Sir Jolyot Anstey, who strolled across the room to greet his acquaintance, several large books tucked under his arm.

"May I join you," he asked, "in a cup of tea? Ah, I'm glad to see you take milk in yours. Too much of this deplorable lemon habit nowadays, particularly among women, I've noticed. A thoroughly pernicious idea. Vitamin C is rarely lacking in the modern diet, whereas the calcium in milk is not only highly necessary but neutralizes the action of any tannic acid that may have been liberated from the leaf by overbrewing."

Vachell was feeling too hot and tired from a fast drive over bad roads to respond.

"I came in to secure some text-books on ecology," Anstey continued undismayed. "One would hardly expect to find books of that type here, but really it is wonderful what the Carnegie scheme does in small places like this. I am starting a small series of experiments with the object of studying plant succession on forest soil after burning and cultivation—the recent fire provides a chance to do this which may never recur. A detailed study of the order of colonization by plants on land where a climax vegetation is suddenly entirely destroyed has, so far as I know, never been made in this part of the world."

"Sounds interesting," Vachell remarked dutifully, spreading jam on his third scone.

"My object is to correlate this plant succession—the types of vegetation which succeed each other on cleared and then cultivated land—with changes in the soil fauna, which I'm convinced holds the key to the problem of the fertility of tropical soils," Sir Jolyot Anstey went on, warming to the task. "You see what I'm aiming at, of course?"

Vachell smiled, and leant back against a cushion. He felt weary and relaxed, and Anstey's words were like the smoke from his cigar—a pleasant cloud hanging overhead, indeterminate but soothing.

"I'm afraid not," he admitted. "But go ahead just the same."

"The real problem of tropical soils is their rapid loss of fertility," the ex-surgeon began, "in contrast to the soils of North-West Europe, whose ecological climax was also closed forest, though of a very different type. In the case of European soils, persistent working for generation after generation has enormously increased their fertility; their original productiveness was not high. Tropical soils, on the other hand, are at their maximum fertility before, and not after, the plough or the digging-stick are brought to bear. Soil microorganisms have done the work of generations of patient serfs. The native system of shifting cultivation . . ."

He broke off, and looked at Vachell with a comical expression of dismay.

"My dear fellow! I beg your pardon, I really do. Here am I, riding my hobby-horse and boring you to distraction when you are no doubt exceedingly weary after a long day, and in any case quite uninterested, and naturally so, in the biology of tropical soils. I'm afraid it is quite unforgivable. . . . Well, I hear you have made an arrest, so I suppose you consider your work in this district at an end."

Vachell looked up in surprise at the sudden change of subject. The news had got about quickly, in spite of his warning to Prettyman to keep it quiet.

"How did you know?" he asked.

"I met Norman Parrot in the street a short time ago. The poor fellow is almost distracted. He feels that a great mistake has been made."

"So Parrot's back." Vachell nodded, and pulled a cigarette out of its pack. "The news fetched him, then. Where is he now?"

"He was on his way back to his own farm when I met him. He'd been to see Mrs. West, but the askaris refused admission absolutely. I myself tried, on the chance that I could be of some service to Mrs. West in regard to legal defence, but was told that no one was allowed in." He glanced at Vachell over his cigar, and there was the hint of a twinkle in his sharp eyes. "You are, I suppose, quite satisfied that no mistake has been made?"

"I'm satisfied that Mrs. West's detention was necessary in the interests of public safety."

"Dear me! A very official-sounding reply. I apologize, Mr. Vachell, if my suggestion has given offence." There was no doubt, now, about the twinkle in his eye. He got up, collected his armful of books, and added:

"I must be getting home. I do not believe, if I may say so, that you are quite so foolish as you appear to be." With the parting shot he was gone, hurrying out of the room as if he were late for an important meeting.

Vachell paid for his tea, retrieved his car, and drove out along the now familiar road with Parrot's farm as his goal. But when he came to the Munsons' turn-off he swung the wheel, on impulse, and headed the car's nose up the short hill leading to the homestead. He had better make sure everything was all right.

Mrs. Munson had recovered so completely that she had gone out to see to the farm, he learnt. He found Anita Adams on the living-room sofa, her knees wrapped in a rug, reading aloud to Theodora in the fading evening light.

"Mrs. Munson's amazing," she said. "Really she is. I'm all right now, but I don't feel a bit like walking about. Mrs. Munson has been out since after lunch, seeing to things on the farm."

"She's a tough baby," Vachell agreed. "I came to tell you Dr. Lawson and I are ready to back you in getting the children away for a spell. It's a hell of a place for kids just now, they've had a couple of bad shocks, and we reckon it would be best if you got them out for a week or two."

Anita Adams' thin, sallow face took on a new look of animation. The poisoning hadn't improved her appearance; there were dark circles round her eyes and her hair had no lustre, like the coat of a sick animal; but she pushed it back with a gesture of relief and smiled.

"That would be marvellous. You've no idea what a release it will be—what it's been like here the last week. I could take them to my sister in Marula—even to the coast. I'm not feeling awfully bright to-day, but to-morrow, perhaps . . ."

Vachell nodded. "You can call it a rest cure. The danger's over now. The murderer's under arrest."

Anita Adams stared at him with widened eyes.

"You mean—who?"

"Janice West."

The girl jumped to her feet, throwing off the rug in which she was wrapped. "I don't believe it! You're playing some kind of joke! *Janice* didn't do it—she couldn't, you know she's not that sort of person. You're making a mistake. You're . . ."

Vachell shook his head. "There's no mistake. I've got proof, and I'm going to get more—from you."

Anita Adams sat down again heavily on the sofa. Her voice was flat and hard. "I don't understand."

"You took a message to Munson from Janice West. To meet him in the pyrethrum shed early in the morning—she had something to say. You gave him the message, and that's why he went."

The girl was watching him with a set face and wild eyes. She shook her head slightly. "No, no, no. You're wrong."

Vachell shrugged his shoulders. "The prosecuting council will pull it out of you on the stand. He'll unwind you like a bandage. You don't have to tell me now."

Anita Adams ran her tongue over dry lips. "I've got nothing to tell."

"You can tell Mrs. Munson about the arrest. It's nice to be the bearer of good news." Vachell took up his cork helmet with the police badge in the band and made for the door. He turned in the doorway and looked back. "You'll have to put on a better act if you want to convince a jury. You gave Munson that message all right. You may get orchids for loyalty to friends but for perjury you can get five years."

Anita Adams answered: "I've got nothing to say."

CHAPTER 25: THE CORPORAL IN CHARGE CAME
up to report as soon as Vachell left the living-room. Mrs.
Munson, he said, had not been out of his sight all day. She
had spent the first part of the afternoon supervising the boys
who were working on the leopard trap. Then she had returned
to the office. She'd had tea in the house, gone out to a near-by
bail to inspect the milking, checked the cream after separa-
tion in the dairy, and now she was out with the white turkeys,
giving them their evening feed. Extra precautions were being
taken because of the leopard, the guard added. Miss Adams
had ——

The man broke off as a shrill shout came from the direction of the chicken-houses. Vachell jumped and began to run,
but when the sound came again he realized that it was not
fear but anger. The voice was Mrs. Munson's, shouting for a
boy. He found her outside the pen which housed the white
turkeys. Her black eyes were gleaming dangerously and her
face was set. She glared at Vachell, and spoke directly to the
boy.

"You, what sort of poultry-guard are you?" she asked furi-
ously. "Where is the gobbler, the white gobbler? Where?"

The native looked helplessly at the turkeys, as if hoping
to see the missing male appear out of the ground. He counted
them over with his eyes.

"Are you dumb?" Mrs. Munson insisted. "Is it not your

240

task to look after these turkeys? Where has the gobbler gone?"

The native shook his head in obvious bewilderment and despair. "He was here at four o'clock," he said. "At four o'clock I went into the pen to fill the water-troughs and scatter cabbage leaves for food. The big male was here then. I went out and closed the door and I don't know ——"

"You fool, you left the door open," Mrs. Munson exclaimed. Her voice was shaking with rage. "That is what you did. That gobbler is a valuable bird, very highly valuable, and through your foolishness he has run away. Go and look for him at once! Call the others! Go, all of you, search the paths quickly, before it is dark."

The boy hurried off to call his friends and to start the search. There was not much time. The sun had gone down behind the mountains and shadows had faded abruptly into the grey-blue mists of early dusk.

"Was the pen door open when you got here?" Vachell asked.

Mrs. Munson turned her eyes on him. "With two of your askaris camped on the place," she observed, "yesterday a murderess comes to this farm attempting to poison me, and leaves unmolested. To-day my pocket-knife is stolen and now a valuable turkey, an imported bird. Can't you even recover a stolen turkey? If you did, it would be the first time for the police to find anything stolen or lost in their history, so far as I know."

"Governments just hate a guy to set a precedent," Vachell observed. "But I'll risk a try." He waved to the corporal, and by a flick of the hand indicated that the askari was to stay close to Mrs. Munson. When he had gone a little way he looked back and saw the native following her only a few yards behind. She might as well try to get rid of her own toenails as of Corporal Abdul. Native policemen might not be unobtrusive shadows, but they stuck.

The turkey had probably escaped from the pen and just wandered off, he thought. All the same it was a little queer that only one should have disappeared, and that one, apparently, the pride of the flock. Vachell moved his shoulders impatiently and dug his hands into his pockets. He was getting jittery, seeing bogies behind every bush. The sense of strain, the expectation of dangerous events, was getting him down. Even a turkey couldn't take a walk without a lot of sinister ideas showing their prick-ears through the long grass, like a pack of hunting dogs around a sick beast.

Although he knew his fears were foolish, he couldn't leave the Munsons' now until the insignificant mystery was solved. He followed a narrow native path from the turkey pen past the pyrethrum shed and across the pasture to the forest's edge. Here it branched. One fork went left towards a dam and some cultivation, the other crossed the broad ride that marked the boundary between farm and forest, and plunged into the green depths. This part of the forest had escaped burning, but gaunt blackened branches stood against the skyline to the right as a stark reminder of the havoc of fire.

He sauntered along the path leading into the forest, keeping an eye open for the turkey, but preoccupied mainly with his own thoughts. He went over his conclusions for the hundredth time, and found no loophole. The path, he noticed, seemed to have had a lot of recent use. The underbrush on each side bore signs of bruising and breaking, as though something heavy had been dragged along. The path itself, however, grew fainter; a game-track only, he thought. It was growing dark; the heads of the tall creaking junipers were clear against a dark-blue sky, but only the faint blur of their thick boles was visible beneath.

Something loomed ahead in the path, black and solid. Vachel froze in his tracks. In an instant he thought of rhinos, buck, leopards. . . . Of course, the leopard trap. This was where the boys had set it. He stepped forward to examine it closer.

It was a solid cage of cedar posts planted in the ground. They were set at an angle sloping inwards, their tops interlocking to form a tent-shaped structure. The far end was closed. The open end faced the path, and above it was poised a heavy door made of cedar logs.

The opening which confronted Vachell was black as a buffalo hide and the trap unsprung; but as he went down to peer inside there came to his ears a sort of desperate breathing sound, and then a high-pitched gurgle, like a man caught by the throat. He felt a cold tingle up his spine and the hairs rising on his scalp. There was something inside in the trap, something alive, something that was moving, invisible in the blackness.

His right hand stole round to the holster on his hip and clasped the comforting butt of his revolver. The sound came again—a noise of struggling, a sort of shuddering rather, unlike anything he had heard before. He pulled out the gun and stepped forward to peer into the trap. Something white caught his eye, and the darkness was full of a sound of fluttering. He lowered the revolver and laughed aloud. The missing turkey gobbler was found. The head man who'd made the trap had taken it for bait—combining, Vachell supposed, a little quiet revenge on his employer with the execution of her instructions to bait the trap. He grinned in the half-darkness; it was a neat trick.

The beam from his flashlight, playing over the trap's interior, showed that the bird lay trussed on its side, unable to move anything except its wings, and tied to the posts at the back of the trap. To reach it the leopard must go completely in and tread on, or otherwise dislodge, a stick laid across the floor and held loosely in position at each end by two nails. A string attached to the centre of this stick ran up to the roof, a thin white perpendicular line, and thence along the trap's exterior to the front, where it supported the whole weight of the poised log door. Once the stick was knocked out of position the string would be released and the door would fall. Thus the leopard would be securely caught inside the little cage.

It all seemed straightforward enough, and yet there was something wrong. A turkey as bait for a trap. Did leopards eat turkeys? Vachell didn't know. Of course, they might. Or the natives might have put it there as a joke on Mrs. Munson, knowing she'd find it missing when she shut in her turkeys for the night, or, perhaps, reckoning that she'd find it there when she went to see whether the trap was properly set. . . . He gave a low whistle and felt the familiar thrill of excitement he always experienced when, like a ranging hound, he came on the scent. He bent low and dived into the trap's mouth, stepping carefully over the loosely secured stick that released the door. The gobbler renewed its struggle with a desperate gurgle of fright. He knelt down and played his flashlight over the turkey's bound legs and over the back of the trap, to which the bird was attached by a piece of strong twine. If you wanted to release the captive you'd cut the twine, but if you hadn't got a knife you'd have to untie the knot where it was fastened to one of the logs forming the back of the trap. And to do that you'd have to fumble at the knots with both hands close up against the posts. . . .

Vachell thrust his flashlight against the cedar logs and directed the beam on to the knot. In sharp relief the light picked out something that he already knew was there: two nails, driven through a log just above and just below the knot. They projected perhaps an eighth of an inch above the surface of the wood. They did not shine in the light. Their tips were coated with a black substance that dulled the glint, making them invisible against the dark, wooden logs. They were neatly placed; you could not have untied the knot without tearing your flesh, however slightly, on their poisoned points.

The turkey, which had been temporarily quieted by hope of release, started to struggle again. A big useless wing, flapping in panic, caught Vachell in the face and stung his eyes. Involuntarily, and still kneeling, he fell back and put out a hand to steady himself. It met the ground behind his feet, and something gave way. He heard a click and then a loud thud as the heavy door of the trap, released from suspension, crashed down into position and blotted out the last of the twilight. For the second time, Vachell laughed aloud. He'd never played leopard before. It was a new experience, to be caught in a trap.

He felt the first twinge of misgiving when he wondered if any more doctored nails had been planted, just for good measure, in the woodwork of the trap.

The second twinge came when he put down his flashlight and tried to lift the door. He couldn't make it budge. He tried again, bracing one knee against each wall and heaving with all his strength, but there was nothing to get a grip on with his fingers, and the door would not yield. He went on till the sweat broke out on his forehead and his chest felt like bursting, but it was no good. From outside, the door would be easy enough to shift—you could get a leverage on it, and there was a crossbar to grip—but from the inside there was nothing to hold on to but the smooth vertical logs. When he stopped he was panting, and alarm was beginning to chill his blood. Trapped in a leopard trap. It sounded funny, but it didn't feel that way.

He sat back on his heels to think it out. Darkness was complete now in the forest, and dense in the tent-shaped trap. The hoarse, raucous croak of a plaintain-eater sounded from a near-by tree, and died out in a fading cackle. The turkey started to struggle again, croaking in agitation. Night had come.

The trap wasn't more than half or three quarters of a mile from the Munson homestead, Vachell reckoned. If he fired his revolver the corporal would probably hear, and send a man to investigate. Or, in any case, Mrs. Munson might come out to look at the trap. Or the head man might want to be sure it was properly set. Or ——

The thought made Vachell remove the hand he had already put to his revolver holster. It wasn't comfortable in the trap, and soon he would be very cold, but he could stand that. It was best to wait. The person who had baited the trap might return to see what sort of game had been caught.

Vachell grinned ruefully at the extent of his preparations for the night. There was nothing to be done about the turkey. It lay in the corner, calmer now, but still restive. At intervals it rattled its wing feathers against his back. There was no room to stretch his long legs. He put the revolver on the ground beside him next to his flashlight, ready for use. Already the damp, cold night air was beginning to make him shiver.

There were six cigarettes left in the pack. He lit one gratefully; no chance of visitors yet awhile. Best let his thoughts roam where they wanted; no need for concentration yet. They came to rest quickly enough. Janice West's face appeared before him as clearly as if she had been standing there. He could see her deep eyes, the colour of peaty water, the smile that lay a little behind her lips, the high cheek-bones that gave her a wild, sculptured look when the light fell from certain angles. He sighed, and reflected: a hell of a thing to think about in a leopard trap. The whole situation was screwy, if it came to that; a policeman shut in a trap with a turkey gobbler in a forest in the middle of Africa, waiting for a killer who went around smearing nails with native arrow-poison, thinking about a woman who went around with sadistic Nazi roughnecks and neighbouring farmers and any one who came along, while her husband was driven half crazy. It didn't make sense whichever way you looked at it.

Time dragged by very slowly. A cold wind swept insidiously through the undergrowth, rustling leaves and branches. It pierced Vachell's thin clothes like a million tiny needle-points of ice. His limbs became stiff and frozen. He could barely move his fingers, and all his joints ached. Every position became unbearable. It was impossible to lie down or stand up, and his knees were tortured with bending. His breath came in little gasps and his stomach was a dull ache of emptiness. A dozen times he thought: the hell with it, this is a sucker's game, I'm getting out of here; and reached for his revolver. But each time he put it down again. It was the last chance. If the killer came and he could swear to the identity, then that would be some sort of proof.

Strange rustlings and groanings came out of the forest all around. The natives, he remembered, believed the forest to be haunted. "A very bad place," his boy had once remarked, "there are spirits there." "Of whom?" Vachell had asked. The boy had shrugged his shoulders. "Of bad men. In the old days little hunters lived there, in holes in the ground, like moles. They lived on the blood of wild beasts, and at night their spirits come out of the ground, to hunt again." Vachell had laughed at their superstitions. They were foolish, of course, but somehow their ideas didn't seem so fantastic any longer.

The sharp crack of a twig plucked his tautened nerves as

a finger twangs the string of a guitar. Vachell's hand groped
for his revolver, and closed around it. Slowly he raised the
gun and listened, holding his breath. A sound like a low moan
made his spine tingle. A painful, muffled groan, as if wrung
from a throat. It came again, and Vachell lowered the revolver and slowly expelled his breath. His nerves were getting jumpy; this wouldn't do at all. The sound was only the
creak of a cedar as it stirred a little in the wind. Curious how
like it was to a human in pain. No wonder the natives believed the forest to be full of spirits. And the crack was
probably a bushbuck moving about in the darkness, going out
stealthily to feed.

A rustling in the bushes to the right made him jump a little
and grip the gun. A long silence, and then the rustle again, a
little farther away. The bushbuck, probably, moving cautiously, smelling for danger. He wondered if ——

The night was broken by a sharp grating cough, like the
sound of a saw against wood, broken off abruptly. It was
quite close. An icy chill crept up Vachell's back and the hand
of fear gripped his heart tightly so that he felt it couldn't
beat. The leopard: here in the forest, near at hand. He'd
almost forgotten about the leopard. Suppose it came up to the
trap, smelling meat. Well, if he couldn't get out, the leopard
couldn't get in. He breathed more easily, but then the noise
came again. Nearer this time, much nearer. The prickles were
busy again in his spine. A primitive impulse to leap up and
run itched in his legs. He fought it down, but still wished himself a hundred miles away.

The leopard's call came again, the most cold-blooded sound

he'd ever heard. Then there was silence, and he wished frantically to hear it, to know which way the leopard was moving. It might be coming closer, right up to the trap, perhaps. Between chinks in the logs he could see leaves against
a star-spangled sky, and a black wall of living darkness.
He wished feverishly that he could know. The hand gripping
the revolver was damp.

Behind him, in the forest, came a sharp, frightened cough,
and then silence again. A bushbuck warning its mate, probably. Those soft sensitive black nostrils had caught a whiff of
death's scent in the air. A frantic chattering broke out, a little
while later, and there was a stirring in the foliage as if a sharp
gust of wind had blown. Baboons or monkeys, giving warning
to all other beasts that the dreaded shadow was passing with
silent footfalls below. Then silence again, but a silence full of
small, indeterminate sounds.

A hundred dramas of the night were being played all around
him, Vachell thought; moles burrowing softly underground,
hurrying ants quartering the surface for food, nervous twitch-
nosed dikdik courting in the undergrowth; tree-hyraxes coming out of their hollows in the trunks to feed and mate and
serenade the stars. And the leopard, prowling in his nightly
quest for blood. To all this, Vachell thought, man's ears are
sealed, his nose insensitive, his eyes blind, his senses dumb.
Only his brain is keener than theirs, only his ingenuity can
protect him.

A soft rustle just outside the cage made him hold his breath
again. He put his eye to a chink and thought he could detect
a movement in the dark undergrowth beyond. He listened almost actively, trying to force his ears into sensitivity. The

rustle came again. He was certain something had moved. The leopard, come to investigate, perhaps. It wasn't ten yards away. A violent sound behind made him jump. The turkey had come to life again suddenly, and started to flap its impotent wings. Something had scared it, all right. The shape Vachell had been staring at had disappeared. It *was* the leopard, then. He swallowed hard, and tried to steady his hand on the gun. The posts no longer seemed solid. They seemed a flimsy protection, and the chinks between each post yawning gaps.

Nothing happened, after that, for some time. His ears grew more accustomed to the shrill, loud cry of the hyraxes, the creak of junipers, the rustles of moving animal life. He lit his last cigarette with a steadier hand, and smoked it through. The aches in his stiff, cold limbs grew painful again, and he tried to warm his hands under his armpits, then by sitting on them, but with little avail. His teeth were nearly chattering and he had pins and needles in his feet.

A sound which seemed somehow different, came to his ears. He didn't know why it was an alien noise, but it was. The sound of rustling, then of a stick snapping suddenly, then a branch whipping back into place. He realized that all the other sounds of the night, save the creaking of cedars, had ceased abruptly. The hyraxes had stopped their screeching, a buck whose soft progress through the forest to his left he had been following half unconsciously had ceased to move. Another stick cracked, and a tense silence followed. The sounds came from straight ahead. From the path. He caught his breath, and gripped the revolver again. This was it, at last. Some one was coming, very cautiously, very slowly, along the path.

CHAPTER 26: THROUGH THE CHINKS OF THE

door Vachell could see nothing but blackness; there was no moon. He could not see the figure that crept closer by stages, moving skilfully over the rough forest path. But his ears, made keener by the long silence as eyes are made sharper by the dark, could follow the approach. Rustle, swish, and then quiet. Something too soft for a footfall, too loud for the fall of a leaf. A gradual closing in.

Vachell waited, every muscle rigid, gun in hand. The figure must be close to the door. Close enough to see that the trap was shut.

There was a long pause. The beat of his heart sounded like hammer on anvil, the blood in his ears like a waterfall. He scarcely dared to breathe. He could feel the presence of another human as clearly as he could feel the butt of the gun in his hand. A new element had come into the air. Something electric, magnetic—no word could describe it. The presence of a human, as definite a thing to him as the smell of a leopard to a bushbuck. He could feel his mind encountering another mind in the darkness as two buck might lock horns. Behind his tense concentration, a part of his mind wondered whether it was indeed some latent unconscious sense of smell, a dim inheritance of the primitive, that warned a man when any of his kind was near.

A sudden commotion stabbed the tense, fierce silence like a

knife. The turkey flapped its wings and rattled its tail feathers with a noise that sounded in Vachell's ears like thunder. An instant later a white blinding light assaulted his eyes. He fell back involuntarily, as if he had received a physical blow. The light came through gaps between the posts in long shafts. Beyond the posts he could see nothing at all. He pushed the barrel of the revolver into a chink of the door, his finger ready on the trigger, aiming at the light. He realized with sickening clarity that if the killer had a gun he was finished. He couldn't see his target, but the killer could.

The voice, when it came out of the darkness, sent a thrill of horror through his heart. It was a hoarse, rasping whisper— a crazy whisper, the whisper of an insane degenerate in the grip of the thing that had overthrown the balance of the mind.

"I can see you," it said. "Keep still. You are going to die." The hand holding the light moved around in a wide circle, and the beam dodged through the cracks to find Vachell's eyes. "So it's you, then. You will die too. I don't mind. She must die, and then . . ."

The whisper petered out hoarsely, but the flashlight went on describing its crazy, senseless curves.

Vachell started to speak quickly in a low, urgent voice.

"I've got you covered with this gun. You can't shoot through this timber, but I can get you. One of my men is just behind. Switch off that flashlight and ——"

The sixth sense that warns of desperate danger made him break off and jerk his body back. There was no other warning. Something flashed past in front of him from the left, missing his chest by a fraction of an inch, and flashed back the way it had come. Simultaneously he fired at the light. Before the roar of the report had died out among the startled trees the light went out.

For a second there was no sound. Then a low, hideous laugh sounded almost in Vachell's ear. His own flashlight sprang to life and lit the rough cedar posts of his prison with a blinding illumination. He swore violently and switched it off. The chinks between the posts were too narrow. Threads of light struck through, but reflection off the posts blinded him and the light threw his own position into sharp relief. And from outside the killer was jabbing through the gaps with a pointed stick, whittled down to pencil thinness. A stick whose tip, he knew, was coated with black poison.

The turkey was beating its wings in a frantic paroxysm in the corner. Vachell cursed it aloud. All other sounds were drowned by its thrashings. He was sweating with terror, feeling the pricking of the stick's point on his flesh in a hundred places. Arrow-poison—no antidote. The thought swelled like a balloon in his head.

He heard the rattle of wood on wood to his right. In a chip of a split second he switched on the flashlight, saw a black point coming towards him, flung his body forward, felt the sleeves of his coat rip open and something rough brush against the skin of his arm. He didn't known whether it had cut the flesh. He dropped the flashlight and with a twist of the body brought his left arm round underneath, rolled over as far as he could go, and made a desperate grab for the stick. He caught it as it was being jerked back and felt his flesh burn as it tore across his palm, and his hand close on air. He pushed up his right arm and fired three times through the cedar posts to his right. Then he heard the laugh again, low and crazy.

Now he was panting and sweating with fear. The inside of the trap was flooded with light, and smoke from the gun-powder danced in notes across the beam. He picked up the flashlight and jabbed it against the posts, trying to shine the beam through the chinks. A long thread of light picked out leaf mould, earth, a tangle of thin branches. It was no good.

Panting still, he sat back on his heels, flashlight in one hand, gun in the other. He put down the flashlight and re-loaded the gun, trying to keep his hands steady. From behind he could feel in imagination the prick of the pointed stick all down his spine. He bent quickly to one side, swivelled his wrist, and fired behind him through the back of the trap. Silence closed in after the crash; and then, from the direc-tion in which he'd fired, he heard again the hoarse, low-pitched laugh.

His ears ached for the faint sound of wood grating on wood. Before it came, another sound broke the stillness from in front. A long shout, repeated, and then the distant crashes of a body hurling itself through the undergrowth towards the trap. Vachell, sick with hope, fired again into the posts at his back. Now he could hear the running feet. He shouted with all the force of his lungs. A moment later the askari burst through the thicket ahead and pulled himself up against the door of the trap.

"Watch out!" Vachell called. "Shoot what you see!"

He heard the askari's panting and the slap of his hand against the rifle butt.

"There is no one, bwana."

Vachell swore. "Let me out. Quickly, lift the door. . . ."

At last he stood erect outside, his cramped knees aching painfully. He took a deep, glorious breath, and swung the flashlight around. It showed thickets, brambles, vast mysterious pillars immobile in the darkness, the thick boles of towering trees. Behind the trap some leaves on a branch were swaying slightly. The flashlight picked them out in sharp relief. The whole scene looked unreal, cut out of paper, like a stage set.

"Gone!" he exclaimed. "You followed?"

"Yes, bwana," the askari's face gleamed with sweat. He spoke in a quick, excited voice. "To where the path forks, but then I did not know which way. I waited, hidden in the forest, because I . . ."

"Yes, yes! This path—where does it go?"

"A little way, to a place where wood is cut—that is all, bwana. It does not continue. No one can escape that way."

"They can circle back. The house and the road are guarded?"

"Yes, bwana. Corporal Abdul is there. Capture is certain, unless . . ." The askari clicked his tongue against his teeth. "Perhaps . . ."

"What? Quickly!"

"The motor-car—if it could be reached. No one guards it. One askari only. . . ."

"Go," Vachell ordered. "Run like a cheetah, tell Corporal

Abdul to seize whoever moves and guard the car. But do not shoot."

The askari clicked his heels, saluted, turned and ran back down the path in long, loping strides. Vachell pushed his way into the forest through a gap where the quivering leaves hung. The path was very narrow. Fallen logs lay across it, a branch hung low. The flashlight picked out the obstacles in vivid black and white. The gun was ready in his hand.

But the quarry had vanished into the forest and the dark. Vachell came to an old clearing, full of mossy stumps and slippery, rotting logs, and retraced his footsteps past the trap. The white turkey still crouched in a corner, bemused with fear. No sounds but those of his own progress came to his ears.

He felt like a man released from a lightless dungeon when he came out of the forest and stood in the open, a star-strewn sky clear and untroubled overhead. The air was cold as sleet on his face. Half running, half walking, he reached the Munson homestead, breathless but warm at last. The corporal and the other askari were patrolling the buildings on bare, silent feet.

"Not yet, bwana," the corporal reported. "But, whoever comes, we shall see."

Vachell nodded, crossed the lawn to his car, and got in. He pulled a flask out of the dashboard pocket and took a long drink. The whisky spread out inside in a warm, sharp flood. He found a packet of cigarettes and lit one, frowning at the match. The hand that held it was shaking like the leaves that had trembled over the forest path. He blew out the smoke with a deep, grateful breath. His blood was tingling from the whisky in his hands and toes and ears.

He was jerked back into action by a shout from the direction of the hen-houses, a distant, shapeless mass in the pale light. He was half-way across the lawn when the shot came. A second later a ghastly screech, a cross between a cry and a bellow, brought him to a halt. Once he had shot a monkey; it had fallen from the tree with a cry like that, and he had never fired at another. A half human, half animal cry. He plunged on, rounded the corner of the hen-houses, and saw both askaris bending over something on the ground.

The corporal stood erect when he reached the scene.

"Bwana, I shot at the leopard," he exclaimed. "I saw it come, it was creeping round the corner and the house of the chickens. I did not think—I did not know—what man walks like a leopard, bent low?"

Vachell knelt down and turned the body over. The shot had torn through the chest. The head lolled back, and the lifeless face—white, distorted, the lips drawn back from the teeth, the jaw hanging loose—stared into his own. Vachell felt a twinge of sorrow for Anita Adams, possessed by a madness that could be concealed but not conquered, diseased in mind and yet pathetic in futility, as he let her body sag back on to the ground. The corporal was jittering by his side, fearing rebuke. Vachell stood up slowly, and wiped his hands on a handkerchief.

"It was a good shot," he said.

CHAPTER 27: THE SUDDEN SNAPPING OF THE
tension that had stretched their nerves to breaking-point during the past few days made them all a little light-headed. Norman Parrot, looking true to life again in his old burberry, his
blond hair dishevelled and curly, had been rolling about on
the lawn in a violent game with Bullseye and the red setters.
He was hot and panting and covered with bits of grass. Janice
West was lying back in a garden-chair, a glass of beer at her
side. Her eyes were still tired and haunted but she was smiling at Parrot's antics. It was the first time there'd been anything to smile at, Vachell thought, for what seemed like half a
lifetime, or more.

Parrot abandoned the dogs and came over to join them
in the shade of a tree. A bed of delphiniums between them
and the view made a brilliant patch in the sunlight, and a
syringa in full blossom scented the air.

"I need beer," he remarked. "I could drink enough to
waterlog the Queen Mary."

Janice West waved a hand towards the table, bearing bottles, and said: "Help yourself."

"You know, Vachell, I owe you an apology," Parrot remarked. "I'm sorry I had to spring on you like a jaguar and
then bat you on the bean with a torch. Highly irregular, I'm
afraid, and I dare say I shall get ten years in chains. The
trouble was I didn't know who you were till the damage was
done, and then it was too late to explain."

Vachell rubbed the back of his head reminiscently. "I bought it," he admitted. "I should have known enough to look behind the door."

"I heard you outside Munson's room and only just had time to slip out of sight, ready for the pounce. I thought it was Wendtland, of course. You could have knocked me down with a feather when I saw I'd laid out the pride of the Chania police."

"It was smart to know where to look," Vachell observed, "to find Munson's horde of nuts."

Parrot glanced across at Janice, and smiled. She shut her eyes and leant her head back, her hands linked behind her neck. Vachell helped himself to more beer and tried to fix his mind on Parrot, on the report he'd got to write, on anything to stop him thinking how tired she looked, how wrung out by emotion, how after to-day he would not be seeing her again.

"A little bird told me," Parrot said. "A bird of fine plumage and sweet song, and, if one can apply the phrase to birds, of considerable guts."

Vachell put down his beer and reached for a cigarette, lit it, and leant back in the chair.

"You mean . . . ?" he began, and stopped; he couldn't press Parrot for a reply.

"Didn't you know?" Parrot asked. "Oh, I thought you'd realize that Janice was working in with me as soon as you tumbled to my little game. (I owe you an apology about that, too; I ought to have warned you what I was up to when all this started, but I thought you'd be certain to know, as

Armitage had the information. Just like the old fathead not to pass it on. I wonder if he forgot or thought it too secret to mention out loud?) Anyway, Janice was helping me in this show. When I say helping, she was doing it all, I just sat back and used the information. It's a dirty game, at times."

Janice opened her eyes. "If I'd known how dirty I wouldn't have played. It's like swimming, it's too late once you're in to worry about the water being cold." There was a touch of bitterness in her voice.

Parrot walked over with a beer bottle to fill her glass, and touched her hand lightly with his own.

"It's over now," he said. "It worked, and it didn't have anything to do with—with the other business, and Dennis being killed."

"I know." She shut her eyes again and smiled faintly, and stroked a setter that rested its chin on her knee.

"You mean," Vachell said slowly, "Mrs. West was stringing Munson along to get information on Nazi activities, which she passed on to you?"

Parrot nodded. "Unpleasant, isn't it? Definitely allergic to the old school tie. Why anybody ever thought that worming information out of reluctant foreigners, nine-tenths of it useless anyway, was a romantic sort of job, God knows. It's all done by bribery, or else by taking advantage of some rather unpleasant bloke's weaknesses, so it's a cad's game either way. Janice would have driven Munson off long ago, but I propositioned her to keep him on a string and find out all she could about the doings of this precious Bund. And I must say, she did it proud. Here's to Olga Pulloffski, the beautiful spy."

He raised his glass to Janice, but although his tone was facetious there was an almost dog-like look of devotion in his eyes.

Janice sat up and reached for her drink. "Thank you for telling him, Norman," she said. "I didn't know if that would be allowed." She looked across at Vachell and some of the animation returned to her face.

"It wasn't so bad as it sounds," she said. "Munson was easy to handle, I didn't have to lure him on in a *négligée* over supper for two with caviare and iced champagne, or anything. He liked to talk about himself. I kept the seduction on a reasonably platonic level, but it got in my hair to have him around at all."

"And he told you where to look for the papers Wendtland wanted?" Vachell asked. He felt light in the head, as if a ten-ton weight had been taken away.

"Not exactly, but he told me that he'd hidden them, and one day he said: 'Every night I lie on my back in bed and see the hiding-place of the bomb to blow Wendtland up, and I think, ah-ha,' or words to that effect. So Norman figured they must be behind the ceiling somewhere, and the first chance he got he went over to grab them before Wendtland and Mrs. Munson tore the house apart."

"And brained Vachell in the process," Parrot added. "Munson was using them to blackmail Wendtland into giving him back the leadership of the Bund. Of course, Wendtland had taken over under orders from Berlin. He'd been down in South Africa for a couple of years, helping to organize the Sudafrika Bund, and got himself into a nice mess down there.

The dark-eyed non-Aryans of Jo'burg were too much for him, he got a girl into trouble and in due course a little non-Aryan with a storm-trooper for a poppa was born. Somehow Munson's sister dug it all up and got a statement from the girl, and some letters Wendtland had written to her, which proved the thing beyond doubt. As you know, Aryan boy mustn't meet non-Aryan girl in the Reich or its outposts, and I suppose if loyal members of the Party had raised a stink, the personnel department would have to sit up and take notice to kick Wendtland out of the Bund."

"The information wasn't much use to you," Vachell suggested.

"No, not directly, although it's all gone off to the right quarters in Berlin, on the general theory that anything which upsets an apple-cart is a good thing. That was why I had to disappear so suddenly, by the way; I had to get it off in Munson's name before the news of his death got back to Germany, and the channel doesn't, so to speak, open out from here. However, there was some other stuff with the proofs of Wendtland's little slip—lists of active Nazis here, and one or two other documents Munson evidently hadn't wanted to hand over to his successor. He wasn't a very loyal Nazi, I'm afraid."

Vachell looked across at Janice over the rim of his glass. "I owe you two apologies," he said. "One for getting you all wrong—if I hadn't been a sap I'd have guessed how it was between you and Munson—the other for having you forcibly abducted by one of your sincerest admirers, Inspector Prettyman. At least you didn't have to go to jail."

Janice looked down at her hands resting on her lap and said: "It seemed a little harsh. I thought you really believed that I'd killed Karl Munson and then Dennis. That was tough, you know."

"Yes," Vachell said. "I gave Prettyman the job. I couldn't take it. I was afraid you wouldn't agree to leave the farm at my suggestion, and I couldn't explain—I had no proof. I figured you'd think I was nuts and stay where you were, right here, and that was another thing I couldn't take—the knowledge you were in danger."

Janice looked up at him in surprise. A slight touch of colour had come to her cheeks. "I don't understand," she said. "Why should Anita—that poor girl, I can't possibly realize she was that crazy, and I never knew it—why should she want to hurt me? We were always very friendly, she seemed to like me well enough, she never gave any sign . . ."

"Sure, she liked you," Vachell answered. "You had everything she hadn't and never would have—looks, poise, and whatever it takes to turn level-headed guys like Parrot here and me into soft-headed saps who'd pull out their eye-teeth if you wanted them for souvenirs. She could admire it, she was kind of fascinated, she liked to watch and talk with you, and the more she did so the more a festering sort of jealousy grew in her twisted, abnormal mind. When those crazy spells attacked her things came up out of the subconscious like sea-beasts from the ocean bed after a marine earthquake. And, among them was a blind and ghastly sort of jealousy because you had all the things she wanted and never could have, whatever she did."

Janice shook her head. "I can't believe it, even now. She was a pathetic creature. I can see how she was all tangled up inside, with no normal home life and the sort of treatment the Munsons would give a governess, but it's the violence I can't understand."

"I can't understand much of it either," Vachell agreed. "It's the sort of case a psychiatrist would go to town on, but it's over the head of an ordinary cop. From what Anstey said, it seems she wouldn't remember much of what she did when these spells were on her, after they passed off. They were all attempts to injure you. Remember you told me, right at the beginning, you felt there was something malicious trying to get at you? I reckon she wanted to make you suffer for the injustice done to her, to give you hell because you had everything when she'd been cheated of it all. She tried to hurt you through the things you cared for—your prize flowers, your dogs—but she might not have kept going that way. She might have turned on you. That was why I was scared."

Janice shivered a little, and said: "It's horrible. Anything turned inside out, that one can't understand, gives me the heeby-jeebies. If only I'd known . . ."

"There wasn't a thing you could do. Her mind was diseased. Once she'd started on an orgy of murder she couldn't stop. I reckoned the only way to play for safety was to get you right out of it, with Prettyman and a couple of police askaris guarding you with fixed bayonets and drawn swords."

Janice smiled wryly: "Thanks," she said. "It would have been nice to have known that at the time. It isn't so good to be locked up in an eight-by-eight bedroom with a cop by the window and another outside the door, even though Inspector Prettyman was the soul of courtesy, and so embarrassed, poor boy. But I still don't understand. These crazy spells are one thing, but brewing arrow-poison and smearing it on nails is something else again."

"Sure, there wasn't anything exactly crazy about that part. That was a scheme built by her conscious mind, I guess, not a sort of outbreak of criminal lunacy, like tearing off the heads of ducks. But it was the product of an abnormal mind, just the same. It's hard to draw a line between the two."

"What I can't understand," Parrot interposed, "is why she decided to bump off Munson, particularly. He was a nasty piece of work, and any one might have wanted to get him out of the way, but after all if she didn't like him (and who shall blame her) she could always have pushed off and got another job."

"Not without leaving the children. That's where the crazy part comes in. She loved those kids, they were the only living creatures she had to love, and the only ones who showed her any real affection in return. And they weren't hers. That was what burnt her up—they weren't hers."

"You mean she killed Munson in order to get the children to herself?" Janice asked incredulously.

"I'm dealing with supposition here. But I've talked with Anstey, and he says it has a basis of possibility. It's the same kind of feeling she had toward you—a violent unreasoning jealousy, with its roots in God knows what complexes and maladjustments. The kids were hers, she took care of them and loved them, but all the time they belonged to the lousy Munsons, whom she hated, and not to her. The injustice swelled up to the size of a monster balloon in her mind. So she decided to clear the tracks, to rub out both Munsons and get the kids for her own. They'd be hers for keeps, then.

"It was a crazy scheme, the product of a crazy brain. She got the Acocanthera from Arawak, the old Dorobo mole-catcher—at least that's my guess. We haven't pulled him in yet, but when we do we'll get that loose end tied up. She stewed it in an old gasolene can, which she subsequently planted over here so if it ever got found it wouldn't be traced to her—that was another crack at you—and stuck a doctored nail through the sole of Munson's shoe."

CHAPTER 28: "BUT WHAT MADE YOU EVER suspect Anita," Janice asked, "at all?"

"You did." Vachell poured out some more beer and grinned at her across the froth.

"But I had no idea . . ."

"Two little pointers gave me a line, but if it hadn't been for something you told me, I'd never have doped out just how she lied in regard to her alibi for the time when the poisoned nail was taken out of Munson's shoe."

"Couldn't you begin at the beginning and go on from there?"

"Okay. I'll take the two pointers first. We figured, very early in the case, that the reason Munson went into the pyrethrum shed was to keep a date, and that the date was probably with you. If that was so, you must have sent either a note or a message, since Munson's place isn't on the phone. I couldn't get to hear of any note, but Anita Adams had been over here to tea the afternoon before Munson was killed, and she could have taken a message back if there was any message to take.

"That was the set-up. There was another angle. Anita could have given a message to Munson from you that didn't come from you at all. She could have invented one. That was only a possibility, and I had no proof, but I kept it in mind."

Janice nodded, a slight frown of concentration on her face.

"So that was it. And the other pointer?"

"Anita Adams told me how the pigeons had their heads torn off, one night, over at the Munson place. She said Mrs. Munson and herself had the only two keys to the pigeon pen, and the lock hadn't been forced. It didn't seem likely any one would steal a key for the sort of screwy crime that wasn't premeditated but the result of a sudden mania to kill and destroy. That looked as if it was either she herself or Mrs. Munson that had torn off the pigeons' heads."

"Mrs. Munson might have been a good bet," Parrot suggested.

Vachell shook his head. "She wrote the anonymous note smearing Mrs. West with the murder. When that didn't seem to register she even poisoned herself with cattle-dip in the sherry (as well as Corcoran and Anita Adams) and then pulled a phony story of how she'd seen Janice snooping around Corcoran's room, and found her alone in the living-room with the sherry. She made the house-boy, Mwogi, back the story and say he'd seen Mrs. West, too.

"She was another one half eaten up with jealousy and a desire for revenge. She had only one idea, to get her claws into the woman who'd been carrying on with her husband, and rip like hell. I reckon she really believed you'd done the murders, Mrs. West, but whether she believed it or not, she meant the police to. If we wouldn't arrest you on the evidence we had, by God she'd give us the evidence. So she tried to frame you by making it appear that you'd sneaked over to the Munson place and spiked the sherry with a shot of cattle-dip. It was clumsy as the devil, but Mother Munson is not a subtle woman. How did she know you used a sleeping-draught, by the way?"

Janice frowned in thought. "I don't know. Wait a minute, though. I lent a bottle to Anita one day, when she complained she couldn't sleep. It had my name on the bottle and Mrs. Munson may have seen it in Anita's room."

Vachell nodded. "That would be it. She wrote the note on Mrs. Innocent's machine when she went in to Karuna the afternoon of Munson's death. At that time she didn't know how Munson died. She guessed he'd been poisoned, but guessed the wrong kind of poison. We found afterwards that chloral hydrate didn't come into it at all, and that put her in the clear, unless she was being more cagy than I gave her credit for. Anyway, after the night Bullseye got slashed, I knew it couldn't be her."

"Because she isn't agile enough to jump the fence and get away from the askari," Janice said. "I thought of that too. Up to that point I thought she might be the one who'd been doing these crazy things, but after that I knew it couldn't be. That was a terrible night. I couldn't sleep, and I went out for a stroll, just when the maniac—Anita, I can't get used to the idea—must have been around, I guess, because I'd only been back in my room maybe five or ten minutes when the askari fired and all the commotion began. I was so scared I told you I'd been in my bedroom all the time, and then you found the mud on my mules, and it nearly killed me."

"You didn't consider letting me in on the story?"

"I was too scared. The way you'd been looking at me, I thought you suspected I was the guilty one. And then Dennis—I knew what he thought, I knew he wouldn't believe that I'd just gone out to take a walk. . . . And now it's too late to explain."

Her voice was so low it was almost a whisper, and she kept her eyes on the head of the setter that rested on her lap.

"That wasn't suspicion, that was the look a guy keeps for women who can trample all over him and have him come back for more," Vachell said lightly. "I was telling you how you showed me the crack in Anita Adams' story. It has to do with eggs."

"Eggs?"

"Eggs. It wasn't possible to check on the times during which the killer could have driven his doctored nail into Munson's shoe, but it *was* possible to narrow down the time when the nail must have been taken out. We got it down to half an hour, between a quarter to seven and a quarter after. I checked on every one's alibi during that time. Wendtland was on his own farm thirty miles away. You, Parrot, seemed out, for the same reason. Corcoran was with a whole gang of natives, sowing oats. Mrs. Munson was in the office, but she was ruled out for other reasons, and Anita Adams was doing the morning chores in the poultry pens. One of the jobs a poultry-keeper mustn't skip is to turn the eggs in the incubator night and morning—isn't that right, Mrs. West?"

"I wish you'd stop calling me Mrs. West. Sure, that's right. They have to be turned twice a day."

"Anita Adams said she'd done the chores as usual between six-thirty and breakfast at seven-fifteen. But she hadn't turned the eggs."

Janice stared at him with eyes that were startled out of

their preoccupation with her own tragedy. "For Heaven's sake, how do you know that?"

"When you show me something, it sticks. You showed me how you mark one side of the eggs with a cross and leave the other side bare. Anita Adams used the same technique. The eggs had a cross on top when I looked into her incubators around noon the day before Munson died. I saw them again the following afternoon. In the interval they should have been turned twice, evening and morning. That would have brought the crosses back on top. But the bare surfaces were on top. That meant the eggs had been turned once instead of twice in the last twenty-four hours. Unless this could be explained away, it meant that Anita Adams had skipped her normal routine that morning. She'd skipped it because she was waiting around within sight of Munson's bedroom door for a chance to jump in and grab the nail. She got the chance, but not until nearly seven, and by that time it was too late to turn the eggs."

Janice stared at him in amazement. "Well, for the Lord's sake," she exclaimed. "If that doesn't take some beating. You mean to say you built up the whole case on Anita's failure to turn the eggs?"

"No," Vachell said. "There were lots of other things. It was obvious we were dealing with a person well on the road to the nut-house, some one as full of repressions and psychological kinks as a sheep is full of worms. Mrs. Munson and Anita Adams seemed to be the only two mentally unhealthy people mixed up in the whole business, and Mrs. Munson could be ruled out for the reasons I gave. That just left Anita Adams; but it didn't leave any proof.

"This has been a hell of a case, there never was enough proof to make a grass-blade tremble. Right now I haven't a shred of proof that she killed the Commander. I reckon he came on her during the fire, just at the moment when the bushbuck calf had bumped into her legs, and the sight of something scared and helpless aroused the rage in her to destroy, so she cut its throat. Most likely she was carrying a shot of arrow-poison around with her in case a chance arose to get at Mrs. Munson's bloodstream. All we know is, he dropped his axe, maybe to grab hold of her, and she struck him. Anita Adams caught up with Janice—and came out with the rest of the party. My only chance to pin anything on her was to close in during the attempt I knew she'd make, if my calculations were right, on Mrs. Munson. I encouraged her to think she could take the kids away, so she'd figure her big chance had come and go ahead and make her play. I was in a spot: if she'd succeeded Mrs. Munson's death would have been at my door, and the sort of murder you can commit by leaving a nail or splinter around for the murderer to scratch a hand on is kind of hard to stop.

"Right here I got the breaks. Anita Adams figured Mrs. Munson would be certain to look over the leopard trap last thing to see it was properly baited. She always saw to things like that herself. So Anita fastened the pride of the turkey flock in the trap, so Mrs. Munson couldn't help but wound her hands when she went in to rescue the bird. Anita was thorough, too. She even swiped Mrs. Munson's knife so the string couldn't be cut, and Mrs. Munson would have to undo the knots. If I hadn't happened to take the path into the forest last night the trick would have worked, I guess.

"There was one more piece to the plan. I reckon Anita Adams intended to return later and open the trap so Mrs. Munson's body would be leopard's bait, and next morning another of those deaths that looked like accidents and couldn't be proved to be anything else would be discovered. Then Anita Adams would be free to take away the kids, with no one to kick. And there'd still be no proof, even that Mrs. Munson had been murdered. It was neat, but the wrong sap fell for the turkey gag, and when she came back later that night she found a live body instead of a dead one in the trap. She tried to put things right, even at that late stage, and if it hadn't been for the askari who followed her down I guess she'd have had her third killing after all."

"It was lucky the corporal fired that shot," Parrot observed.

"Sure was," Vachell agreed.

They sat in silence for a little, watching the wide view below them trembling in the midday heat, ponderous clouds resting on the horizon, and sunbirds flashing with metallic brilliance among the flowers. The dogs had quieted now, and lay, panting gently, in the shade. After a little Norman Parrot got to his feet, stretched, and picked a battered old felt hat off the grass.

"Well," he remarked, "thanks for the beer, Janice. It hit the spot. I must be getting along."

"Stop to lunch," Janice said.

Parrot shook his head. "I'd like to, but I've got to pack

and fix things up for the farm to carry on. You'll have a rest from my ugly mug for a while."

Janice sat up in her chair in consternation and surprise. "You're not going away?"

Parrot nodded. "For a bit. One job is over, there's another to come. Onwards and upwards is our motto. All the little pyrethrum flowers will bow their heads, the cows conceive in sorrow and the tassels of the mealies wilt, but, nevertheless, I must leave them to their fate. It's a hard life."

"But you'll come back?"

"Oh, rather," Parrot said cheerfully. Janice got up and he shook hands, started to say something, and then changed his mind. He looked embarrassed and unhappy, like a small boy going back to school. "I shall pop up from time to time," he added. "But it isn't exactly the sort of job one can settle down in, if you know what I mean. One day I shall retire on to the Stock Exchange with a cosy little flat near Marble Arch and marry my cook, if she'll have me, and spend a week-end at the Metropole at Brighton now and then. That's always been my secret ambition."

"Oh," Janice said, a little blankly. "We shall miss you. It won't seem the same."

Parrot rammed his hat on to the back of his head and managed a grin. "Time, the great healer, already has the situation in hand," he remarked. "Any one who can handle a scythe and an hour-glass at once, plus a long beard, can fix anything. Besides, you've now got the devoted personal attention of the Chania Police. Make the most of it—exploit it to the full. Thanks for everything, Janice, good-bye and good luck."

He shook hands quickly with Vachell and muttered awkwardly: "You'll do all you can? I mean, she's on her own, and things have been a bit harassing. I wish I could stay. Well, so long, and next time you want to make a study of African wild life don't do it in a leopard trap." He looked back from the other side of the lawn and waved his hat as he climbed into his dilapidated car.

"That's one swell guy," Vachell said, looking after him, "with a tough job. He has to travel light."

"He's a good neighbour," Janice said.

Vachell looked at her across the table where brown bottles caught gleams of sunlight that shone down through the tree. Wild thoughts and hopes were rushing around inside his head like a flock of madly excited birds. None of them paused for long enough for identification.

"I thought maybe he was more to you than that," he said. His mouth had suddenly gone dry.

Janice glanced at him and he looked straight into her eyes. He lost all sense of time and place; he felt as if he were swimming in . depthless pool between high rocks. There was a hint of a smile at the corners of her mouth.

"Listen," he said, and his voice seemed to be coming from a long way off. "This is a hell of a time to say it, but I'm madly in love with you. Ever since I first saw you, since the night you asked me up to dinner, I've been so damned much nuts about you I haven't been able to think of anything else. It's like being drowned in the sea, and never quite going under.

Now you can throw me out on my ear, but I had to say it before I go. The trouble is, I don't want to go. I want to stay right here and look at you, I want to help you out of this jam. I don't want to leave you like this, alone."

Janice smiled, but it was a weary smile, and her eyes were sad.

"Everything moves too quickly," she said. "I'm sorry, I can't keep up any more."

Vachell stepped forward eagerly, a new and brilliant idea filling his mind. "Look," he said quickly, "you can't stay here alone, no one to help out or anything, even Parrot gone. It's impossible, it's absurd. All I want is to be some use to you, that's all I care about now. I'm no farmer, I don't know yet what it's all about, but I can learn, and in the meantime I can take care of the labour and fix all the business side and see the boys don't start to chisel now there's no boss. I could move into Parrot's place for the time being and maybe one day when . . ."

"Have you gone entirely crazy?" Janice demanded sharply. She looked amazed. "Have you got a touch of the sun, or have I, or what? Or have you just been pretending all this time to be a superintendent in the Chania police?"

"None of those things," Vachell said. His eyes were shining with excitement. He seized a bottle of beer off the table and waved it in the air. "I've just given birth to the only swell idea I've ever had. I'm sick of this police racket. I've been feeling that way for months, only I didn't know it. I've held down one job long enough. I'm through with the whole darned thing. I'll call up Major Armitage right now and tell him I'm quitting, and nuts to him. I'll stay up here for a while and help straighten things out, and when you're ready to say the word we can pull stakes and go places I've always wanted to go—China, maybe, and the Dutch East Indies, there's islands in there that still haven't been explored, and New Guinea, where the head-hunters are; we'll explore it all together and we'll keep a place here so we ——"

He broke off and put down the bottle, abashed and suddenly calm. "I'm sorry," he said. "I guess you're right. I'm nuts—it must be the sun. This is a hell of a way to talk, when only two days ago . . . I mean it, though. I'll wait ten years if I have to; but one day you're going to marry again, and when you're ready I'm going to be on hand, and if you won't have me at least I'll be the first guy you turn down. Janice, tell me something, will you?"

"You make me dizzy in the head."

"You haven't got Norman Parrot on your mind?"

"No, of course not, I ——"

"Nor any other guy?"

"Will you please not talk this way? Do you think it's even decent, when Dennis ——"

"I'm sorry, Janice, you'll have to forgive me, this is the biggest thing that's ever happened to me. Does it get you down to run this place single-handed? Do you need help?"

"Of course, but I decline ——"

"Do you hate to be alone?"

"What *is* this? Will you ——"

"Do you want to go places and see things? Do you like to act crazy, to go as far as your money takes you and then find a job that pays you some more? Do you think of the hell it would be to stop in one place all your life and never see all the things you want to see? Of course you do. I knew it the first time I met you. I read it in your eyes, the way you spoke, and everything about you. Janice, I ——"

She was looking bewildered, annoyed and exhausted at the same time; he had brought a slight flush to her cheeks with his words. He stepped forward quickly, and took both her hands in his own.

"We're going to have fun together," he promised. "Whenever you say." She drew back quickly, but there was no anger in her eyes.

"I don't know," she said. "It's too soon. You must give me time."

A flood of the kind of happiness that made him want to shout and sing threatened to sweep the last of Vachell's sanity away. "All the time in the world," he said. "What's time for? I've lived a thousand years in the last half hour. I could spend another thousand looking at you."

She looked at him in silence, smiled and picked up her hat. A boy was crossing the lawn with news of lunch.

"Of course, you're nuts," she remarked. "But I guess even a tornado would be a distraction in the middle of an epidemic in which all one's family was dying of bubonic plague. You'll stay and have some lunch?"

"I'd be glad to," Vachell said.

THE PERENNIAL LIBRARY MYSTERY SERIES

E. C. Bentley

TRENT'S LAST CASE
"One of the three best detective stories ever written."
—Agatha Christie

TRENT'S OWN CASE
"I won't waste time saying that the plot is sound and the detection satisfying. Trent has not altered a scrap and reappears with all his old humor and charm."
—Dorothy L. Sayers

Gavin Black

A DRAGON FOR CHRISTMAS
"Potent excitement!"
—New York Herald Tribune

THE EYES AROUND ME
"I stayed up until all hours last night reading *The Eyes Around Me,* which is something I do not do very often, but I was so intrigued by the ingeniousness of Mr. Black's plotting and the witty way in which he spins his mystery. I can only say that I enjoyed the book enormously."
—F. van Wyck Mason

YOU WANT TO DIE, JOHNNY?
"Gavin Black doesn't just develop a pressure plot in suspense, he adds uninfected wit, character, charm, and sharp knowledge of the Far East to make rereading as keen as the first race-through." —Book Week

Nicholas Blake

THE BEAST MUST DIE
"It remains one more proof that in the hands of a really first-class writer the detective novel can safely challenge comparison with any other variety of fiction."
—The Manchester Guardian

THE CORPSE IN THE SNOWMAN
"If there is a distinction between the novel and the detective story (which we do not admit), then this book deserves a high place in both categories."
—The New York Times

THE DREADFUL HOLLOW
"Pace unhurried, characters excellent, reasoning solid."
—San Francisco Chronicle

END OF CHAPTER
". . . admirably solid . . . an adroit formal detective puzzle backed up by firm characterization and a knowing picture of London publishing."
—*The New York Times*

HEAD OF A TRAVELER
"Another grade A detective story of the right old jigsaw persuasion."
—*New York Herald Tribune Book Review*

MINUTE FOR MURDER
"An outstanding mystery novel. Mr. Blake's writing is a delight in itself."
—*The New York Times*

THE MORNING AFTER DEATH
"One of Blake's best."
—Rex Warner

A PENKNIFE IN MY HEART
"Style brilliant . . . and suspenseful."
—*San Francisco Chronicle*

THE PRIVATE WOUND
[Blake's] best novel in a dozen years . . . . An intensely penetrating study of sexual passion . . . . A powerful story of murder and its aftermath."
—Anthony Boucher, *The New York Times*

A QUESTION OF PROOF
"The characters in this story are unusually well drawn, and the suspense is well sustained."
—*The New York Times*

THE SAD VARIETY
"It is a stunner. I read it instead of eating, instead of sleeping."
—Dorothy Salisbury Davis

THE SMILER WITH THE KNIFE
"An extraordinarily well written and entertaining thriller."
—*Saturday Review of Literature*

THOU SHELL OF DEATH
"It has all the virtues of culture, intelligence and sensibility that the most exacting connoisseur could ask of detective fiction."
—*The Times* [London] *Literary Supplement*

THE WHISPER IN THE GLOOM
"One of the most entertaining suspense-pursuit novels in many seasons."
—*The New York Times*

Cyril Hare

AN ENGLISH MURDER
"By a long shot, the best crime story I have read for a long time. Everything is traditional, but originality does not suffer. The setting is perfect. Full marks to Mr. Hare." —*Irish Press*

TRAGEDY AT LAW
"An extremely urbane and well-written detective story."
  —*The New York Times*

UNTIMELY DEATH
"The English detective story at its quiet best, meticulously underplayed, rich in perceivings of the droll human animal and ready at the last with a neat surprise which has been there all the while had we but wits to see it." —*New York Herald Tribune Book Review*

WHEN THE WIND BLOWS
"The best, unquestionably, of all the Hare stories, and a masterpiece by any standards."
 —Jacques Barzun and Wendell Hertig Taylor, *A Catalogue of Crime*

WITH A BARE BODKIN
"One of the best detective stories published for a long time."
  —*The Spectator*

Matthew Head

THE CABINDA AFFAIR (*available 6/81*)
"An absorbing whodunit and a distinguished novel of atmosphere."
  —Anthony Boucher, *The New York Times*

MURDER AT THE FLEA CLUB (*available 6/81*)
"The true delight is in Head's style, its limpid ease combined with humor and an awesome precision of phrase." —*San Francisco Chronicle*

M. V. Heberden

ENGAGED TO MURDER
"Smooth plotting." —*The New York Times*

James Hilton

WAS IT MURDER?
"The story is well planned and well written."
  —*The New York Times*

Elspeth Huxley

THE AFRICAN POISON MURDERS
"Obscure venom, manical mutilations, deadly bush fire, thrilling climax compose major opus.... Top-flight."

—*Saturday Review of Literature*

Francis Iles

BEFORE THE FACT
"Not many 'serious' novelists have produced character studies to compare with Iles's internally terrifying portrait of the murderer in *Before the Fact,* his masterpiece and a work truly deserving the appellation of unique and beyond price."　　　　　—Howard Haycraft

MALICE AFORETHOUGHT
"It is a long time since I have read anything so good as *Malice Aforethought,* with its cynical humour, acute criminology, plausible detail and rapid movement. It makes you hug yourself with pleasure."

—H. C. Harwood, *Saturday Review*

Lange Lewis

THE BIRTHDAY MURDER
"Almost perfect in its playlike purity and delightful prose."

—Jacques Barzun and Wendell Hertig Taylor

Arthur Maling

LUCKY DEVIL
"The plot unravels at a fast clip, the writing is breezy and Maling's approach is as fresh as today's stockmarket quotes."

—*Louisville Courier Journal*

RIPOFF
"A swiftly paced story of today's big business is larded with intrigue as a Ralph Nader-type investigates an insurance scandal and is soon on the run from a hired gun and his brother. . . . Engrossing and credible."

—*Booklist*

SCHROEDER'S GAME
"As the title indicates, this Schroeder is up to something, and the unravelling of his game is a diverting and sufficiently blood-soaked entertainment."　　　　　—*The New Yorker*

Thomas Sterling

THE EVIL OF THE DAY
"Prose as witty and subtle as it is sharp and clear...characters unconventionally conceived and richly bodied forth . . . . In short, a novel to be treasured."
　　　　　　　　　—Anthony Boucher, *The New York Times*

Julian Symons

THE BELTING INHERITANCE
"A superb whodunit in the best tradition of the detective story."
　　　　　　　　　—August Derleth, *Madison Capital Times*

BLAND BEGINNING
"Mr. Symons displays a deft storytelling skill, a quiet and literate wit, a nice feeling for character, and detective ingenuity of a high order."
　　　　　　　　　—Anthony Boucher, *The New York Times*

BOGUE'S FORTUNE
"There's a touch of the old sardonic humour, and more than a touch of style."
　　　　　　　　　—*The Spectator*

THE BROKEN PENNY
"The most exciting, astonishing and believable spy story to appear in years.
　　　　　　　　　—Anthony Boucher, *The New York Times Book Review*

THE COLOR OF MURDER
"A singularly unostentatious and memorably brilliant detective story."
　　　　　　　　　—*New York Herald Tribune Book Review*

THE 31ST OF FEBRUARY
"Nobody has painted a more gruesome picture of the advertising business since Dorothy Sayers wrote 'Murder Must Advertise', and very few people have written a more entertaining or dramatic mystery story."
　　　　　　　　　—*The New Yorker*

Dorothy Stockbridge Tillet
(John Stephen Strange)

THE MAN WHO KILLED FORTESCUE
"Better than average."　　　　　　　—*Saturday Review of Literature*

Henry Kitchell Webster

WHO IS THE NEXT?
"A double murder, private-plane piloting, a neat impersonation, and a delicate courtship are adroitly combined by a writer who knows how to use the language."　　　　—Jacques Barzun and Wendell Hertig Taylor

If you enjoyed this book you'll want to know about
THE PERENNIAL LIBRARY MYSTERY SERIES

Nicholas Blake

☐	P 456	THE BEAST MUST DIE	$1.95
☐	P 427	THE CORPSE IN THE SNOWMAN	$1.95
☐	P 493	THE DREADFUL HOLLOW	$1.95
☐	P 397	END OF CHAPTER	$1.95
☐	P 419	MINUTE FOR MURDER	$1.95
☐	P 520	THE MORNING AFTER DEATH	$1.95
☐	P 521	A PENKNIFE IN MY HEART	$2.25
☐	P 531	THE PRIVATE WOUND	$2.25
☐	P 494	A QUESTION OF PROOF	$1.95
☐	P 495	THE SAD VARIETY	$2.25
☐	P 457	THE SMILER WITH THE KNIFE	$1.95
☐	P 428	THOU SHELL OF DEATH	$1.95
☐	P 418	THE WHISPER IN THE GLOOM	$1.95
☐	P 399	THE WIDOW'S CRUISE	$1.95
☐	P 400	THE WORM OF DEATH	$2.25

E. C. Bentley

☐	P 440	TRENT'S LAST CASE	$1.95
☐	P 516	TRENT'S OWN CASE	$2.25

Buy them at your local bookstore or use this coupon for ordering:

HARPER & ROW, Mail Order Dept. #PMS, 10 East 53rd St., New York, N.Y. 10022.

Please send me the books I have checked above. I am enclosing $ _____ which includes a postage and handling charge of $1.00 for the first book and 25¢ for each additional book. Send check or money order. No cash or C.O.D.'s please.

Name _____

Address _____

City _____ State _____ Zip _____

Please allow 4 weeks for delivery. USA and Canada only. This offer expires 2/1/82. Please add applicable sales tax.

Gavin Black

☐	P 473	A DRAGON FOR CHRISTMAS	$1.95
☐	P 485	THE EYES AROUND ME	$1.95
☐	P 472	YOU WANT TO DIE, JOHNNY?	$1.95

George Harmon Coxe

☐	P 527	MURDER WITH PICTURES	$2.25

Edmund Crispin

☐	P 506	BURIED FOR PLEASURE	$1.95

Kenneth Fearing

☐	P 500	THE BIG CLOCK	$1.95

Andrew Garve

☐	P 430	THE ASHES OF LODA	$1.50
☐	P 451	THE CUCKOO LINE AFFAIR	$1.95
☐	P 429	A HERO FOR LEANDA	$1.50
☐	P 449	MURDER THROUGH THE LOOKING GLASS	$1.95
☐	P 441	NO TEARS FOR HILDA	$1.95
☐	P 450	THE RIDDLE OF SAMSON	$1.95

Buy them at your local bookstore or use this coupon for ordering:

HARPER & ROW, Mail Order Dept. #PMS, 10 East 53rd St., New York, N.Y. 10022.

Please send me the books I have checked above. I am enclosing $ _____ which includes a postage and handling charge of $1.00 for the first book and 25¢ for each additional book. Send check or money order. No cash or C.O.D.'s please.

Name _____

Address _____

City _____ State _____ Zip _____

Please allow 4 weeks for delivery. USA and Canada only. This offer expires 2/1/82. Please add applicable sales tax.

Michael Gilbert

☐	P 446	BLOOD AND JUDGMENT	$1.95
☐	P 459	THE BODY OF A GIRL	$1.95
☐	P 448	THE DANGER WITHIN	$1.95
☐	P 447	DEATH HAS DEEP ROOTS	$1.95
☐	P 458	FEAR TO TREAD	$1.95

C. W. Grafton

☐	P 519	BEYOND A REASONABLE DOUBT	$1.95

Edward Grierson

☐	P 528	THE SECOND MAN	$2.25

Cyril Hare

☐	P 455	AN ENGLISH MURDER	$1.95
☐	P 522	TRAGEDY AT LAW	$2.25
☐	P 514	UNTIMELY DEATH	$1.95
☐	P 454	WHEN THE WIND BLOWS	$1.95
☐	P 523	WITH A BARE BODKIN	$2.25

Matthew Head

☐	P 541	THE CABINDA AFFAIR (available 6/81)	$2.25
☐	P 542	MURDER AT THE FLEA CLUB (available 6/81)	$2.25

Buy them at your local bookstore or use this coupon for ordering:

HARPER & ROW, Mail Order Dept. #PMS, 10 East 53rd St., New York, N.Y. 10022.
Please send me the books I have checked above. I am enclosing $ _____ which includes a postage and handling charge of $1.00 for the first book and 25¢ for each additional book. Send check or money order. No cash or C.O.D.'s please.

Name _____

Address _____

City _____ State _____ Zip _____
Please allow 4 weeks for delivery. USA and Canada only. This offer expires 2/1/82. Please add applicable sales tax.

M. V. Heberden

☐ P 533   ENGAGED TO MURDER $2.25

James Hilton

☐ P 501   WAS IT MURDER? $1.95

Elspeth Huxley

☐ P 540   THE AFRICAN POISON MURDERS

                                                     $2.25

Frances Iles

☐ P 517   BEFORE THE FACT $1.95
☐ P 532   MALICE AFORETHOUGHT $1.95

Lange Lewis

☐ P 518   THE BIRTHDAY MURDER $1.95

Arthur Maling

☐ P 482   LUCKY DEVIL $1.95
☐ P 483   RIPOFF $1.95
☐ P 484   SCHROEDER'S GAME $1.95

Austin Ripley

☐ P 387   MINUTE MYSTERIES $1.95

Buy them at your local bookstore or use this coupon for ordering:

Thomas Sterling

☐ P 529   THE EVIL OF THE DAY $2.25

Julian Symons

☐ P 468   THE BELTING INHERITANCE $1.95
☐ P 469   BLAND BEGINNING $1.95
☐ P 481   BOGUE'S FORTUNE $1.95
☐ P 480   THE BROKEN PENNY $1.95
☐ P 461   THE COLOR OF MURDER $1.95
☐ P 460   THE 31ST OF FEBRUARY $1.95

Dorothy Stockbridge Tillet
(John Stephen Strange)

☐ P 536   THE MAN WHO KILLED FORTESCUE $2.25

Henry Kitchell Webster

☐ P 539   WHO IS THE NEXT? $2.25

Anna Mary Wells

☐ P 534   MURDERER'S CHOICE $2.25
☐ P 535   A TALENT FOR MURDER $2.25

Buy them at your local bookstore or use this coupon for ordering:

HARPER & ROW, Mail Order Dept. #PMS, 10 East 53rd St., New York, N.Y. 10022.
Please send me the books I have checked above. I am enclosing $ _____ which includes a postage and handling charge of $1.00 for the first book and 25¢ for each additional book. Send check or money order. No cash or C.O.D.'s please.

Name _____

Address _____

City _____ State _____ Zip _____
Please allow 4 weeks for delivery. USA and Canada only. This offer expires 2/1/82. Please add applicable sales tax.